SHADOW OF THE CASCADE

A Post-Apocalyptic Story In The Shadows Of The Coast Mountains

Written by: Kai Hugessen
Cover Illustration by:
Tasi Schneider

Copyright © 2020 Kai Hugessen

All rights reserved

The characters and events portrayed in this book are fictitious. Any similarity to real persons, living or dead, is coincidental and not intended by the author.

No part of this book may be reproduced, or stored in a retrieval system, or transmitted in any form or by any means, electronic, mechanical, photocopying, recording, or otherwise, without express written permission of the author.

CONTENTS

Title Page	1
Copyright	2
Foreword:	5
Prologue	7
I: Overhead	8
II: Outcast	16
III: Renegade	22
IV: Bond	29
V: Apocalypse	35
Shadow of the Cascade	36
1: Undergrowth	37
2: Exodus	45
3: Disruption	54
4: Subspace	63
5: Investment	72
6: Renewal	79
7: Passenger	90
8: Shadows	100
9: Hatching	110
10: Cabins	117

11: Labour	129
12: Backups	137
13: Distractions.	144
14: Evaluation.	151
15: Ghosts	159
16: Seas	169
17: Islands.	179
18: Roots.	182
19: Communication.	190
20: Operation	197
21: Barter	204
22: Inevitability	211
23: Reparations	222
24: Veins	233
25: Downhill	244
26: Vanishings	253
27: Faintly	255
28: Red	266
29: Revenge	276
Epilogue.	285
About The Author	287
Acknowledgements:	289

FOREWORD:

To describe what I've done to write this story, you'd need an entire other book. I've spent hours researching, writing and formatting these words so that they could be the best story I can put forth. The journey that each and every character goes through was a journey I felt I needed to tell. This book was crafted not because I wanted to spin a tale that I could brag about later, or to just make a quick 2$ off of royalties. This book was written because I felt it needed to be written. It's an expression of humanity and our flaws. It's a love letter to British Columbia, my homeland which in my humble opinion is one of the greatest natural wonders of the world. This book, it's more than the sum of its parts to me.

I just hope that for you it ends up being the same.

I wrote this as an understanding that the end of the world isn't really the end of the world. Paradise, it is not, but we as a species are so much more incredibly resilient than I think we give ourselves credit for. That's true for you as well.

In the end, the story within these digital pages is a story about us. As individuals, and as a species, who we are and who we chose to be.

So the question I pose to you is this. Who do you choose to be?

PROLOGUE

I: OVERHEAD

The low humming of a ceiling light tends to go ignored. It loses itself in the dim of conversation and the background of common thought. It's drowned out by the heater, or the air conditioner. It was designed that way, to minimize the amount of attention anyone would give it. It was meant to disappear, while fully living out its purpose.

But right now, the damn thing was all Alex Park could focus on.

His eyes wandered around the room, scanning the drab walls and worn-out conference table. His nose swelled with the stale air of the windowless room, laden with the dusty aroma of the carpet beneath his feet. His hands tapped restlessly on the table, playing some unknown tempo that was far removed from the thoughts that floated through his brain.

The meeting had gone on for hours, but for the entire time, his concentration was on that sound, and he had no earthly idea why.

"Alex!" Even the voice at the head of the table barely made its way through his skull, battling its way through the buzzing to reach some soft part of his brain that hadn't been consumed by the thought of its noise. But barely still makes it.

"Yes, what? Yes?" Alex snapped out of it, focusing once more on all his senses. "Yes, I'm here. What?"

The whole room looked at him. Marge looked at him from the head of the table. Albert looked at him from his right. Isabelle from his left. Half a dozen more from everywhere else. He felt like the main act, who'd forgotten all the lyrics.

"Alex, we need you to pay attention." Marge spoke again, this time managing to catch Alex's attention. "This is important. That goes for all of you. This might be boring, but we need to find a way to crunch these numbers goddamnit!"

She rubbed her temples, sitting back down in her seat. Standing up to make a point seemed to have only worsened her headache. She glanced up at the lights above her, before sighing and looking around the room at all of them. Alex wondered if she heard the buzzing too.

"I'm sorry for yelling Alex. I'm sorry everyone, actually. But if we don't find space in the budget to make our case to corporate, we're never going to get out of this goddamn basement. So please, even if you're the damn PR guy Alex, and numbers aren't your forte, help me out here. Help each other out here. Poke the guy next to you awake if you have to. All hands on deck!"

Everyone in the room nodded and muttered to themselves. Faces blended together in a drour melody of affirmation. Albert glanced over at Alex, leaning in a little, with a subtle air of conspiracy. "Looks like you pissed off Ms. Margey." His eyes flickered mischievously, a small smirk on his lips. "Now we won't be able to go out for recess."

Alex glared at him, running his hands through his hair. "Shut up dude, this wouldn't have happened if you'd helped me stay focused like I asked..."

Albert straightened back up in his chair, giving Alex one last dastardly smile, before turning back to the meeting at hand. "But where's the fun in that?"

Alex shook his head, trying to clear the cobwebs from his mind. Someone was making a suggestion. At least, that's what he assumed. People were speaking and Marge had a look on her face that told him she was about to shoot something down.

"No, that would just... goddamnit, Greg that would increase our expenses, not lower them!" Marge looked like she wanted to slam someone's head into the table. Alex coughed quietly, trying to think something up and hoping it wouldn't be him tasting splinters.

"What about leasing out some of our office space?" Isabelle chimed in. "We could share some desks, right? I mean, it'd halve some of our tied up expenses. Maybe even create a more communal work environment?."

Marge digested her words pensively, looking around at everyone else. She seemed to consider it. She nodded at Isabelle, then cleared her throat. "Any objections?" Several hands went up, each worried about the implications such an action would take on their lives. Crammed desks and shared workspaces weren't exactly a selling point. Alex was among them.

Isabelle sighed, while Marge glared. Alex considered putting his hand down from the sheer intensity of that stare. Several other people did. "You all realize that it's either that, or we stay in this shithole of an office, right? Forever?" The sheer vindictiveness behind the words made everyone but Alex put their hands down. And the concentrated glare that she put on him when she saw his hand was up almost made him do the same. "Well?"

Alex cleared his throat. Suddenly it was as dry as parchment. It was like the fire in her eyes was evaporating the moisture in his throat, turning it to steam that clouded in his head and drowned his thoughts. "I just don't think... I mean, Corporate shot down all our other ideas. Every time we've found a way to cut something out of our costs, they just cut our budget more to keep us down." His speech was over, but all eyes were still on him. "That's just what I think. Mostly."

Marge just stared him down, boring an almost tangible hole through his head before snapping and storming out of the room, slamming the door behind her. The room went quiet. Albert looked around at everyone, then leaned towards Alex again. "Who put shit in *her* coffee?"

Isabelle looked annoyed at the two of them, as Alex tried to shoo Albert away. "I'm going to go after her. You two just... don't make anything worse." She set out after Marge, deepening the silence in the room. Everyone else funnelled out slowly, unsure if this meant the meeting was over or not. The last one out was Albert, who patted Alex on the back and gave him another mischievous grin as he closed the door behind him. Alex was left alone with the empty room and the slow heavy buzz of the lights above. He closed his eyes and sighed, stewing there alone for a moment. The sudden isolation was rather fitting for his mood.

He stood up after a few minutes, putting all the chairs back into place and heading for the door. He glanced behind him at the windowless box that was the conference room, flicking the light off and shutting the door.

Now the buzz from above was gone.

On his way down the hall, he paused a moment. The pipes along the walls hissed softly and the mildew that tended to gather in the air left a pungent aroma in his nose. The sad excuse for an office that they pretended to occupy was nothing more than a 'renovated' industrial basement. It was underneath some old factory, and it maintained all the charm and integrity that an old smog belching hell house could. That is to say, none at all. Ahead, a door opened, and Isabelle appeared. She closed it behind her, striding quickly over to Alex. He opened his mouth to say something, but she cut him off, whispering in an agitated and unhappy tone.

"What were you doing there? Jeez Alex, that was like, the worst timed objection ever!" Isabelle blew air out of her nostrils, something that made her look more worried than angry. "Marge is having a meltdown right now, and she really needed you to back her up in there. I know it's not really the best of times, but it's important that we give her confidence!"

Alex took a step back, a little shocked. "Me? Why me?" Isabelle blinked, raising her voice a little more.

"Because you're her friend! I'm her friend! She's not used to this whole leadership deal, so we need to be as supportive as we can." Alex could hear something in her voice. It was angry, of course, but there was something there behind it. Something he couldn't quite figure out. Remorse? Exasperation? Reading people's emotions had never been his strong suit and the mixed cocktail of feelings on display in front of him left his head spinning.

He straightened up a little, trying to feel less like a scolded child. "Hey, I am not... I mean, we take the same bus home, but..." He trailed off. Isabelle kept eye-contact expectantly. "But... goddamnit, fine. I'll go talk to her."

Isabelle nodded, satisfied, then headed down the hall. Alex sighed, going to the door Isabelle had just come out of. He hesitated a moment, glancing back at Isabelle. She had left, walked off without looking back, and now Alex realized he could just leave. This definitely wasn't in his job description. But he pushed the door open anyway, peaking into the room.

Marge was sitting in the visitor's chair of her cramped office, her back to him. The light was off, and the only natural light in the room came from a basement window that looked out into the street. It was a small square of foggy sky that did little to boost the atmosphere. From where Alex stood, all he could see was the back of her head, her hair a little more frazzled and unkempt than it was just a few minutes ago. She was looking at the wall, where a projector showed the image of her direct opposite. Rather than a murky basement, the woman on the screen was inside a lavish and modern office. Instead of a simple suit and tie, she was dressed in a modestly impressive white sheath dress. And while Marge's shoulders slumped and her posture sagged, the woman on the screen sat upright, looking back at her with an icy and indifferent stare.

There was silence, for a moment, while Alex considered what to say. Fortunately for him, the woman on-screen broke the tension first.

"I will not grant your request, Ms. Bossam." The voice she spoke with was measured and her face was neutral, but Alex could swear he saw a smile at the edges of her lips. It was the look of someone who was tearing something down with the utmost professionalism while enjoying every moment of it. He'd seen it on some of the salespeople when they made a particularly nasty deal. He'd seen it on Marge's face before, at least a version of it. It was the image of superiority. But this woman on screen, she didn't just dominate the conversation, she dominated the look. "Your budget has been cut for a variety of reasons. The situation you and your people find yourself in is entirely within the fault of your own. It was your predecessor's investments that put you in that office, and it's your own job to dig yourself out of that hole"

Alex walked into the room, trying to quietly sidle himself to the side. From this angle, he could see the tears that threatened to break down Marge's face. Her mouth quivered for a moment, as she struggled to find the words to speak. It was unnerving, seeing the sudden change from predator to prey. She gave a glance towards Alex for a split-second, before looking back at the woman on the screen and gathering her courage. "Mrs. Elena, I'm not... I can't be held responsible for the Paradise Valley investment. That was Mr. Donahue's idea, and he's not at the company anymore. He's gone. I just don't see why our branch should be limited like this for what he did."

Mrs. Elena gave her a measured look, then leaned forward towards the camera. "Ms. Bossam, do you know what Mr. Donahue said to me when he pitched the founding of your branch? He said to me: 'There's a place north of Vancouver with untapped potential. All I need is a team and some capital. I can build something that exceeds every expectation. I'll put Macedon Tours on the international map'. I told him that it was a terrible idea. The 2025 recession left our company reeling. We barely got out of it, and here he is not even five years later asking for a huge investment. Now, I advised against it, but Mr. Donahue is well respected. So, we threw him a bone. Do you know what happened?" She paused, seeming to loom over Marge, despite being nothing more than a 2D projection on a screen. "We spent millions turning 'Paradise Valley' into a tourist Mecca. Campgrounds, adventure parks, hiking trails, you name it. And how did it turn out?"

Marge swallowed, rubbing her eyes to try to clear the tears. She looked back at the projection silently. Mrs. Elena met her gaze evenly. "How, Ms. Bossam? How did Paradise Valley end up?"

A tear streaked down Marge's face, starkly visible with its reflective light. "Empty, ma'am. It ended up empty…"

The woman on screen finally smirked fully, seemingly pleased with what was before her. She sat back in her seat, thoroughly lavishing in the sadistic experience. "Empty. So much money pissed away on nothing. I'd worked with Mr. Donahue for years before this, and to tell you the truth I considered him a friend. So, trust me, it wasn't pleasant for me to sit him down and fire him. But he screwed the pooch, Ms. Bossam. He screwed it badly. It's a pure charity act that your branch even exists."

Mrs. Elena finally sat back, reclining in her chair carefully. "So, circling back to the start. I will not be increasing your budget. I will not be moving you out of your current office. I will instead be hoping and praying that you learn from your position and step up to the plate. I will instead be visiting you within the month, to make sure your leadership doesn't crash and burn our reputation even more. Make Vancouver something substantial for Macedon Tours, Ms. Bossam, or you'll be working with Mr. Donahue. At the strip mall."

The projector blinked back to the desktop, accompanied by a pleasant chime and a request for Marge to review the call's quality. She pressed the power button on the projector to turn it off, staying silent as she watched its light flicker out. When it did, she stood up and turned to look at Alex, wiping away her tears in the faint light of the window.

"So… you needed something?"

II: OUTCAST

Alex and Marge sat at the bus stop, waiting for the 232 to take them home. The air was cold, still gripping onto the icy chill of winter, terrified to lose itself into Spring. April was like that in North Vancouver. All signs pointed towards the warmer air of summer, but somehow every year it refused to let go. Alex watched the faint imprint his breath left on the air, seeing it spiral away and fade into nothingness. He watched the traffic go by, slow and uninteresting. At one time, this would be rush hour. An avenue chock full of cars and life. Now, it seems the gray sky had come to the ground and placed its subdued energy upon the earth.

He wondered if maybe it was just a matter of perspective.

"The bus is running late. Or something." Alex looked over at Marge, trying to meet her eyes. She just looked at her feet.

"It's always running late Alex." Her shoulders slumped even more as if the weight of his statement had put something upon them. "When, in the two months since we moved to this shithole of an office, has the bus ever been on time?"

"Once or twice, I guess. Look, you don't have to be a dick about it."

Marge laughed. It was dry and humourless. Pained, even. "I do. Goddamnit, I do. I'm your boss, Alex. That's my job. Being a dick is in the job description." She turned to look at him, wiping her eyes again. Alex could swear he saw the beginnings of a smile there now. "And letting you call me a dick isn't. So watch your mouth."

Alex chuckled nervously, shifting slightly on the seat. "I'm sorry..."

Marge turned away again. The smile was gone. "About what? Calling me a dick, or ruining my meeting?" She rolled her shoulders, staring at the overgrown pavement beneath their feet. "You did both asshole."

Alex started to say something but paused. The bus rolled up in front of them, the brakes releasing a harsh *hiss* of noise. "About both, look Marge..." She stood from the bench and walked to the door of the bus without looking at him.

"I'll see you tomorrow Alex."

***

Alex took that as a hint to not sit next to her on the bus home. He waited a few moments before stepping in after her, giving a nod to the driver and shivering a little from the change in temperature between the chilly air outside and the toastier interior. After swiping his card, he made his way towards the back of the bus, squeezing by dozens of people on their commute home. As empty as the streets seemed to him, the bus was entirely full. There was only one spare handle to stand with, and fortunately for Marge, it was at the opposite end of the bus from her. Alex ignored the sounds and smells of the people around him, closing his eyes and just feeling the bus move beneath his feet. The grime of his riding partners did not reach his eyes. The coughing and chattering did not reach his ears. Here, alone, he was just a wave in the ocean, buffeted around without a word. But like that wave, it didn't matter to him. It was right there, standing in a bus full of his fellow man, after long hours of work and a disappointing day, that Alex was able to find his moments of peace. He was just a cog in a machine, but that machine was humanity. And it was a better cog to be than one inside a corporate slaughterhouse.

But inevitably, as with every day, the moment had to end. The bus ground to a halt, doors opening once more. There was a collective groan all around him, and his eyes shot open to assess what had happened. Not that it was any surprise. A Mountie stepped onto the bus, an honest to God Mountie. A peacekeeper, with the red uniform and the big hat. The whole shebang. He looked almost sheepish, as if he was embarrassed that he had suddenly taken center stage. All around Alex, people began digging into their pockets and coats, looking for something. He began to do the same as the Mountie cleared his throat.

"Alright folks, sorry about this, but we're going to have to do an ID check. I'm sure you all know the drill by now, just pull out your ID's and as soon as we've looked over them all, you can be on your way. Again, so sorry, it's just procedure." Upon completing his little speech, he stepped to the side. Several more traditional officers filed in after him. They had a similar apologetic smile on their faces, but the looks in their eyes showed that they were going to take this seriously.

By now, Alex had his ID out and was just waiting for them to check it. One of the officers eventually reached him, which is when he offered his ID to them. The officer used a handheld scanner, almost like the kind you would see at a supermarket. But instead of scanning his underwear or embarrassingly specific shampoo brand, all it took was a moment before he had his ID scanned and the officer was back on his way.

One or two people were asked off the bus. Usually, it was just a matter of an expired ID or a glitch in the system. It had happened to Alex once, when the scanner had a screwed-up flagging algorithm. He'd had a short talk with the police outside, and when they realized he wasn't a domestic terrorist, they let him go. He had to walk home after that. So far, it had seemed all this system had done was cause annoyance. Something about monitoring tensions and minimizing threats. It was all some sort of political jargon that went over Alex's head.

But once the police departed and the Mountie gave one last embarrassed goodbye, he couldn't help but look back at the people who had disembarked the bus. The likelihood of them being a terrorist or a foreign agent was low, but...

Well, it wasn't impossible. And that brief possibility alone was terrifying.

The bus turned a corner and hid them from view. Alex sighed and closed his eyes again, feeling the rhythm of the bus move beneath him once more.

The bus stopped a few more times, each of which saw more people disembark. Marge was one of them. He didn't open his eyes, but he knew from memory which street her stop was. The electronic voice would chime its tune, and everyone who needed to would get off. It was like a metallic beast, belching people and fumes into the outside world. He also knew from memory that his was up next. He opened his eyes, letting go of the handle and making his way towards the front of the bus. It had emptied considerably, and there were plenty of seats available for him. Regardless, he chose to stand, waiting until the bus rolled to a final stop to set off on his way out. He thanked the bus driver and stepped off the bus, followed by the throng of people behind him, each of which headed off down the block in either direction. He joined one of those throngs, walking for a few more streets until turning into his apartment building. As usual, it was quiet as the grave. His footsteps were the only noise from inside the building, quieted only a little by the ratty carpet beneath his feet. He took a moment to check his mail, grabbing the mess of bills and adverts that tended to plague the small box. He considered taking the stairs a moment. After all, wouldn't the exercise do him good?

As he exited the elevator on the third floor, noise came back into his world. The first door he passed played the sound of rock music, the second of some sort of soap opera. The third had a noise behind it that was best ignored, and the fourth was his own home. He unlocked the door, closing it behind him carefully. He made sure to lock it again, flicking the light on with his other hand. The illumination of his studio came with that click, a welcome sight after a weary day. He set his keys down on the kitchen counter, kicking off his shoes and opening the curtains to his windows.

He took stock of his apartment. Organized, but not exactly tidy. His belongings didn't fit in the storage space he had. Maybe it was a bit of a hoarding problem, but it didn't particularly bother him. He laid down on the bed, turning on the TV and flickering through the channels. Tensions in the North Sea, cooking shows, reality dramas. He passed each of them without much thought, eventually settling on a show about a home makeover. It wasn't the best programming, but he liked to fantasize about what he would do if he had a place of his own. Put in a nice brick fireplace, maybe some exposed beams in the ceiling. It would be nice and homey.

He watched an hour of it. An hour and a half. By the time 7:00 rolled around, he had seen a home and a half be turned on their heads. But the mind-numbing brought about by the TV had to end at some point. He promised himself that. Just one more show.

It was 9:00 by the time Alex stepped out the front door of his apartment building, hands in his pockets. The lights of the street after dark almost made the world seem brighter. Colours of the city now, not of the drab sky. There was something more interesting about the arrays of gray that a concrete wall could provide, contrasted mutely with the tamer shades of a cloudy sky. He set off at a brisk pace, trying to make up for the lost time that had been sunk into Jessica and Emanuel of Halifax and their two-bedroom bungalow renovation. The crowds were heavier now. The shadow of night had brought out the revellers and the destitute, people who shied away from the light of day. Here, he could see people celebrating or despairing, something he tended to avoid for the drama of it all. He weaved through the throngs of people, without a destination intent on his mind. He found a bench to sit on, looking upwards towards the sky.

It was orange now, the clouds reflecting the lights of the city. He figured it sort of morbid that man had made its mark on the heavens. Not in a weird 'outpacing of the natural order' sort of way, but rather just as something strange. A statement about man's mark on the world. Maybe he could use that for an ad. Something about escaping that ever-increasing reach of mankind. His mind pulled itself down from the clouds, crystalizing on something concrete to think about. Ad campaigns, the natural evolution of communication.

Maybe he could even throw in something about the destruction it wrought on nature. Play the card that the wild is only getting smaller. Make Macedon Tours that gateway to a shrinking frontier. He figured that would be good. Of course, he had also figured out the irony of trying to use nature's beauty as a slogan. He'd had to accept that on day one of working this job. By the time he was done waiting for a phantom bus that never came, he had pulled out his phone and written a plan for a series of ads that would maybe do... something. At this point, Paradise Valley was essentially a lost cause, but he hoped that *maybe* he could turn it around.

He knew he couldn't.

But fighting hopelessness, that was something he could do. Alex figured that ideas were something valuable. Even if they're never implemented, or even brought to light, an idea was something powerful. He headed back home, content with the idea of brightening his company's prospects just a little bit more.

III: RENEGADE

Early morning on the next day, Albert seemed to have an idea.

"Rent-a-car-rumble." He looked expectantly at everyone else in the repurposed janitor's closet that they had called the break room. Everyone, Alex included, only gave him a confused look back. Tim, from QC, seemed to object the most.

"You're insane." Albert only smiled back at him in his usual way, like a Cheshire cat. It was mischievous and carefree but undercut with a level of sinister knowhow. Alex didn't like it one bit.

"You haven't even heard the idea, Tom." Tim looked at Alex. Alex shrugged and looked at Isabelle. Isabelle pretended not to notice, stepping closer to Marge.

Marge looked at Albert. "His name is Tim, not Tom."

Albert winked at her, spreading his arms out like a preacher. "Well, maybe if we hung out more, I'd know that. So, Rent-a-car-rumble." Tim just looked around at the other three, then shook his head and left, muttering something unintelligible. He'd had enough of Albert's shenanigans for now.

Alex watched him go, then turned to Albert with a bit of foreboding. "What's rent a car rumble?"

"I'm so glad you asked." Albert clapped his hands, eyes lighting up enthusiastically. "We pool some money together and go rent a car for the day. We can use it to head downtown, check out the sights, do all the cool shit we can't do normally in North Van."

Marge looked at him blankly for a moment, disbelief in her eyes. She blinked twice, then breathed in deeply to calm herself. "Albert. Our branch is trying to scrape by on just existing.

Rental car prices are insanely high right now. Shit, they've been insanely high for half a decade. Fuel shortages and whatever the hell else. It's a shitty idea and I can only guess that you'll somehow get yourself hurt. Worst of all, I'm your boss now, so your idiocy affects my performance ratings. What the hell made you want to propose going nuts with a road-rage anyways?"

Isabelle nodded along to all of this, chiming in at the end. "Plus, I already have a car, so renting one is a dumb idea anyway." The room went quiet each of them turning to stare at Isabelle. Isabelle looked around at everyone, taking in their surprised looks. "What?"

Albert's smile turned into a grin. "So, we don't have to rent one then?"

Marge sighed heavily, facepalming. Alex figured he should say something but chose to keep quiet. The points would click together without him. He shared a quiet look with Marge as Isabelle seemingly realized what Albert was saying.

"No, what? I'm not... I'm not doing that. It's my car, and I don't have a license anyways. I got it from my parents before the market crashed. It's in a storage unit, and I don't want to... look, I'm not giving you my car!"

Albert considered this for a moment. "Ok... what about Marge? Why not let her drive?"

Marge looked surprised, glancing between the two of them. "What, me?" She shook her head, frowning. "I'm not driving you downtown, Albert."

"Then let's not go downtown! Come on, how about West Van? I'm sure it can be fun! You know, cut us out of that daily grind." Albert had a twinkle in his eyes. It was the twinkle of a man whose idea was gaining purchase. It was the twinkle of a conman who knows that he has his mark on the hook. Marge and Isabelle didn't seem to think so.

Alex looked on as they disputed and discussed. He started to daydream. He looked at one of the cracks in the wall, seeing the way it snaked its way down the plaster, like a canyon cutting its way through the desert. The details of the after-work excursion came to rest somewhere unimportant in his brain, as he focused intently on the winding way the crack sought the floor. It only served as a reminder of their dour conditions, and the way the weight of the rusting machinery above them probably didn't do much towards the tensile integrity of their ceiling.

"Alex, what about you?"

He focused again, returning from the walls around him to the people beside him. "Hm? Oh, me?"

Isabelle nodded, looking at him again with a hint of something Alex couldn't quite figure out. It wasn't anger. It wasn't desire. Maybe pity? He still couldn't tell. "Is everyone else going?"

Albert snickered to himself "If by everyone, you mean everyone in this room, then yes. Isabelle has the car; Margey has the license and I have the dashing good looks. We just need a comic relief."

Alex rolled his eyes, putting his hands in his pockets with a shrug. "Well, if you guys are all going..."

"Hell yeah!" Albert made a little fist pump motion and stepped out of the break room. "This is going to be amazing!"

The other three filed out after him. Alex tried to dig up the exact details of what he'd just agreed to from where he'd stored them somewhere in his hippocampus. That was the trouble with having your head in the clouds, sometimes a little vital detail such as their evening plans failed to break through the lid.

Failing to find anything but the vague recollection of West Van, he elected to just ask. "Hey, so where are we going again?"

Isabelle didn't look back at him as she headed towards the exit. "To a storage unit for me! I've got to go make sure the car is ready by the time everyone else is."

 Marge stopped walking for a moment. "Excuse me, what? No

you're not, you're still on the clock Isa!"

Isabelle paused, then turned to look at her sheepishly. "Right… I sort of… sorry, Marge."

As Isabelle hurried back to her desk, Alex turned to Marge. She looked annoyed, which he figured didn't help his chances of getting an answer. "So, where were we…" She stormed off before he could finish, mumbling something angrily about authority. "…going."

***

Alex looked around, rubbing the back of his head. Just a second ago he was cramped for space. He essentially just wandered, heading back to his desk at a meandering pace. He gave a polite nod of the head to his coworkers as he passed, most of them just mumbling something back, with a dishevelled lack of interest as they typed away on their computers. The one notable exception to this was Albert.

"Hey Alex, could you come help me out a second?" Albert was typing on his phone, not even pretending to look at Alex as he spoke. "Do you know where I could find an airhorn on short notice?" He looked up at him, flashing his trademark smile.

The real surprise to Alex was that he didn't know where to get one already. "No… I've never had to buy an airhorn before. What do you even need one for anyways?"

Albert chuckled softly, a jester who'd just thought of a clever act. "That's a secret. It would ruin the fun if I told you, right?" He looked back down at his phone, scrolling down a list of open stores from his search. "You'll find out soon!"

"Dude. You worry me sometimes."

He chuckled again, standing up and grabbing his bag from under his desk. "Hey, I have a job to do. Morale is my corral!" He started walking away towards the exit of the office. Alex followed him, more than a little bit concerned.

"That doesn't make sense. It shouldn't even rhyme. Why are you... why are you going that way? Hey, where are you going?"

Albert looked back at him, then shrugged. "Where do you think? The bank? That's right. Definitely not to buy an airhorn to use in my dastardly schemes!"

"But you're on the clock. You should have seen how Marge just reacted when Isabelle tried to leave."

"I did. And I know! But this is a work project. The airhorn is very important for tonight. And tonight is very important for getting Margey to loosen up. Come on, a night out on the town with moi and two less vital but equally present people? It'll do her wonders!"

"You really have issues"

"Yep. But hey, that's the job." He walked up the stairs out of the office, opening the door and taking a dramatic breath of the open air. "Ah. Smog."

Alex had paused at the bottom of the stairs, thinking. "Hey, wait a second, where are we actually going- "

The door shut behind Albert, leaving Alex staring at the miserable moulding wallpaper that lined the staircase.

"...tonight. Damn it!"

He turned around and headed back to his desk. He'd struck out on finding out what he'd actually agreed to do twice. And as much as the concept of heading straight into the unknown was quintessentially the way this company seemed to be run, he did still want to know what his plans were for the night, and if he had to cancel them. That left him with one choice for who to ask.

Alex knocked on the wall of Isabelle's cubicle, leaning awkwardly against the side of it. She turned in her chair, looking frazzled and defeated. Apparently, it was a common look around the place.

"Hey, so what was that with Marge just now?"

Isabelle's shoulders slumped, and she looked embarrassed. "Well, this promotion has been really stressful for her in the last couple of months. It's a lot of pressure to put on her so suddenly. I mean, I've been helping her try to get it for years, but we just weren't ready for it to be sprung on us after Paradise Valley failed."

Alex nodded. "Mhm, that's noticeable." It was true. Marge had been campaigning for higher positions as long as he'd known her. Something about the corporate lifestyle seemed to suit her. But ever since she actually got as high as a single branch could get...

Well, some would call it poetic irony.

"So, when I just disregard it by almost leaving... in front of everyone outside the break room..."

"That never would have happened under Mr. Donahue." Alex figured he understood now. Solidifying authority, showing a united front, all that political and corporate nonsense he tried to duck his head under. At least knowing about it served to help him figure out why she stormed off like that. "But she seemed to take it really hard. Or, I mean I think so. She stormed off."

Isabelle sank even lower in her chair. "We'd talked about it this morning. You know, about respecting her authority."

Alex considered this. He also considered just how different Isabelle was now in comparison to the fired-up enforcer she was yesterday. She had a sort of spark in her when it came to supporting her superiors. Alex realized she'd make a great second in command. "This really matters to you, doesn't it?"

She nodded, trying to straighten back up and meet his eyes. "Yeah. It's really... it's not fair what corporate is doing to her. And as her friend, I have to step up for her. She's not ready for this Alex. I mean, that's obvious, right? Years fighting for it, and then in one moment... everything? It's just too much."

Alex considered that too. It was true enough. He and Marge were around the same age, and he knew that there was no way in hell he would be able to step up to that position if he got it. "It is. So, that's why we need to help her, right?" Isabelle nodded quietly. "And that's why we're going out tonight? It's not because of Albert, it's because you want to support her?"

Isabelle nodded again. "And that's why you need to come too. I know you already said yes and all but... look, it's not just some 'night out' like Albert wants to think. Marge feels alone, and we have to show her she's not, ok? So... putting up with Albert's idiocy is worth helping her out."

Alex took a deep breath, then nodded. He got it now. Well, he didn't *get it* with fancy italics and directed commentary, but at the very least he figured that he understood. "But hey, Albert isn't that bad. He's just sort of inconsiderate sometimes. A lot of times. He's trying to help this time though. I think. He's hard to read sometimes."

"Which is why you and I need to be extra helpful tonight, ok Alex?"

"Ok. One question though."

"What?"

"Where are we actually... going?"

IV: BOND

The sky above was turning to a victorious orange, the setting sun lighting the clouds ablaze. From the backseat of Isabelle's old hatchback, Alex watched the streaks of light illuminate a fiery diagram in the sky. This wasn't the pale and sickly display that played on the sky from a sombre cloudy night. This was a striking display of energy and power as the sun descended from its perch in the sky, the true reflection of its cosmic presence.

The radio played a quiet melody, turned low and ignorable as conversation flew around the car. Mostly, from what Alex heard, it was a discussion between Isabelle and Albert. Marge drove silently, as the two debated something or other about the plan for the night.

"We're not going to an arcade Albert, ok? So just... please stop asking." Isabelle looked towards the radio knob, looking like she wanted to crank it towards the point of deafness, using the resulting religious ads and alarmist news bulletins to drown out whatever retort Albert had in store.

"Come on. I'm telling you; it would be great! We go out for dinner at... wherever we're going"

"It's an Italian place." Alex recalled Isabelle's information from earlier as he turned his head from where he was looking out the window. "One of those authentic places. With real breadsticks."

"Right. We get some breadsticks, then afterwards we head on down to an arcade and have some fun! It'll be great. I even brought an airhorn!"

"Ok first of all." Isabelle turned in her seat, looking back at the two guys in the back. "We're not going to the arcade. And second of all… actually, you know what, I'd rather not know what the airhorn is for."

"Wouldn't have told you anyways."

Isabelle sighed, leaning on her elbow. "Yeah that figures."

"Hey, could you please be quiet? I'm trying to drive." Marge didn't take her eyes off the road.

Isabelle ducked her head, turning back to look out the windshield at the road ahead and the setting sun. "Sorry Marge…"

Albert scoffed, shaking his head. "What's the point of going out with friends if we don't have fun with it?" He crossed his arms like a petulant child, turning his nose up to the front of the car.

"I'm your boss, not your friend. I'm Isabelle and Alex's friend."

Ouch.

"Well, I'm wounded, Margey. That really hurts." Albert spoke with mock agony, feigning pain to his chest. Everyone else ignored him, which left him looking around at the rest of them in disappointment for not following his antics.

The rest of the ride into the west side of town was quieter. Albert grumbled to himself quietly, Isabelle listened to the radio and Alex watched the sky turn from bright orange to the hazy polluted orange of a city's night. It was a de-saturation of colour, like a printer running out of ink or a light slowly burning out before their eyes. Dusk had overtaken the world, and by the time they reached their destination, even this last vestige of daylight started to fade away.

Marge parked the car near the restaurant, stepping out with a quiet hum. The other three followed after her, the four of them looking into the bright lights inside the restaurant. It had all the signs of an imitation Italian restaurant, menus inscribed in chalk, faux-ivy climbing up a plaster wall built to resemble stone, but the aura of the place was slightly dampened by its position in a strip mall. Albert lead the way to the front desk, opening the front doors dramatically, like a wild west cowboy who's entrance left the piano man dumbfounded and the saloon wondering how he thought so much of himself. Marge and Isabelle filed in after him, Alex pausing a moment to look again at the sky. It was nighttime now, and the transcendent colours of the setting sun had faded away from the sky. It would be another 12 hours before the clouds burst into colour once more, chasing away the faint sickness that permeated them currently. He couldn't help but feel some sense of loss for that, be it for the clouds or the sun itself. After a second or two of sympathizing with uncaring atmospheric trickery, he followed the group in.

They were sat near the back of the restaurant, at the request of Isabelle and the behest of Albert. The noise of their fellow diners that filled the rest of the establishment was quieter back here, isolating them from the generally communal atmosphere that permeated the rest of the place. As they waited to order, a quiet and unimportant conversation started to pass across the table. Inconsequential and uninteresting, the minutes ticked away towards the waiter's arrival. Topics like favourite foods or TV shows. Casual discussions about the politics of the conflict in Northern Europe or the controversial new expansions to martial law put in place by the BC government. Several times Albert tried to chime in with a loud burst of noise, banishing the calm with an outburst of attempted wit. Isabelle never let him get through to dominating the conversation, casually cutting him off and generally redirecting the conversation away from the more disruptive elements of his personality. The minutes ticked by, then the hours. The food was ordered, came and went all the while the world almost seemed to slow. Marge opened up over the course of the meal, sitting straighter and talking the small talk. She was short and curt at first, but by the time the dessert menu was offered, she was involving herself in conversation more and more.

It was actually rather simple to ingratiate herself with the others since it was mostly just an endless heckle of Albert. A non-stop request for him to quiet down or uninvolve himself from the current line of conversation. Albert took it with pride, accepting there heckling as a natural balance of his own chiding behaviour. Still, he found a way to enjoy himself by the time dessert rolled around.

"You didn't…" Marge stared dumbfounded at the giant bowl placed before Albert, filled to the brim with ice cream and fudge. Isabelle and Alex shared equally shocked looks with each other, watching as Albert's eyes lit up in delight.

"I definitely did."

He dug in, sending a smattering of icecream over the edge of the bowl. He was rather content with his oversized delight before being suddenly surprised by another spoon digging into his mess. Marge smirked at the other two, eating her spoonful of ice cream with a shrug. "There's no way he'd finish it alone."

The two continued their dessert with gusto, and by the time the check rolled around, everyone was happy. With one exception.

"Hey, why do I have to pay for it? We split it!"

"You order the ice; you pay the price." Marge smirked at him, getting up and leaving after paying her share. The other two follow, leaving Albert to sputter and complain about the rest of the bill.

**

It was about 25 minutes later and 36 kilometres north when Albert approached Alex. After dinner, the group had decided to take a little detour to a scenic spot up the coast. It was Friday after all, and the dinner had left them in good spirits. On the way up, Isabelle had flipped through radio stations, passing by boring classical and unremarkable world news to find a rock station. They jammed their way up the Howe Sound, following the Sea-to-Sky highway north and eventually parking at a sightseeing spot above the sea. Marge parked the car, almost bumping into the railing after being distracted by laughing at a joke Isabelle had told.

While the two girls headed over to look at the lights over the sound, Albert decided to have a chat with Alex. "So, did I do it, or what?" He had that smug look on his face that a cat tended to have after knocking over a vase.

Alex looked confusedly at Albert, tearing his eyes away from the dark shadows of islands on the sound below. "You did what?" Alex had a sinking feeling that he wouldn't like what he'd done.

"I did it. I got Margey to have fun."

Alex shook his head, smiling to himself. "By making a fool of yourself dude."

Albert smacked the roof of the car, causing the women to look back over at them. "Sorry!" He turned back to Alex, grinning mischievously. "That's the idea." He gestured grandly, winking.

Alex quirked an eyebrow, while Albert snickered. "The idea? You wanted to be the punching bag?"

"Yep." He gestures towards the other two with a smile. "It worked, didn't it?"

"You sly dog."

"Hey, it's a gift. Still, don't let that stop you from praising me as your new overlord!"

Albert blew the airhorn and took a bow, something that Alex found rather funny. Isabelle and Marge came back over to find the two leaning on the car and laughing like idiots. Isabelle shook her head, getting in the car, while Marge tried to grab their attention.

"Hey idiots, it's getting late. We should head back."

After a few more seconds of laughing at the sheer stupidity, the guys got in the backseat. Marge sat in the drivers' seat, turning to look at the rest of them. "Well, as much as agreeing to this was the dumbest thing I've ever done, this has been fun guys. I really appreciate it." She gave them a small smile. "We should do it again sometimes."

Everyone in the car nodded as Marge turned back around and started the car. The radio crackled to life. Isabelle cranked it up, expecting more rock music.

Instead, there was just a flat piercingly loud tone, followed by the words that would change the world.

"Repeat Message: Confirmed nuclear detonations along the Eastern Seaboard. I repeat, there are confirmed nuclear detonations on the Eastern Seaboard. This is not a drill. I repeat this is not a drill. Get to cover, now. A nuclear attack is imminent. I repeat a nuclear attack is imminent, get to cover now…"

The radio went to static after that, and the whole world went silent.

V: APOCALYPSE

Next, there was only a blur.

A cacophony of voices.

A sputtering of engines.

Marge flying northward, Isabelle yelling all the while.

Albert looking back, at the distant lights behind them. Someone else was screaming.

It was Alex himself.

Sirens blaring, going back to the south.

A cloak of trees hiding the sound behind them.

The sound that rent the earth, shattering it from the inside.

And an orange light, that burned the clouds away.

SHADOW OF THE CASCADE

1: UNDERGROWTH

Alex woke up shortly after dawn, head full of fire and brimstone. He was on the pine-strewn ground of a forest clearing. His eyes blinked out of synch, the muscles in his face startled now into waking. He sat up quietly, looking around. Albert and Isabelle were sprawled out around him, both seemingly enthralled in a restless sleep. Marge was leaning against a tree, looking towards the sky in a lost blank agony. Something struck in him and Alex pushed himself to his feet, walking over to her. His footsteps almost seemed to shake the ground, letting Marge know of his presence as she dragged her gaze back down to earth, and to him.

They stared at each other a moment.

"What the hell happened?" Alex's voice felt rough. Raw. He rubbed his throat, wincing at the tenderness within.

"The goddamn world ended. That's what happened." Marge sighed, slumping against the tree. "They blew it up. Perfectly timed too."

Alex could see something had gone out of her. It was the same look he saw in her when she was alone in her office, being faced with the turmoil of her failed experience. It was an empty look. A hollow one.

"I... I know that." Last night's radio announcement rung through his head. But it was a dull sound, distant and confusing. Like listening to someone else's life through a sheet of ice. "But I mean, what happened to us? Where are we?"

"Well, that's a question, isn't it?" She stayed quiet for a few moments, shaking her head. "Somewhere north. I don't know where really. I think we're somewhere around Squamish, that little town at the end of the sound. But screw it, we could be as far as Pemberton for all I know. It's messed up Alex. It's messed up. After the radio came on, something took hold of me. I don't know if it was self-preservation instincts or what, but I just drove. I drove away from Vancouver. Isabelle hated it, started yelling at me about going back. I just… I couldn't stop myself. Couldn't take my foot off the pedal. Albert was out of it. Just kept staring back at the city and whispering. I couldn't hear what he said because of you. You just kept screaming."

Alex shook his head, leaning against the tree next to her. He couldn't really put together what all of that meant. What it was. What had happened. The world had just ended, but here he was anyway. It didn't seem right. In all the movies he watched, all the books he read, the people who survived these sorts of things were the people that were ready. The preppers and the politicians. Everyone else got eviscerated. But him? He survived? He was just the PR guy.

"When the blast hit, the car shut down. I don't know why. Some magic wizard techno bullshit in the bomb probably. The highway was full of people and dark as hell, so I figured it would be better to get the hell out of Dodge. I had to drag Isabelle here, and Isabelle had to drag you two." She shook her head, going back to staring at the sky. "I just knew staying there would be bad. Instinct and all."

Alex joined her in looking at the sky. It was flatly grey. The kind of cloud cover that made you question if there were even clouds at all, or if the sky had just turned off.

At this point, he wouldn't count it out.

But farther south, towards Vancouver, he could see trails of black in the gray. Puffs of ashen smoke that streaked across the sky, settling among the other clouds like a cancer. It was a claw stretching northwards, and Alex could see the gently moving streaks were getting closer.

The two of them gazed at the heavens in silence for a while. Albert and Isabelle woke up in the meantime, but neither tried to disturb their ritual. They had to spend their own time picking up the pieces of what had happened. It was longer than Alex could count before he finally turned to Marge.

"So, what do we do now?"

She turned to look at him, then shrugged. "Find a gun, I guess. It's probably less likely to backfire than jumping off a cliff. Quicker than slitting wrists too."

Alex blinked at her. She blinked back. There was a shocked silence between them.

"You mean... for defence, right?" Alex's thoughts were somewhere along the lines of survival. Defying the odds, eeking out an existence. Doing something to keep himself going after what had just happened. Clearly, Marge thought otherwise.

"No. No Alex, I mean to shoot myself. If I'm feeling nice, I'll shoot you and Isabelle first. What's the point of it anyway?"

Alex straightened up from the tree, taking a step towards her. "Hey, no... don't talk like that. You don't have to do that."

"Uhuh. What else can I do?" She shrugged at him, the blank look on her face boring into his soul. "The world has ended. The kaput. Big Kaboom. Billions of people are dead, what the hells another one?"

Alex mulled it over a second. The wind whistled in the trees, and the cold chill of the mountains carried with it. He peeked through the trees at the towering peaks. Their shale cliff faces stretched towards the mute sky. Howe Sound was flanked on both sides by mountains. The highway followed the coast north, where it eventually cut down the middle of a valley northwards. He stared for a moment at the snow-capped peaks. At the enduring testament of the earth and the monoliths of Mother Nature that still withstood the test of time.

"It's a lot. It's a lot, Marge. You matter."

Marge just looked back at him with the same empty stare. Alex gulped, coughing to try to clear his throat. He waved at the other two to try to get their attention. They looked back at him with the same lost and empty gaze. "Look. I'm not... you guys know I'm not a good speech giver. I try to just sort of... watch a lot of the time. I'm not incredibly involved. But... screw it. I'll give it a shot. Really." Alex paused a moment, trying to figure out where he was going with this. It was pure improvisation, and he was panicking at the realization. "The world... the world hasn't ended. I mean, we're still here. The mountains and trees are still here, right? This... this is messed up. Royally, messed up. But it's not the end, right? We can keep going. It's going to be different. A lot different. Our lives will probably get harder. They'll definitely get harder. But we can't just... give up, can we?"

Isabelle and Albert nodded slowly. The hollowness in their eyes was still there, but there was an edge there now. A sharpness. Not of hope, or of acceptance. But of acknowledgement. The world hasn't ended. They hadn't ended. It made Alex feel... potential. That maybe what he had said was true.

Until Marge walked off into the woods.

"Sure we can. I'm going to go find that gun."

***

It had been an hour since Marge left. Isabelle and Albert were sat in the centre of the clearing, quietly talking about nothing. Words passed between them, but even from his spot at the edge of the clearing, Alex could tell that they didn't mean anything. They were more to fill the air, give life into the unsettling quiet that surrounded them. It was only when he decided to sit down with them that the conversation turned serious.

"We should have gone after her." Isabelle fidgeted in place, shivering a little from the wind. She kept checking back to the spot Marge had left, hoping that she would see her emerge from the foliage soon. "She's not right. What if she finds a gun Alex?"

"I know. I know. But... look, she's not here right now. Mentally and physically. I think if we tried to talk her down, it only would have gotten worse. Made her do something stupid. I... I hope we did the right thing."

"Of course you didn't." Heads turned towards the edge of the clearing as Marge emerged from the undergrowth. "I'm in a dark place right now, and you let me go look for a gun. That's stupid as shit."

"But... you're back?" Alex kept his eyes on her as she worked her way across the clearing and back towards the tree she was leaning against. "So you're ok?"

"Hell no. I'm just better. I cooled off and whatever the hell else." She shook her head. "Still pretty reckless of you to bet on that. I figured out where we are by the way. And it's royally screwed up."

"Royally how?" Alex looked in the direction he'd seen Matge go. He assumed that some sort of town must be that way, but he couldn't identify it through the trees, and the usual telltale signs of humanity were gone. No sound of the highways and no honks of horns. Only the wind in the trees and the scattered chattering of birds.

"I think it's better if you saw it for yourself."

"That's dramatic." Albert smirked, but it was a pained smirk. The usual charm was gone, scattered like the wind that whistled through the spruce trees. He brought himself to his feet, digging his hands into his pockets and shrugging. "Lead the way then."

Marge shrugged, beckoning the other two to step in line after Albert as he followed her into the forest. "Follow me, and be careful, alright? I'm not sure how safe it is."

Their footsteps were quiet on the soft earth beneath their feet.

The trees above cast a shadow onto the group below, hiding them in the darkness of the shade. It was a relatively short walk, but it seemed to drag on a while. Alex couldn't tell why. Eventually though, they reached what Marge had wanted to show them. Ahead, there was a wall of foliage, an unkept hedge of bushes and berries that reached almost up to the start of the leaves on the trees. Between them, a small sliver of gray, the distant sky peeking between the green.

Marge ducked between the bushes, gesturing for the others to do the same. Alex and Albert followed, moving next to her. Isabelle stayed back.

On the other side of the undergrowth, there was a small hill rolling down to a road. Or at least, that's what Alex thought was supposed to be there. About a quarter of the way up the hill was water.

"What the hell is... where did the town go?"

Marge pointed farther out. Buildings peaked out of the water, monuments in a sea of dirty and clouded water. The town was underwater

"We're definitely in Squamish. It's right on the sound, so when the shockwave hit the water..." Marge turned to the other two, gesturing with her hands to imitate an explosion. "It must have sent a monster of a wave down the sound. Flooded the whole downtown area."

"Damn... what should we do?" Alex tried to see if he could locate anyone in the town. A survivor, somebody who needed help, anyone. "I don't see anyone, but..."

"What do you mean what do we do? It's a flooded town, there's nothing to do but watch the funny little waves be where they aren't supposed to be."

Marge ducked back out of the bushes, followed quickly by Albert. Alex spent a few more seconds surveying the wreckage of the town, before ducking back into the wild in the same way. He'd hoped that they could have helped somehow, but all they'd seen was water and a dead town. It wasn't the most inspiring of scenes.

Alex digested this rather cynical outlook while Albert shook his head. "This made you hopeful Margey? Shit, I think it's doing the opposite to me."

Marge winced. "Not more hopeful, no. But... realistic, I guess. Damn it, I don't know. I just know that seeing all that made me realize that Alex is right. They might be screwed, but we're not. Yet. We have the luxury of giving up so we damn well better not. So, what do we do?"

Alex looked at Albert, then at Marge. She furrowed her brow. "I think... I think that's your decision. I mean, you are the boss, right?" Alex shifted slightly where he stood, alternating pressure on each of his feet.

"Alex, what? No, I'm your... I'm not the boss anymore. I don't think the corporate chain applies to post-nuclear hellscapes." Marge didn't look offended. Or angry. She just looked confused. Alex did realize that it was perhaps a little silly to consider the corporate ladder when making decisions after what had just happened, but it made sense to him.

"Well... you lead us here, didn't you? You kept going while the rest of us panicked. I just figure maybe it would make sense if you stayed in charge."

"Well, I think that's the dumbest shit ever. You gave the inspiring speech, why the hell don't you lead us?" When Alex didn't say anything, Marge spread her arms theatrically. "In that case, I guess we don't have a leader, and that's ok. So with that settled, who the hell has any ideas?

"Paradise Valley." Everyone turned to Albert. He raised his eyebrows and spread out his hands. "Makes sense, right? It's north of here, so we'd be farther away from whatever heeby jeebies are crawling out of Vancouver. Plus it's pretty damn empty, and it's got all those amenities we spent millions of dollars screwing around with. Like that salmon hatchery we invested so much in, remember?. It just makes sense."

"Was… was that a good idea from Albert?" Marge looked at the other two with shock, raising an eyebrow.

"Hey, don't be like that. I'm trying to think here while you two jabber. So, are we going, or not?"

"Well, it's a good option and all." Marge looked towards the north, or at least towards what Alex assumed was the north. "But maybe we should consider other options."

"No, I'm… I'm pretty sure he's right." Alex stepped over towards Albert, nodding. Isabelle stayed quiet but went to join the boys. She hadn't said much so far, and clearly the idea of having something to aspire towards mattered to her. Now only Marge was left opposing the idea.

"Fine! Fine. I guess we'll go to Paradise Valley. Because that's a reminder I needed in my life."

Without another word, she set off. Albert shrugged at Alex with a small grin, then followed her into the woods, flanked by the other two.

Paradise, here they come.

2: EXODUS

The valley that stretched north of the Howe Sound was covered in a thriving evergreen forest, cut down the middle by a winding highway that wound it's way north. Only a few towns sprung from this highway, intersecting across it in a criss-cross pattern. Squamish, Whistler and Pemberton were all in a rough line north along the thoroughfare before it cut east and inland just after Pemberton. Aside from these limited settlements, the rest of the area was wild, inhabited and dominated by nature. It was only natural then, that the group would choose to follow the road until they reached Paradise Valley. They walked through the forest at an angle, heading northeast rather than just north. When they neared the highway, the silence of the surrounding world began to shatter. Shouts came first. Then the crying of children. By the time they stood behind the foliage that separated them from the rest of the world, regular conversation could be heard from beyond. Upon poking their head through the bushes, they knew why.

A steady stream of people made their way north along the highway. They weaved between fried cars and trucks, intent on their purpose. Most of them looked exhausted; ragged and confused as they moved their way up the road with a distant look and a steady pace. It was like a scene from a horror movie, a parade of lost souls on their way to meet Charon.

"What the..." Alex stepped out of the bushes. Isabelle and Albert followed. They stared, shocked, at the tide of refugees, before being pulled back into the woods by Marge.

"What the hell are you guys doing?!" Her whisper was quiet but frantic. She peeked out through the foliage as she spoke, eyes wide and paranoid. "Don't go out there!"

Alex gently pulled himself away from Marge, looking questioningly at her. "What? Why? It's just a bunch of people." Admittedly, they were rather dour people, but still, Alex couldn't quite understand Marge's panic. "They must be refugees, like us."

"Exactly. Shit, think about it! That is a whole highway full of desperate people!" Marge almost hissed now, eyes flaring up with energy. "Jesus Alex, Vancouver just goddamn exploded! They've lost everything! Who knows what they'd be willing to do?"

"Why are they like that?" Isabelle was peeking through beneath the others, and Alex followed her gaze to a pair of squabbling guys who seemed to be arguing over an improvised wooden club. "They seem... off."

It was true enough. It must have only been hours since the end of the world, but these people seemed like they'd spent weeks somewhere darker. It wasn't a physical abnormality or even one that would be noticed without a certain level of attention. It was something with the way they carried themselves, like the weight of the world was on their back and it was getting to the point where they might as well collapse. It was a hollow look.

"Well, we can't walk through the forest forever, can we?" Albert crossed his arms, snapping Alex out of his analysis. "I say, we give the dirty unwashed masses a shot!"

"We *can* walk through the forest, and we will, Albert. I'd rather do that than figure out why they have those clubs." Marge turned and walked off again, expecting the rest to follow her.

They did, but not before Albert snuck in a snide comment. "I thought she didn't want to lead?"

Marge led them through the forest on the side of the highway, keeping close enough to follow the noise and maintain their heading. Progress was slow, with the bushes scraping and cutting at their skin with shallow swipes that made their skin itch. From time to time, an outburst could be heard from the highway, shouts that mixed with sickening thumps and crunches, unpleasant noises that indicated a struggle. Curiosity got the better of him and Alex made the mistake of trying to see one of these fights. All he managed was a glimpse of someone's jaw being broken on a divider before Marge pulled him back into the woods. He didn't try to peek again.

After about 10 minutes of silent and sullen traversal, the forest cut short, falling into a gully that separated the highway from a commercial zone. The bottom of the gully was pooled with water, and it was a struggle to convince Albert that wading into the knee-deep water was better than the parade of psychos on dry land. In the end, they had to drag him in, something that resulted in a good measure of splashing and a few glances from the refugees. Fortunately, as of now they were too preoccupied with their own struggles and nobody disturbed them, and they made it halfway down the gully before Albert kicked up a fuss again.

"Look, as much as I love wading through this mud, I think maybe we should try walking on land. Like people. This whole thing is idiotic."

"Albert, shut up! This is what we're doing, ok? Now stop drawing attention to us!" Marge spoke in the sort of shrill whisper that somehow sounded as loud as a shout. It barely did the job of keeping a low profile.

"I thought you weren't in charge?" He started climbing up the side of the gully, flashing a cheeky grin at Marge. "So I don't really see why I have to listen to you."

"Albert!"

But it was too late, Albert was already on the shoulder of the road. He looked down at the rest of them and winked, walking dramatically on the land. Marge was fuming, and she looked like she was about to jump up there and strangle him. Alex just kept trudging, hoping Isabelle would calm the two down. Just keep walking, and don't look back. If you can't see the argument, it doesn't exist at all.

But hearing the argument grow from whispers to shouts has a way of escalating the situation. Alex turned filled with trepidation and already a good bit ahead. Someone from the highway had come over to Albert, yelling something unintelligible. Now Albert was back in the ditch, and the woman had pushed him in. She screamed at them, cursing their names and threatening to bash their heads in with the rusty tire iron that she had somehow procured. Spittle flew from her mouth, her eyes no longer hollow but angry and paranoid. Something incited in her as Alex trudged back to the other three, something basic and primal. Someone else, another woman, tried to pull the attacker away, but after a moment of hesitation, she jumped into the ditch and started swinging.

It was madness, a three against one with no space to spare. But the other three were taken by surprise so badly by the sudden turn of events that Albert was hit hard twice in the elbow and Isabelle was jabbed once in the stomach before Alex was able to jump at their assailant from behind and wrestle the weapon away.

He held it close to him, moving so he was between the crazy lady and the rest of the group. She hissed at them, backing up down the gully clumsily.

"Bandits! Wood people! You've come to prey on the rest of us! Hiding in the shadows so you can pick us off one by one!"

"Wow Albert looks like you found a keeper. Great job asshole." Marge's words dripped with sarcasm, and Albert didn't respond. Alex didn't particularly care about intra-personal politics right now, focusing more on the raving madwoman in front of them. She hadn't moved, still staring them down with an intense glare.

"We don't want to hurt you! Seriously! Just... leave, please. We just want to keep going."

What followed was probably the strangest possible thing. She giggled. "Oh no, that's not true. You're hiding in gulches, pulling women into the mud! Hellfire wasn't enough for you!"

Marge shouldered past Alex, trying to grab the tire iron from him. "Give me that Alex. You attacked us bitch! Leave us alone or I'll leave you in the dirt!"

Alex held onto the tire iron trying to hold Marge back. "No! Come on, please. We can solve this without anybody needing to get hurt."

"More hurt! That bitch hit Albert and Isa! That shit's not ok!"

Isa clutched her stomach, trying to step up next to Marge. "Marge it's ok. Just let her go, alright? She's just scared. Watch..."

The woman looked between the two of them, spat on the ground, then scampered back up the side of the gully. Alex let out a big sigh of relief, dropping the tool into the murky water at their feet. Marge sighed, glancing back at Albert, who was clutching his arm and moaning.

"Maybe stay in the gully next time?"

It was another 10 minutes of slogging before they reached the end of the gully. At one point, it was crossed by a road that cut off from the highway, which was intermittently crossed by refugees seeking shelter in town. Even after the assault, Albert and Alex weren't willing to crawl through the drainpipe that passed underneath it to avoid them, so they had to wait for a few minutes until there was barely anyone crossing the road.

While they waited, they spoke in hushed whispers, watching the trickle of people stumble into town. Albert kept rubbing his arm, grumbling to himself about it. "What was that anyway?"

Marge shook her head, keeping a close eye on each of the passing people. "That was someone not listening to me. Didn't I tell you that these people are on edge? I mean, goddamn, look at us! We've already resorted to crawling through ditches, and we weren't direct witnesses to God's express delivery of hell."

"You made us crawl through the ditch Margey. You're the one one who's lowering the bar here."

"Because everyone else is. Hey, maybe we can take the road next time, so Albert can break his other arm. Those are desperate goddamn people, ok? We need to avoid them because desperate people do desperate things."

"It's not broken. I'd be screaming more if it was."

"Could you two just… shush for a moment?" Alex checked the road. It looked clear, and the next few people who could cross it were a while back. "Let's go, now."

Once on the other side, the gulley resumed, as did their slog. They finally collapsed once they were in the forest again. A small boulder gave them enough space to all sit and rest while letting Isabelle and Albert look at their wounds.

"Damn, that hurt…"

Isabelle nodded. "Yeah. I guess you shouldn't have jumped up there, huh?"

Albert laughed. It wasn't a happy laugh, more tinged with regret that humour. "Yeah, that's on me huh? Guess I'm paying for that."

Isabelle shook her head. "We're both paying for that."

"Well sure, but maybe me just a little bit more? I got hit twice!"

While the two of them bickered, Alex looked for some sort of sustenance. He found some blackberries and started picking the ripe ones. He used his jacket as a basket, grabbing as many as he could for the group. They hadn't eaten since last night, and he didn't think the adrenaline would keep them going forever.

Marge joined him after a little while, helping him pick. "There's a little road up ahead. It's got trees on both sides, and I didn't see any people on it so it's probably safe."

"That's what you said about the gully."

"Hey, screw you! It would have worked fine if Albert hadn't been an idiot. It's not my fault he decided to ignore me." She scoffed at him, picking a little clumsily and cutting herself lightly on a thorn.

Alex backed off, shrugging his shoulders meekly. "Whoah, calm down. I was just joking. Trying to lighten the mood a little."

She picked a berry angrily, yanking it from the stem and depositing it in his makeshift basket. "Well, save it. I have to deal with Albert's nonsense, I don't want to deal with yours. You can't exactly lighten the mood when the mood is a goddamn black hole."

Alex shrugged. "I think that's exactly when you should lighten the mood."

"Whatever. The point is this is a serious situation. A serious, goddamn situation and I don't want to put up with his chaotic neutral jester act. I just wish he'd shut up and listen to me."

"Like a leader?" Alex raised an eyebrow at her. "You don't get to tell him not to do that if you aren't."

"You're an asshole Alex. What do you want from me? To say I want to be a leader? This isn't some corporate ladder that I had to climb with wits. This is survival. I don't want that. I'm just a take-charge sort of person."

"Right... well, I think..."

Marge cut him off before he could even get his thoughts in line. "I don't want to know what you think! This is bad enough without you trying to elevator pitch a democracy!" She had that look in her eyes he remembered from the board room. The kind of look that demanded the silence of anyone who opposed what she thought. The irony easily registered for him.

"...I was going to say, I think we picked the bush clean." He gestured with his head at the jacket full of blackberries.

"Oh. Right. Uh… shit, let's just get back to the boulder."

**

The berries went over well. By the time they were ready to move on, the flat grey sky had brightened and Alex's jacket was covered in berry stains. When they started walking again, Isabelle had to lean on Albert's uninjured arm for support. She grimaced a little, still clutching her stomach.

"Maybe you shouldn't have let the muscle tighten up." Alex walked on her other side, vigilant in case she ended up needing more support.

"Yeah. Ow. Definitely."

They broke through the treeline again, emerging onto a mercifully empty road. It was just like Marge had described, surrounded by forest and so peacefully and wonderfully bare.

They hobbled their way down the road, talking quietly among themselves.

"So, remind me again why we're not growing third arms right now? Where's all the radiation?" Albert was struggling a little less than Isabelle, using her for support almost as much as she was using him. "That *was* a nuclear bomb, right?"

Isabelle winced, nodding. "I guess maybe we're far enough away?"

Alex shook her head. "From the blast yeah. The actual explosion probably wasn't powerful enough to send radiation this far north. And since the wind is blowing southwards, we'll… probably be ok."

"Well, that's really comforting." Albert snickered to himself. "So I won't start glowing?"

Alex shook his head. "The radiation we'd get would probably be more long term than immediately deadly. Cancer, genetic disorders in our kids… that sort of thing."

"Bold of you to think of kids right now dude. I admire the player in you." Albert smirked, looking back towards the way they came. "But hey, there are two of us, two of them. Repopulation isn't an OW!"

Marge had smacked him on the back of the head. She looked thoughtful, glancing at her feet. "What about the water?"

"Uh… I'm not sure." Alex scratched his head, trying to remember what he'd learned about radiation. It wasn't much that was applicable, and he could only barely remember anything at all. "I mean, the wave started at the blast wave… so it might have carried some nuclear material with it. I don't know. I'm basically bullshitting here from best guesses."

"You know, you sharing your best guesses would have been good before I got knee-deep in that ditch water. Just for future reference." Albert now also glanced at his feet, more worried this time.

"…let's just say it'll be fine." Marge shook her head quietly. "We have enough to worry about."

"Repression, great. I got plenty of that going on here." Albert stopped and the end of the road. It lead to a three-way intersection. To the right the road started to wind a little through the trees, running alongside a swollen river before intersecting again at a bridge over it. To the left, a road that led down a hill and into floodwaters.

Most notably of all, straight ahead of them was a raging fire.

3: DISRUPTION

A series of apartment buildings were meant to be there. At least that's what the signage out front said. From where the group was standing, it seemed there was only fire. Several people ran around, sprinting over to the flood's edge and grabbing buckets before running back and spilling the water onto the blaze. It was essentially hopeless, and there was a pause in the little group as they watched them struggle.

"We should go. Paradise Valley is up over that bridge, and we're still pretty far away." Marge pointed at the intersection and started walking. Alex, however, stood still. He watched the struggle for a moment, seeing the way the people scrambled. How they ran and ran, carrying the small hope of salvation with them and promptly spilling it all over the pavement.

It struck him, and even as the battle grew more and more fruitless, as the blaze grew higher and higher, all he saw was more determination and effort to put it down.

One of the scurrying people eventually sat back on the blacktop, watching the way the sparks flew up towards the cloudy sky. His arms were limp, fruitlessly realizing the futility of the situation. He locked onto the sight of his home burning and wept. He was a pitiful figure, played against the dark ground like the centre of a tragic renaissance portrait.

"Hey Alex, hurry up!"

Alex waved dismissively, distracted by the presentation in front of him. "Just a minute..." He walked over to the man, crouching next to him and ignoring the protests of his group as he did so. He touched the man on the shoulder, trying to get him to acknowledge that he was here. It didn't seem to work at all. The man just kept staring forward at the fire, lost to the world as it enveloped everything he knew.

Alex looked around for a moment, finding the discarded bucket on the ground. He picked it up, looking it over and running things through in his head. He could admit the futility of the attempt, throw the bucket away and try to talk sense into the man. Or...

The man on the ground found the bucket thrust into his hands. His grip tightened around it, looking confusedly up at Alex. "What... what are you doing?"

"Telling you not to give up dude. You've got this." The words spilled out of Alex's mouth, and he wasn't even sure why. "You can't give up.

"I-I have to. It's all burning, and I can't do shit." His eyes permeated an emptiness. It wasn't like the refugees from the highway, it wasn't shock or surprise. It was simple and utter defeat.

"The only reason you can't do something is because..." Alex paused. He tried to remember some famous quote about fear, or defeat. "... is because you give up on doing it."

The man nodded slowly, wiping his eyes and picking himself up to his feet. He took a deep breath, turning and running towards the floodwaters once more. Alex watched him go, smiling to himself until Marge yanked him away.

Marge waited until they were at the bridge, away from the smoke clouds and the crackling of the fire, to lay into Alex.

"What the hell was that? What the hell were you doing?"

Alex shook his head, mumbling an apology. He didn't really know why he did that. It was just something about the scene, something about the way the man was so broken and distant that made him try to step up and push him back to his feet. He realized now that it was a stupidly risky move. The man could have done anything when he showed up. The refugees just how quickly can snap. Very."

"What if they follow us? I mean, goddamn Alex, you could have just screwed us all over. Jesus Christ…"

All he could do was take the abuse. Eventually, Marge cooled off enough to take the lead again, leaving Alex trailing at the back of the group as they crossed the bridge.

Once on the other side, the group cut down a path that wound over a cliff next to the river. Usually, it was a steep slope that lead to the river's edge, but the flooding had raised its banks so high that it threatened to lap at the edge of the path.

"Ok… so I think this is the right way." Isabelle gazed into the cloudy river, rubbing her neck. She was walking on her own now, no longer needing Albert for support. "If we follow this path, it'll take us to the intersection that leads off to Paradise Valley. I think. From there, we just need to pass through Cheekye…"

They spent around an hour walking the trail. By now, thirst had also begun to take its toll. Berries were picked and their juices used as a supplement for water, but it just wasn't effective. There were mutterings about trying the river water, but nobody was eager to drink the swirling vortex of dirt and water. Alex had a burning feeling in his lungs by the time they reached the end of the trail. Unfortunately, it ended by going straight into a freshly upturned swamp.

"What?" Isabelle stepped to the edge of the water, right where the trail descended underneath the waterline. "Oh no… the flood, it…"

"It sunk the trail. Well hell, of course it did…" Marge took a deep breath, closing her eyes and collecting her thoughts. "Ok. Damn it, guess we're getting our feet wet again."

Albert crossed his arms, wincing as he remembered his injury. "Hell no! You heard what Alex said, the shit could be full of radiation or something! I'm not walking through all that!"

"Well, what then? Go around? That'll cost us an hour, and we're already losing daylight here. No, we have to go through."

"Well then Margey, if you want to tell us what to do, but not be the leader, I guess we have to put it up to a vote." Albert smirked at her, winking at Alex.

"Fine. Let's vote then. All in favour of taking the longer and harder route, raise their hands" Marge put her hands on her hips, scowling expectantly at them.

Alex took one look at the swirling waters of the newly upturned swamp and decided that going around would be safer. He and Albert both raised their hands. Isabelle tentatively raised hers, then lowered it again. Finally, she seemed to make up her mind and held her hand up.

Marge stared at her, astonished. "Isa?" This was the first time that Alex remembered seeing her so surprised, and more so seeing Isabelle so conflicted.

"I'm sorry Marge, it's just... I think Albert is right. What if it's radioactive?"

"Oh, so we're listening to Albert now. I see how it is. Well, let's go then. Through the goddamn woods of darkness and into the place with all the crazy skeleton people. Sounds like a fun time."

***

As they headed off the path and into the forest, skirting the edge of the water, Isabelle shook her head. "I'm sorry Marge..."

"Oh, you will be when you get your face mauled off by a cannibal or something once we intrude on their territory. I'll be sorry too; they'll use my damn bones as a seasoning!" She slumped her shoulders, muttering angrily to herself.

"Why are you so paranoid, Marge?" Alex walked in line ahead of her, glancing back. "It's not like the bomb flipped a switch or anything... these are still just regular people. Sure, there are some bad apples, but… I mean, what would you expect from people who just went through that? Who knows, we might even find help in town."

"Alex, this isn't goddamn Happy Days. This is the end of the goddamn world. Everything that anyone ever knew just disintegrated. The good Samaritans of this world have snapped for Christ's sake. If you show up to someone's door, begging for help like candy on Halloween, you're going to get chased off like a rabid dog." Marge spoke with venom in her voice, seething with some sort of inner rage.

Alex really didn't like the sound of it. "We could at least try. If you're right, you're right, but I don't think people are that far gone…"

"Go ahead." Marge rolled her eyes. "But I won't feel bad when someone is wearing your face as a party hat."

Isabelle sidestepped to walk in between them. "Can we not fight, please? Really, it's… making me uncomfortable."

"You and Albert fight all the time. About stupid shit. This is a real issue Isa." Marge tried to cut ahead of her. "And stop trying to get ahead of me."

Isabelle was firm in standing between Marge and Alex, even as the bushes and undergrowth they walked through became thicker. "Me and Albert bicker over nothing. It's… just how we small talk. It's not an argument, and it's definitely not a fight."

"Oh, side with them then, you've already done it before. Why break the goddamn streak?"

"Marge, this isn't about sides, ok? We're all in this together, right?" Alex slowed down a little, putting less focus on trailblazing and more on looking back at Marge. "Cooperating is how we're going to get through this. Everyone but you thought this was the right way to go so… sorry, but it's what we're doing."

"You're really shitty at apologies Alex."

Alex sighed, continuing to cut through the woods. The difficult terrain continued for a while, causing even more scratches and cuts on their arms and legs. Even worse, it started to rain, with the drops falling quick and thick down upon them. It was a miserable hike, and Marge was sure to smile smugly every time someone complained. At one point, Alex pushed a branch out of the way and let it go without thinking, wincing when it cut back whipped Isabelle in the face.

He ended up having to apologize profusely.

By the time they reached civilization, they were soaking wet and exhausted. Even worse, they hadn't cut into a road. Instead, all they were met with was a line of backyard fences.

Albert crossed his arms with a *hmm.* "Well, that's not good." Everyone looked at him. "What?"

"Let's just follow these until we find the path again. Or maybe we should invade someone's backyard? Let's put it to a vote." Marge was really just being a pest now, and it was getting on everyone's nerves.

Even Albert's. "Oh, shush Margey. You were right, no need to rub all our faces in it."

"In your case Albert, there's plenty of need."

The brown picket fence was rather constant. It stretched for quite a while, leading off as the edge of suburbia. As they walked, the sounds of struggle permeated over the rooftops and through the cracks between houses. Shouting, glass breaking, gunfire. It ruptured the air abruptly from time to time, breathing manic insecurity into the air. The fence separated them from chaos, the struggle of a world recently turned on its head. Alex's heart sank as he realized that maybe Marge had a point. He occasionally glanced over the fence at a few of the houses they passed, hoping to find evidence to the contrary. Some of them were empty, others filled with light and noise. Alex was tempted to leap over the fence a couple of times, try to see if he could talk to some people to find or provide help, to prove that the world hadn't suddenly turned into a mass of bloodthirsty monsters, but Marge's constant pace kept him moving.

"See that assholes?" Marge pointed at one of the houses, watching as someone through a chair through the back window with a blood-curdling scream. "That shit's why we need to hurry up. It's a madhouse."

The very next house was calm, occupied by a family watching a movie on their TV. The difference was striking. Alex paused, trying to think of something to say to point out the normalcy to Marge. He started to speak, but his words dried up in his mouth when he saw the shotgun that was laid next to the couch they sat on. His face drained of blood, making him shake his head and keep moving. Marge seemed to be right about the danger.

"How do these places have power?" Isabelle walked with a slump, holding her jacket tight around her to try to protect from the rain. "Where are they getting it from? Wouldn't that weird pulse thing that took out all the cars turn it off?"

"Most of the valley's power comes from a dam upriver from here. They rehashed the system a few years ago to protect against E-M pulses. They even integrated the same sort of protection into a few of the more vulnerable household items." Albert scratched his neck, looking at one of the lit-up houses. "Maybe they figured that something like this would happen."

Silence.

"Albert, what the hell?" Marge looked a little shocked. "How do you know that?"

"That's my job?" He raised his eyebrows. "Or it was. I worked on the infrastructure, remember?"

"*That's* what you did? I always thought you were the on-site jackass!" Marge shook her head. "So that's why it was so hard to fire you..."

"I do things. Smart things." He grinned, winking. "Most of the time."

"So that means we'll have power in Paradise Valley?"

"Eh… sort of. Why do you think I suggested it? We've got to have a way to watch our MTV, don't we?"

"And now the jackass is back. Great." Marge sighed. Alex and Isabelle looked at each other and shrugged, not knowing what to make of it.

By now, they had reached the end of the fences. Ahead of them was a small stretch of woods, then a clear cut stretch of land that surrounded a straight line of sizable powerlines. After a brief excursion, they fought their way through the brush onto a gravel trail that ran alongside them.

"Huh. I think this might actually be a better route." Isabelle traced the direction of the powerlines with her finger, pointing the way forward. "If we follow these, it should take us to the substation. From there, we just follow another set of lines to Paradise Valley."

"And it would avoid any civilization?" Marge looked interested, raising an eyebrow.

"Well, there's Cheekye… but that's just a couple of houses really. We'll be fine."

"Famous last words?" Albert snickered a little. "Or would you prefer 'I think we're going to make it'? That one is fun"

"Actually, I think my famous last words will be 'Oh no, I accidentally stabbed Albert.', so I can get one good thing out of it." Isabelle bit back. She was right, they *did* bicker.

"Ok, shut up with your shit. We've still got to walk, so Alex… Alex?"

"Huh?" Alex had gotten distracted, watching the way the water fell down the tower that held up the powerline. The small droplets cascaded down towards the earth, trickling into puddles and pools that competed for purchase against the slick gravel of the path. "Yeah? What?"

"My God man get your head on straight. Let's go already" Marge looked at him in the weird way people sometimes did, it was the look that told him he was a grade-A dumbass. He preferred not to dwell upon it as the group treaded their way north. By now, the sun was getting lower in the sky, starting to approach the peaks around them. Within an hour, the peaks were painted gold in the setting sun as dusk came towards the world. It was the end of the first day since the apocalypse, and soon the night would come.

4: SUBSPACE

The group had just entered Cheekye when the sun disappeared behind the mountains. Cheekye was a village that constituted little more than a couple of residential buildings and small businesses; surrounded by wilderness and cut through by a single road. Only one of them was lit up, the bright lights of its ground floor windows accentuating the dark shadows over the rest of the town.

It was by this light that the group made their way into town, staying quiet as to not alert the residents. They took cover inside of a derelict gift shop, sifting through the empty shelves and discarded merchandise. Alex found a camping light, fumbling around in the darkness with knobs and buttons until flipping a switch and bathing the room in its eerie glow.

The other three flocked towards the underwhelmingly stark light like moths, using it to find their own handheld lights. With these new beacons, they fully explored the discarded and defunct items that had been abandoned a long while ago.

"So, Albert, why do these work?" Isa gestured at her lamp, simultaneously poking at a small electronic display of the river that was meant to light up and play a sound when someone pressed the button. "Wouldn't they be messed up like the cars and things?"

"I know why, actually." Alex peered over at her from between the shelves. "When we set Paradise Valley up, we wanted to encourage tourists to buy from associated businesses like this one instead of unaffiliated competitors. So, we decided to market these as 'Survival Lamps'. Means they're pretty tough."

"What, so this place was run by Macedon Tours?"

"They were on contract." Marge rummaged through an ice-cream freezer, trying to find something that wasn't long melted and spoiled. "Cheekye was supposed to be the gateway to Paradise Valley. Macedon Tours sponsored a couple of shops and put up some signs. Might have grown the town to something bigger if we'd succeeded."

"Instead...?" Albert grinned to himself as he looked at her through a small pair of binoculars he'd found.

"Instead, we crashed, the town crashed, eventually the world crashed, and very soon your nose is going to crash if you bring it up again." Marge smacked the binoculars out of his hand, sending them clattering to the floor.

"Sheesh... fine. I'll be in the can if you need me. I've been busting all day."

Alex laughed, inspecting a silvery foil package. "I saw an outhouse when we came in... I don't think there's a toilet."

"Well shit. Literally."

The little bell dinged over the doorway as Albert went outside. Alex came over to Marge and Isabelle, holding up what he'd found. "Do you think this camping food is still good? I'm starving."

Marge took the package from him, turning it around in her hands. "I'd say so. It's not going to be really good, but it's better than..."

The three were interrupted by a flash of light, a bang and a scream all at once, coming from behind the building. In just a moment, the three discarded their findings and ran outdoors into the pouring rain and towards the sounds of a struggle.

Behind the building, illuminated only by the light of Albert's camping light, they found him wrestling with another man. Dark blood stained the ground as the man put his hands around

Albert's throat and started to squeeze. Beside them was a semi-automatic hunting rifle, tossed down onto the wet grass carelessly. Alex froze up at the sight, barely able to understand what he was seeing. Isabelle screamed, the sound piercing the night like a dagger. The man turned upon hearing the sound, face contorted into a maddened rage.

His turning coincided right into the sole of Marge's shoe as she kicked at his face. He stumbled back on the grass, clutching his face before jumping at Marge in a rage. He yelled obscenities at her, crashing her to the hard ground. "I TOLD YOU SONS OF BITCHES TO STAY OFF MY LAND!"

Marge barely managed to hold him off, trying to push the man away as he lifted his fist to punch her across the face. "Help me goddamnit! Don't just stand there!"

Alex looked between the two grappling on the ground. He looked at Albert, struggling for breath and holding his shoulder. He looked at Isabelle, as frozen as he was, eyes locked on the battle. And finally, he looked at the gun, laying alone and abandoned on the ground.

Before he even knew it, he had stumbled over to it and grabbed it. Clumsily, he found the trigger, nearly pressing it pre-emptively in a panic as he tried to aim the gun at the man. He finally got a good grip on it, hand almost slipping from the rain.

"Stop! Back off! Back... back off of her! I don't want to shoot you!"

The man ignored him, finally managing to land a blow to Marge's face. She screamed, kicking up at him ferociously and fighting back with fury. His hands locked around her throat, and she coughed in his face, struggling to breathe. "GODDAMNIT, SHOOT HIM ALEX!"

Alex shook, trying to steady himself. He pointed the barrel at the man's body, trying to steady it and failing badly. "Please! Please just back off!"

Marge's struggle started to become weaker. He saw the way his hands clutched her throat, the way her face contorted in pain and rage. And he knew that he had to stop it. In that last moment, he thought he saw the man turn to him, realize what was about to happen.

There was a flash of light, the kick of a gun, and the man fell to the side, dead.

For a moment, there was silence, only the patter of the rain on the soaked grass to make a sound. Albert sat up, still clutching his shoulder which leaked a semi-constant stream of blood. "Well Margey, I think we found that gun you wanted…"

***

Things flashed around Alex. Shapes and colours that ended up being meaningless. Sounds that mixed with each other in tormented and unfocused ways. Lights swinging in the darkness, sickly with their glow over the grass. He ignored it. He couldn't see it. Just the hole he'd left in the man's head, gushing blood like a waterfall that fell to the earth and painted its core crimson red. There was a hand on his shoulder, pulling him away and prompting him to walk. He walked. He walked until the corpse was out of sight, but not out of mind. The distant tinkle of a bell was the crashing of a gong, a cue that reverberated through him eternally. He sat on the cold hard ground, squeezing his eyes shut and hoping that it was thusly the end.

***

Morning came with a bright sunstrike over the mountains. The clouds were illuminated gold for a moment, hanging heavy on the valley with the promise of more rain. The long trails of ashen smoke had settled into the rest of the sky, dotting it like pepper flakes and working their imperfection on a canvas of nature. Alex sat unfocused and unresponsive at the display window, peaking through the boards in front of the shop at the world outside. People shifted around behind him in the darkened interior of the shop, groaning and talking to each other.

To him, it didn't really matter. Other things were lodged in his mind, fighting with his conscious to take precedence.

He'd killed a man. Shot and killed someone with a rifle in the dead of night. Murder. Even the golden light above the peaks and clouds couldn't wash away that stain. It spread through him like the ash above, deepening the shadows within himself.

Isabelle looked at him from where she sat. She looked at Marge, covered in red marks from the impact of yesterday's fight and still trying to bring together anything that could be useful. She looked at Albert, sleeping restlessly with his shoulder wrapped haphazardly in the gauze they'd found in the back room's first aid kit. She looked at herself, shaking in the half-light of the sunrise and sitting uselessly on a sleeping bag, unable to do anything at all for the rest of them. She sighed.

Marge looked up at the sound, trying to shove another packet of camping food into the backpack she'd found. She grumbled something about Isabelle's uselessness, wincing in pain from the blows she'd taken to the head last night. The pain helped her focus, everything around her being crisp and clear as day. She hooked the rest of the first-aid kit into the handle of the backpack, using a rope to tie the rifle they'd picked up onto the side. She wasn't particularly happy with the results, and the groans of dissatisfaction reached Albert's ears as he woke up slowly.

His vision was blurred, eyes heavy with exhaustion. Pain throbbed through his shoulder, arcing tendrils of lightning that worked their way through him with unrelenting and uncaring force. He tried to sit up, gasping with the pure expression of agony that coursed from the wound. What a world he figured it was, where a man could be shot trying to go to the toilet. He flashed back to the night before, the way the world had unfolded before him. One moment, things were better. They had shelter and food. The promise of a Paradise to come the next day. Now, he was injured. Alex was broken. A single roadblock had shattered them, dragging them down to the earth. All he could do was laugh at the way things worked.

His laughter seemed to snap everyone to attention. Isabelle sat next to him, Marge looked over and even Alex snapped out it just a little bit. He pulled himself away from the window, stumbling towards the other three. The dead man had not left his mind, and really, he realized he probably never would. But for now, he could focus on what was right in front. The people around him and the task before them.

Marge spoke first, and with an expectedly bitter tone. "Well, that was the goddamn worst."

"For me maybe." Albert winced, shutting his eyes tight and blinking them back open. "You didn't get shot on the shitter."

"No, yeah, you're right, I wasn't idiotic enough to get nearly killed by someone with a cowboy hat."

"Did he have a cowboy hat?" Alex tried to remember. But that just conjured up images of his face and the bullet wound that went into it. He shook his head. He wasn't going to think about it. "That's... look, we're all alive. Ok? All... alive." Damn it. Now he was remembering again.

"Alex. Hey, Alex." Isabelle shook his arm, trying to bring him back to the present. "Don't think about that. It's not your fault, you were just defending Marge. He started it, not us."

Alex shivered, wishing they wouldn't look at him that way. "What makes you think I'm thinking about it?"

There was silence for a moment. Albert snickered. "It's pretty obvious dude. And that's coming from the guy with a hole in his arm. That messed you up."

"Yeah, yeah, we can deal with Alex's inevitable trauma later. He did good. Probably saved all our lives by grabbing that gun before that asshole choked us all out." Marge nodded at Alex, grateful. "But we have to figure out what the hell we do now."

"What do you mean 'figure out what we do now'? Aren't we

going to Paradise Valley?" Isabelle wiped her eyes, looking at the rest of them. "Wasn't that the plan?"

"Sure. But that was before we got ambushed by the nutsack with a gun, so I'm not really comfortable hitting the road until we're sure there aren't more threats out there."

"Wow, Margey isn't sure of something? Woah, stop the presses. This is freaking revolutionary!" Albert rolled his eyes. "Seeing as the rest of you haven't been, you know, shot, I think I'm an authority here. So, I say, we get out of Cheekye as fast as we can and hightail it up to the land of nuts and salmon. Sound good? Alright…"

"Can you walk?" Alex pointed at his bandaged wound. "I mean, you got shot, dude. There was a bullet in your body…"

Albert snickered, wincing. "Nah, it went clean through man. Right out of there. I was thinking of taking it as a trophy."

"So, even if we want to keep moving, I think we might be stuck here until Albert can walk that far." Marge gestured at him. "It's not like we can drag him all the way up there without getting bitched at the whole way."

"Oh, sure I can. It was the arm, not the leg, remember? Who needs all that blood anyways?" He winked at Alex, smirking.

Marge rubbed her temples sighing quietly to herself. "God, you'd think losing a quart of blood would make someone less of a jackass." She inhaled deeply, then gestured at the pack of supplies she'd prepared. "I put together some supplies, but I think we'll need more. I doubt there's that much still up there."

"Supplies? How are we going to get supplies?" Isabelle glanced at the window and across the street. "I don't think anyone else is here to borrow from… that mortgage place is closed, and I didn't see any lights at that general store. I think their owners are back in Squamish."

"I'm not saying we ask, Isa." Marge's expression was blank, but even Alex could figure out what she was suggesting.

"You... want us to loot? You want us to loot people's businesses?! Their places of work?!" Isabelle's tone raised the sound of the conversation. "Marge, that's stealing!"

Marge shushed her, furrowing her brow angrily. "It's not stealing Isa, it's borrowing. They're not here, and they're probably goddamn dead based on what we heard in Squamish. Shit, that guy back there *is* dead. It'll be weeks before anyone will be able to come up this far, and by then all the good shit would be spoiled or forgotten. We need it now if we want to survive."

"I... I can't believe you. Marge, you're better than this! You're a better person!" Isabelle looked like she had tears in her eyes now, still shocked.

"Hey, Isa?" Albert raised his hand with his good arm, like a kid trying to get the teacher's attention. "Margey has always been an asshole. Whole-time. This is just a natural part of her evolution."

Marge scowled at him. "Dig a ditch and die in it Albert."

"Love you too Margey. Anyways, I agree with her, as much as the thought of that makes me die a little inside. We're not getting any younger here, but the shit we find around town could help us get older."

Isabelle turned to Alex, desperately searching for an ally. He blinked at her, looking and feeling like a deer in the headlights. "I... uh..." He scratched his head, trying to think of a solution. Darker thoughts brewed under the surface, things about life and death that he didn't want to consider. About the people around him. Behind him. Behind the building. "Okay... okay... how about this. We can look around for supplies. If we find anyone, we hand them over. If we don't... we find a way to take them up to Paradise Valley."

"I think..." Marge looks at the rest of them, gaze measured. "That's the definition of compromise. None of us are happy, but none of us are pissed. Right, Isa?"

"Right. Right… but I'm not helping you steal Marge! You can take Alex, but I'll be here taking care of Albert. He needs to rest."

"Fine. Alex, let's go." Marge stood up with a groan, wincing and walking out the door. "And hey, while you're at it Isa? Bury the guy. It's the least you could do for doing jack shit to help."

"She doesn't mean that…" Alex quickly stood up, burying his thoughts as the tinkling of the door-chime played him out of the dank and dusty giftshop.

5: INVESTMENT

Alex followed Marge across the street, to the front door of a little establishment called 'Cheeky Mortgages'. He caught up with her when she stopped just short of the entrance, looking over the cheap ads and uninspiring slogans that covered its windows. "Hey, what the hell was…"

Marge shushed him, brushing by him brusquely and heading down the street. "I can already tell this place is going to be useless. We shouldn't even bother with it."

Alex shook his head and followed after her, glancing at the mortgage office as he did. "Ok, sure, but don't you think…"

"I don't want to talk about it Alex. At all. Drop it."

"But Isa… I mean, the entire time I've known her she's just been trying to help you out. Why were you so mean to her?"

"She turned on me, back at the swamp. That shit isn't ok." She rolled her shoulders dismissively, trying to relieve some of the tension. "Why does it matter to you anyway?. I couldn't care less."

They stopped again, this time in front of a rickety little building that said 'General Store' on its sign. Marge seemed more impressed by this one, going up to the window and peaking inside. "Besides, I don't need that help."

"But you do Marge. This… bender you've been on, it's not healthy. Ever since… well, yesterday morning, you've been acting… weird."

"Mhm." She tried the knob on the door, finding it unlocked. She made a little hmph of surprise, heading inside. Alex followed, combatting the unusual feeling that he was just talking to air.

"You keep flipflopping between not wanting to be in charge and wanting all of us to just… fall in line with you. It's weird."

"I don't want to be in charge." Marge walked between the shelves, reading the words on the cans and boxes that lined them, taking each into consideration. She looked around a moment, spotting a tote bag on the cashier's counter. She grabbed it and started emptying the shelves into it without much thought or discipline. "But somebody has to make decisions, and who the hell else is going to do it? None of you have the balls. Isabelle is too soft; Albert is an idiot and you can't finish a sentence without pausing to think about what platitude you'd like to use. I hate being the one who has to corral you idiots together, but clearly, I have to, since I'm the only one with any goddamn drive around here."

She finished filling the bag with food, heaving it onto the counter. She started looking around for another bag, while Alex just stood there. "This isn't drive Marge… it's… it's insane. You're acting crazy and unreasonable."

"Alex, could I remind you that it's your fault that I'm still kicking? You and your stupid speech are what made me keep going. The flood didn't do shit, I did. Because you're right, I'm still here. And you're also right, maybe I'm a little bit insane. Because that's what it goddamn takes." She tosses him another bag. "Now stop complaining about how badass I am and get to work."

Alex shook his head, staring at the ground and starting to collect supplies from the shelves. He felt guilty about it, constantly glancing up and expecting someone to show up to chastise him. It was a dirty feeling, but once his bag was weighed down with supplies, he realized it might be a necessary one.

After a few more minutes of guilt-ridden scavenging, he regrouped with Marge at the counter. She looked at the bags with a frown, then shouldered one of them with a groan. "You'll have to carry the other two. I'm too beat up for another." Alex tried to object, but she raised her finger and shushed him quickly. "I don't want to hear it. This wouldn't be a problem if you shot that asshole sooner. Giddyup."

She barged her way out of the store, heading back to the gift-shop with a grimace and an intention. Alex followed after her, but not before taking a moment to look back at the now-empty shelves of the store. He felt like they were missing something, maybe even something important. He spotted a travel guide, picking it up and looking it over. He pocketed it quietly, following Marge into the dusty darkness of the gift shop once more.

"Where the hell is Isa?" Marge peeked between shelves, gesturing at Albert who was only really half paying attention. "She should be taking care of you, not wandering around."

"Out back, digging that grave. Like you asked her too." Albert shrugged with one shoulder. "I'm fine anyways. Alone. Sitting in the dark. Hearing little girls singing in the distance. The usual."

"She can't just goddamn abandon you. That little shit, she needs to get her priorities straight."

"But… you told her to do it. You wanted her to dig that grave." Alex set his bags down next to Albert, peeking around the aisle at Marge.

"Not by abandoning Albert I didn't. I'm going to kill that bitch…"

"For following your orders? Marge…" Alex intercepted her on the way out the door, stepping in front of her the way a matador did a raging bull. "Marge! You can't just get mad at people for doing what you asked. She's trying to help."

"I don't need her goddamn help Alex! Did I not already say that?" The stress was getting to her. She was shouting now, and the shrill sound of her voice was disrupting the otherwise silent woods. "I'll dig that grave! I'll take care of Albert! I'll… shit, I'll do everything!"

"You need to sit down Marge…" Alex still faced her down, even as she tried to brush past him. "Just please sit down. Relax. We're not going to die if you just… take a break."

"You can't… tell me what to do Alex. I'm… shit, I'm… I'm going to go lie down."

Just like that, the bull was pacified. The fight left Marge nearly instantaneously, causing her to slump down to the ground and lean against a shelf. Exhaustion seemed to overtake her instantly, sapping away her energy and leaving her empty and shrivelled. She was snoring within the minute.

"How much did she sleep last night?"

"Margey?" Albert looked thoughtful for a moment. "Not at all. Spent the whole night rambling and planning. Kept me up all night. Or maybe that was the excruciating pain. Could be either really."

"So that's why she's been like this? She's just been riding the adrenaline high from last night all the way until now?"

"Your guess is as good as mine dude. I think she's always been a bitch, only this time she was a bitch with a vengeance." Albert adjusted how he was sitting a little bit, trying to get comfortable despite the throbbing pain in his shoulder. "That's why it's so fun to piss her off."

"That… doesn't really make sense."

"Hey, I've been shot. Can't expect everything I say to be gold."

The bell at the front door tinkled. The two guys looked over at the sound, seeing Isabelle enter with a muddy shovel. She tossed it aside, pausing a moment to look disdainfully at the bags of supplies before sitting with the other two.

"What's wrong with her? Is she ok?" She blinked concernedly at Marge. "Did something happen?"

"What happened, was that she got knocked the hell out." Albert smirked at Isabelle. "Good for you Isa, because she probably would have knocked *you* out if she'd kept going."

"Wh- me? She'd knock me out? Why?"

"She got mad at you for leaving Albert to… you know." Alex shivered a little, trying to suppress the thought of grave digging. Of bodies. Of death. Even mentioning the concept felt like bringing him back to last night. "Anyways, it didn't really make sense."

"Of course it didn't! She asked me to do that."

"No shit, that's what we said." Albert chuckled softly, a slightly unsettling sound. "But she's not really in the best of mental states. Alex here thinks it's something big, but hey, when is Margey not pissed?"

"A lot of the time. Just never when you're around." Even in her confusion, Isabelle bit back. "I think Alex is right, there must be something wrong…"

"What, like the apocalypse?" Both of them looked blankly at Albert. He raised an eyebrow. "No? You don't think nuclear armageddon might cause a few psyche issues?"

"Well, yeah, but…"

"But nothing. Margey is a Type A middle-management bitch. Of course she's going to go a little nuts when the world ends. It could be worse. Could be the bitch that nearly broke my arm. Could be the asshole who *did* break my shoulder."

"Albert, why are you so observant about this?" Alex was perplexed. What he was saying made sense, but… people didn't change that easily, did they?

"It's how you get good at insulting people. You gotta read them dude. I'm good at that. But shit, it doesn't take a genius to figure out that this whole "nuclear hellfire" thing might cause a bit of a disruption." He gestures vaguely in the direction of the highway. "Like Margey said back there, people crack. Sure, we didn't see Vancouver go up in smoke, but goddamn it's something we know happened. Margey is just trying to get ahead of the curve of post-apocalypse, but she's so far past the curve that she's circled back behind it."

"Since when are you defending Marge?" Isabelle blinked in surprise, considering the situation. "That's usually what I do... but now, you're doing it? *You* Albert?"

"Isa, sweetheart, did you hear a thing I just said?" Albert tried to lean forward for effect but ended up having to recline back when the pain of the wound shot through him again. "Everything is different. All of it. Dynamics, personalities, whatever the hell else. Get it in your head."

Isabelle was quiet after that. Alex looked over at Marge, shaking his head and diverting his attention to look around for something that looked like a blanket to tuck her in. There was nothing, not even a sleeping bag. Which was an unfortunate side effect of the gift shop being abandoned.

"Albert, are you alright watching Marge alone? You won't... drift off or anything?" Alex peeked out the window at the street. "I think we should see if either of those houses has someone we should give these supplies to..."

"Well, I'd probably be fine. That is if I didn't know you were going to sell out all our hard work. Come on dude, really? Giving away our stuff?"

"Hey, it's my hard work! And Marge's..." He paused, glancing at her sleeping form. "Look, that was the deal. Ok? If anyone is here, we give them the stuff. Right, Isa?"

"That's right. But... shouldn't we tell Marge about it?" Isabelle scratched her ear, looking cautiously at the still snoring Marge.

"Do you really want to wake her up right now?"

"We should at least let her know... I feel bad about leaving her in the dark."

Albert snickered to himself. "Yeah, but you won't tear the

boards on the windows down, so dark is all we have in here. Come on Isa, as much as this is a terrible idea, it's a terrible idea she doesn't have to hear."

"But- "

"Isa, please. Let's just… hurry up. If we don't find anyone, we won't have to worry about it."

Alex stood up clumsily, heading for the door. Isabelle followed him, unfocused and still looking back at Marge.

6: RENEWAL

The sun was higher in the sky now, peeking down through the blackened clouds above. Their colour was concerning, a deeper shade of grey than before. The ash was almost invisible now, so thoroughly integrated into the scenery that it had taken over the vista of the covered sky. The wind picked up, blowing pine needles off the asphalt and onto the wet ground to the side of the road. It smelled like rain, and the swirling clouds above promised that yesterday's downpour would only be the start.

"I hate the rain…" Isabelle pulled her jacket tighter around her. "It's cold and wet. Like the ocean."

"So… you don't like the ocean?" Alex scanned the street, looking between the two houses.

The closer one was a traditional ranch style, boring in design with drab colours and flaking paint on the shingles. It seemed out of place, and the surrounding nature agreed, covering it with moss and pine needles as if hoping to claim it as it's own. It was the house that had lights on in the windows the night before, so Alex expected it to be occupied. The other one, sitting nice and pretty next to the general store, was a more modern bungalow, better maintained and more fitting with the local theme, made of pine and stone in a modernist northwestern architectural statement. Alex nodded towards the ranch house, walking towards it quietly.

"No, I don't like the ocean. It's cold… like rain." She smiled a little at her own joke.

Alex shook his head smiling in the same way. "Maybe you should have moved out of B.C then. Go somewhere warm, sunny and completely inland."

"I might one day... or... I guess I would have. I don't think I'll be able to exactly book a flight anytime soon." She frowned a little, pausing before knocking on the front door. "But I shouldn't think of that. It's a bad idea to think about... things that can't be done anymore."

"Probably." They both wait a while, watching the door. Alex glanced inside. It was dark, curtains blocked out most of the light and the dirtiness of the windows didn't help any. He shared a look with Isabelle before she knocked again, waiting to see if anyone would answer. Nobody did. "Is it unlocked?"

Isabelle tried the handle, surprised when it turned easily inward. They stepped into a darkened mudroom, peering around in the dim. After only a moment of hesitation, Alex stepped through an ajar door that led into the living room. He stepped over to the curtains and drew them open, turning around to look over the room.

It was a dirty unhappy place, with various bottles of half-finished booze and pizza boxes of various origins scattered around the floor. The furniture was stained, the upholstery rattled and the whole place felt like a garbage dump masquerading as a household. But none of that mattered to Alex when he spotted something that chilled him to his core. A picture frame jumped into his frame of vision, sitting on a cabinet at the other end of the room. Quickly and shakily he strode over to it, ignoring Isabelle as she peeked into the room. He picked it up with a trembling hand, staring at the smudged impression behind the frame's glass.

It was a man. The one from behind the gift shop. The one he'd shot. He glanced around, noticing a fireplace on the far wall. Just like with the picture, his eyes were drawn to it almost immediately. There, just above the mantle, twin iron hooks where a gun could sit. His heartbeat raced, his eyes tearing back down to the picture. It seemed to pop at him, vibrating in his hand like an angry spectre. Sweat formed on his brow as his vision blurred. He tried to squeeze his eyes shut, but the man in the photograph stayed imprinted there, on the dark side of his eyelids. He dropped the frame, trying to erase it from his mind. The hole in the head, the sound of the gun. It all came up at once, threatening to swallow him like a black hole in his heart.

Someone shook his shoulder. He whirled around, expecting it to be the man, coming back for revenge. A ghost, summoned by his fear. His eyes bulged in terror as he stumbled back, barely catching himself on the cabinet. It took a moment to concentrate and come back to reality.

Isabelle looked at him in concern, hand still on his shoulder. "Alex? What happened? Why did you…"

She glanced at his feet, noticing the picture and gasping. "Is that…" She looked back at him and nodded slowly. "You can head outside. I'll handle this."

Alex nodded gratefully, bolting for the door. He paused on the steps up to the porch, sitting down and breathing heavily. His vision swam and his hands trembled, the face of the man he'd killed infected his mind. He tried to bury it but it refused to be ignored, staying there somewhere near the forefront of his concentration, swimming at the edge of his vision like a woeful apparition.

Sitting there was like a time-lapse. The world moved around him, wind blowing and clouds swirling eternally. It was quiet, the creaking and shaking of windows and doors providing a muted encore to the solitude. He lost track of time, working to collect thoughts that didn't threaten to send him screaming back into that moment. It could have been minutes, or hours or even days until he next came back to reality.

In that time, he watched. The towering evergreens bristled in the wind, shaking ever so slightly over the meagre stretch of mankind. It was one road through nowhere, an outpost of mankind at the edge of the world. This was what Macedon Tours had tried to encapsulate. The singular and insignificant feeling that you got by sitting alone in nature. It's what he'd wanted to capture for them. To be so far away, but still so close to what humanity had become. The clouds began to pour down, drizzling a small helping of water onto his unflinching face.

Philosophy did no good here now. It was wasting time really, stuck in the realm of beauty and opinion. But Alex much preferred the moody world around him to the darkest memories that plundered his mind. The dead man's face. The fire stretching towards the sky.

The end of the world, awash with a relentless neon blaze.

***

The door to the house opened behind him eventually, allowing Isabelle to sit next to him with a bag of things. There was silence for a moment, the porch creaking under their weight.

"I cleaned out what I thought we'd need." Isa gestured at the bag, rustling it a little. "Mostly comfort things but… yeah."

She trailed off awkwardly. There was an aura around Alex, almost seeming to demand silence. It was uncomfortable, filling the air with a weight that closed the throat and froze the tongue. He knew from the look on Isabelle's face that she was struggling to break through it.

"I think he lived alone. All of his photos were of just him and some woman. She's not here and she looked a lot younger so… probably his daughter or niece or something. I don't think she lives here."

"Isa, can you please stop talking about his family?"

"Oh, I'm… I'm sorry. I'm just not really sure what to say that can help right now."

Alex stood up, dusting off the mud that had stuck to him when he sat down. "I think we need to just keep going… right? I don't want to think… or talk… or… anything really. At least not about that. So let's just... see if we can find anyone in the other house, ok?"

Isabelle nodded, standing up and patting him on the back. It was an inadequate, token gesture, but one that he appreciated nonetheless. They set off towards the bungalow without comment, chilled not only by the cold air but also by the emptiness that hung within it.

The bungalow was cute, with a little garden and a little gravel path that lead up to the door. A small doorbell was to the right of the entrance, flanking the solid and polished slab of wood that served as a functionally modern door. Alex tentatively poked it, waiting for the sound to play. Instead, the silence stretched on. He pressed the button again, waiting. Nothing happened. He glanced at Isabelle, shrugging. He decided to knock, leaning to the side to try to get a peek into the house.

Nothing.

Slowly, he reached for the single silver door handle, opening into the entrance hall with a small click that seemed far louder than it should have been. He quietly stepped into the house, feet making a sharp sound on the stone floor. The hallway ahead was short, holding only two doors. He glanced inside of one, seeing a neatly kept bedroom. He glanced through the other, spotting the flickering static of a TV screen and the silhouette of a man on a couch.

"Hello?" He paused at the threshold to the room, opening the door a little bit more. "Sir? Are you awake?"

There was no response. Alex glanced at Isabelle. "There's a guy in there, but I think he's asleep..."

"We should leave then... we're intruding on him."

"No. No, we can do this now... or later, with Marge."

Alex stepped into the room, heart beating faster. For some reason, his throat was tight. The static on the screen was the only sound, it's soft hiss drowning out his footsteps. He reached out to tap the man on the shoulder from behind the couch, but thought better of it; Instead moving around to the front, between the man and the TV. He paused, eyes widening and throat tightening even more. Isabelle stepped up next to him, turning to face the man and screaming.

The man had a distant and forgotten gaze, looking towards a horizon that wasn't there. His skin was pale and lifeless, spread like a blank tapestry across his bones. A streak of blood dribbled from his jaw, leading to the floor where it pooled just to where they stood. He was dead, shot and left to rot with a gun in his own hand.

**

Alex broke a little. Just a little. The human mind can only take so much in a short time. Violence, debauchery, barbarity. Enough of it, and the mind cracks in certain ways. It's different for everyone, and the way a mind will break is never the same. Today, for him, it meant finding a ladder and climbing up to the roof of the gift shop. It meant sitting in the rain with a silent gaze towards the sky that didn't falter. Down below, he could hear the other three talking. Arguing, plotting, planning and everything else. Isabelle was probably recounting what they had seen, Marge was probably fuming about them having seen it. Albert was recovering, all the while cracking jokes and providing small tidbits of conflicted wisdom.

But Alex didn't care. The words that would pass around below him were words that would be lost. They might stick in the minds of others, but for him?

All that existed right now was the sky above, the rain on his face and the sounds of voices that might as well have been a million kilometres away. He could stay forever, accepting no truth but that of his surroundings. Slowly, the clouds cleared, and the rain let off, leaving him with the dripping sounds of the forest. Even still, he kept his gaze on the frozen cloud cover above.

It was a few hours before he climbed back down inside. In the time he had thought and wandered, the sun had traversed the sky and now painted the peaks with a dusky glow. He paused at the entrance to the gift shop. With just a glance, he went over to the display windows. Carefully at first, he started ripping the wood from the windows. He pulled them free from the nails, sending the pieces flying to the side of the road. With each board, he stopped being careful, ripping the rotting planks from their perch and tossing them aside with fervour. When he was done, he took a deep breath, looking into the shop. It was flooded with the light of the setting sun, casting it's blinding rays onto the other three. They blinked at him, shielding their eyes as the sky faded towards night.

Albert shook his head. "Dude, how many splinters do you have?"

***

After using the rest of the first-aid kit to pull all the wood out of Alex's hand, the group broke our dinner. Alex hadn't eaten since yesterday, but the scattering of his mind throughout the day's events had left that oddity at the back of his mind. Sitting there on the blankets that Isa had acquired, the meal of cereals and soon to be rotten vegetables ended up being a far cry from the fancy Italian of just a few days past. It was a silent dinner, with Marge hawkishly watching the rest, Albert struggling quietly to eat the food placed before him and Isabelle equally as quietly helping him.

Alex had to be the one to break the ice since it was clear that no one else would. He didn't want the silence anymore. This sort of silence was different. Unhelpful. Where before the silence was a way to concentrate on what was around him, now it drew inwards, towards the darker corners.

"I'm sorry about... tearing down the boards."

Marge wiped her mouth with her sleeve, shaking her head. "It was too dark in here anyways. Not like there's anyone else in town to peek in on us, is there?"

"So Isabelle told you what we found? The..."

"The Empty house and the dead guy?" Marge chewed another bite of food, swallowing it and setting down the box she'd been eating from. "Yeah. I heard about your little 'expedition'. I'm just glad you two didn't find anything worse. Like someone alive."

"Someone being alive is bad?" Isabelle blinked at Marge, seemingly struggling to reconcile what she just said. "That's..."

"Terrible, yeah, yeah. For them, not us. There's no way we were going to give away those supplies. I just didn't want to have to argue with you about it. And now that we know we don't have to argue with anyone else over it, I'm relieved."

"Marge..."

"I don't want to hear it." She glared at Isabelle, making it clear that she was putting her foot down. "I may not be as angry as yesterday, but I'm sure as hell just as goddamn jaded. So let's just agree that what's happened has happened and we're not going to dwell on it."

Nobody really knew what to say to that. Even Albert remained silent on the subject for once.

"I'll take it the silence means 'Yes Marge, I'll keep pushing forward!', right?"

They nodded slowly.

Marge nodded, visually pleased that they were falling into line. Alex was concerned. Yesterday's Marge was unhinged, running and raging like a bull. This Marge seemed more like a snake, calmly waiting for a moment to strike.

"Albert, can you walk?"

Albert snickered. "Sure, to the bathroom. I won't be walking to Paradise Valley, that's for sure."

"Well, we're not carrying you, and I want to get up there and secure it before anyone else does. So, unless we want to leave this jackass behind, do any of you have any ideas?" She looked towards Alex and Isabelle, expectant for an answer.

"Secure it? What do you mean secure it? Who else is going to take it from us? Isn't that the point of going up there?" Alex grew more concerned. The fire went out in Marge, but not the drive. The dedication towards an unflinching goal that seemed to separate from reality and toil on ideals.

"I mean, Alex, that we need a place to stay that isn't a gift shop. We need a place to survive this damn apocalypse, that isn't a stone throw away from the nearest pack of raving lunatics. It's not like we can just commute down to North Van and snuggle in under all that radioactive rubble." She leaned on the counter, scanning the room with a cold look in her eye and an unflinching smile on her face. "So let's do it right. Ideas?"

Isabelle shifted in place, clearly not a fan of the direction Marge was taking. "We could go find a wheelbarrow? We'd need one anyway for all the... supplies"

"That's a surprisingly good idea, traitor. Any others? Alex?"

"Wait, traitor?" Isabelle looked less shocked, or even worried. Now she just looked hurt. "I'm not a traitor..."

"Sure, sure. You definitely haven't consistently let me down. Shit, Albert's been more useful to me lately. Anyways, Alex, ideas?"

Alex fidgeted a little, looking towards Isabelle. "I think her idea is good... and she isn't a traitor Marge."

"Wheel-barrows it is! Head on out to find them. Chop-chop."

"Marge, it's after dark. We're not going out there in the middle of the night." Alex tried to be firm, but there was something so determinedly unsettling about the way Marge was directing them. It felt like a parent scolding a child. Alex felt like he was doing something wrong, evil. Like Marge could count down from three and he'd bend the knee immediately.

But he had to try.

"Oh, right. Here, take these. Bye now!" Marge passed them a couple of camping lights, waving goodbye theatrically.

"Someone's maaaaad. You two are in trouuubllleeee." Albert snickered to himself, watching the show and munching on cereal with marshmallows in them.

"You're goddamn right I'm mad! But, now I'm channelling that anger into bitter humiliation of my subordinates to make up for their insult and insubordination. So if you want me to stop being angry, get me a goddamn wheelbarrow!"

And with that, Marge stormed off behind the counter and sat down, backs to the rest of them.

"She's... she's lost it. Marge has lost it. I don't know what to do with myself." Isabelle shook her head. "I want to help but... she's lost it."

"Margey hasn't had it for months. I've been saying that this whole time." Albert popped the last of the marshmallows in his mouth, shrugging. "You guys just never listen to me."

Alex gently set the lamp down on the floor, staring at the outline of Marge's head that peeked over the counter. Isabelle was right, Marge had lost it. But...

"We've all lost it." He slowly slid to the ground, resting his head on his knees. "Everything. I can't even begin to... it's just too much."

"Don't be a crybaby Alex." Marge peeked over the counter. "You can save it for your diary."

"No, Marge... no." He took a deep breath, leaning back against a shelf. "I think I get it. We're all... primal. Operating on our functions or drives. We can't think about it. We don't... consider. It's the most basic goal, survive."

"No shit?" Marge shook her head. "I thought that was pretty obvious."

"That's what I've been saying!" Albert tossed his cereal box in the air, showering the rest of them with sugar and crumbs.

"But I mean… Marge, look. You're on a drive. You can't stop. It's not because you're insane… it's because you're trying to cope. We all are. I'm losing myself in the dark, Albert's being… more Albert and Isabelle is trying to keep it all together. We're… caricaturing ourselves, since that's what we think we need to do. The bomb has made us realize we're going to be in a world that isn't meant for us… so we fall back on our defining features to try to rationalize our existence."

"Alex, what in the hell are you rambling about? You're a goddamn PR guy, not a shrink. Just shut up until morning. Even better, grab us a wheelbarrow! Like you're supposed to! I can't deal with your psycho-centric nonsense right now."

Marge ducked back behind the counter. Albert and Isabelle had deflated a little from Marge's shutdown. Alex could tell that they were starting to grasp what he'd realized. About what was happening to them. About survival. But Marge had taken that realization from them, snatching it from the cusp of common consciousness. Everyone around him fell to sleep, their breaths and snores filling the empty air with a quiet drone. But Alex's mind was abuzz. Not with memories, or dark thoughts. Now, it was abuzz with speculation. Pondering, so to speak, as he gazed wistfully at the ceiling of the gift shop.

Who was he now that everything he used to be was up in smoke?

7: PASSENGER

The next day, at around noon, the group departed from Cheekye. Alex and Marge had spent the morning making sure nothing was amiss. They found two wheelbarrows behind the ranch house, one much older than the other. After another sweep of the general store to be sure they hadn't missed anything, they dumped most of their loot into the older, rustier wheelbarrow. Alex specifically avoided entering either house, wincing quietly and ignoring Marge's eye-rolling whenever he glanced towards the bungalow. Even still, she also gave the place a wide berth, unwilling to see what she knew had given Alex and Isabelle such a spook.

As they grabbed the last of the mints and candy bars from the general store, Isabelle was busy securing Albert to the wheelbarrow in a way that he could comfortably sit for an extended time. He would adjust positions, then wait for her to start pushing. A little way down the road, he would tell her if it was comfortable or not. Really, it was just killing time, but Albert was intent on insisting it's vitality for his comfort. Alex paused, leaning on the mortgage office and watching them. Isabelle was smiling and Albert was laughing in his mysterious sort of ominous way.

Marge came out from behind the mortgage office, slinging the last bag from the general store and putting it in the wheelbarrow. "Ok, which of you is pushing Albert and which of you is pushing the groceries?"

"Well, Isa already has Albert so… I guess we could split pushing the other wheelbarrow between us."

"What?" Marge scoffed at him. "I just got my face smashed in, and you want *me* to push?"

"Come on Marge, just a turn or two. You'll be fine. If it gets too bad, I'll take over, ok?"

She blinked, then grimaced, nodding. "Fine. Asshole."

She strode over to the wheelbarrow, picking up the handles with a bit of a struggle and starting to walk down the road. Isabelle followed her, pushing Albert gleefully while Alex hooked the survival pack that Marge had made over his shoulder. He ignored the gun strapped to its side, refusing to acknowledge it's presence even as the weight settled on him. He looked back as they walked the road, crossing a bridge out of Cheekye with the muddy waters of the river below swirling peacefully. The pine needles still blew across their path with a relaxed determination, scattered like sands and time. Cheekye was empty now, nothing but nature, ghosts and the wind.

But now, the wind was blowing northwards.

***

The walk to Paradise Valley would bring them through a quiet stretch of pine and fir. Here now, there was no civilization. It was a silent, peaceful walk, even as storm clouds brewed above their heads. Alex gave them some thought, glancing occasionally towards the sky with lingering dread. He preferred not to mention what he'd noticed about the heading of the wind. It was a weight on his own mind, one which was better kept out of the concerns of others. If the winds blew north, so too would the fallout. The ash and dust of a fallen city would wind it's way north with vicious intent, and Alex shuddered to imagine what was in the air. It was like a great oozing wound, working its way north through the land and desecrating this virgin forest. And worst of all, none of them would be able to see it.

The time would come where he'd have to deal with the issue. For now, he kept his mind on the path, and on the trees with their evergreen leaves.

The first signs of Paradise were the large roadside billboards that broke between those leaves, overgrown now but familiar enough to spark recognition. Marge paused at the first one, nodding at it. "Look at that people. Just a kilometre to Paradise Valley! Wow! I wonder if they sell any souvenirs."

"We couldn't find a proper mascot, remember? Mr. Donahue…"

"That was sarcasm Alex. Sarcasm. Take a look behind that thing to see a fantastic prize for realizing that! Then, take the wheelbarrow. My back is *killing* me." Marge set down the wheelbarrow, leaning back on her hands to crack her back. Alex, meanwhile, stepped off the side of the road to look behind the billboard, curious at just what Marge was referring to.

A little way off into the woods, a decrepit building stood starkly off the ground. Made mostly of glass and wood, it crept in the woods like a macabre see-through coffin, held up by thick pillars of concrete and paint. Some of its windows were shattered, and the natural foliage of moss and vines had begun to encompass its façade. Alex ducked back from behind the billboard, looking back over at Marge with a questioning gaze.

"It used to be the Cheakamus Centre. You know, one of those dumbass venues for marriages, events, whatever the hell else." She slouched a moment, letting her back work its way through the process before standing back up straight. "We had the free capital to run it out of business, but not enough to tear it down."

"So you just… covered it with a billboard and left it there." Alex shook his head and stepped back to take a better look at the billboard, trying to see past the foliage and overgrowth to find out what it said beneath. 'PARADISE VALLEY'. It was emblazoned with big green letters, stark against a once vibrant yellow. 'THE 1# FAMILY NATURE PARK NORTH OF THE 45TH PARALLEL'. He remembered brainstorming the motto, trying to decide what combination of appeal and legal security would work best for the attraction. It seemed so far away now, that world of board meetings and focus groups. Like a dream far removed from this post-apocalyptic dawn.

"What's with all the nature and shit on it?" Albert readjusted in his wheelbarrow, sitting up to look at it. "It's only been what, like a year? Nature isn't that aggressive; it takes years with an s to do that."

"Mr. Donahue wanted us to go with a... natural marketing plan." Alex pointed towards almost completely concealed holes in the edges of the design. "We had people put some vines and brambles in those holes, let them grow naturally. It was supposed to be part of the aesthetic."

"And that's Paradise Valley for you all." Marge kept walking, putting her hands in her pockets. "We'll invest millions in a land grab, hundreds on gimmicky advertising and shit all on getting rid of what we didn't necessarily need to."

Isabelle pushed Albert along, following after Marge. Alex paused looking towards the billboard one last time. "We also included pinecones with all our physical advertising. You could get an information packet with a personalized cone."

"Macedon Tours marketing squad everybody! Give it up for the futility!" Marge clapped dramatically, reaching the third and final bridge over the river and entering Paradise Valley's outskirts.

***

Paradise Valley was not it's own valley, separate from the rest of the land they had just crossed. Rather, it was a continuation of the valley that slowly closed off from the Howe Sound. It was surrounded on each side by highlands that merged into the mountain peaks, spreading their bases wider and wider until the once broad valley petered out into a rocky end through which the river ran through. This stretch of land between the river's turn and the end of the valley was thusly given its own identity, Paradise Valley, a place far removed from the relatively bustling town of Squamish.

The wind picked up after they crossed the river, blowing into their backs with a driving of rain and cold. But Alex's worries of the northward wind were soon realized when the rain started falling blackened, darkened with soot and ash and cold as night. He yelled something incomprehensible, dropping the wheelbarrow and starting to run. The other three paused, looking at him and exchanging confused glances. It wasn't until they took a moment to see the puddles forming on the ground, and the way a black stain spread between them that they caught wind that something was wrong.

Soon enough, the two women were running with him, Isabelle roughly pushing Albert's wheelbarrow forward as the rain started to hiss against their clothes and skin, imprinting a burning sensation on their skin as the acid rain peeled into their clothes. Up ahead, a welcome centre stood off to the side, next to a guard gate with a drop-arm that functioned as the entry to Paradise. The centre offered a safe shelter, the group ducking into it's quiet inside without a second thought. As Isabelle set the wheelbarrow down and slammed the door shut, Alex fumbled with his pack, finding his camping light and switching it on. The sudden gloom of the storm had turned the airy design of the centre into a dusk-like shadow. Flat advertisements, scenic pictures and dusty informational flyers surrounded him as he sat down with the rest of the group.

"Alex, what the hell was that, why the hell was it raining acid and why in God's name didn't you say anything?!" Marge did not look pleased, pulling off her jacket and trying to avoid contact with any of the water it brought in.

"I think… I think that was acid rain. From the blast. The wind just turned, which sent all the crap in the air from the bomb north." Alex rubbed his face, going to the window and trying to peer through the glass at the outside. "So… all the aftereffects of the bomb must have screwed with the water in the clouds. Or something. I don't know, I'm not a scientist."

"Really?" Albert snickered, rubbing his arm and struggling for breath after the ordeal. "I thought you were a neuroscientist after I heard you use the term 'Aftereffects.' This is shocking to me."

"Sorry, I'm doing my best. I saw a few movies. Read a few books. I'm not a scientist, I'm just trying to guess here. I have no idea why anything is happening, it's just what makes sense."

"Well that's comforting. Our resident radiation expert is neither an expert nor radiation. A plus job there, real proud of you Alex." Marge shook her head, pulling herself to her feet and shaking herself off. "At least we're finally here. Thank God for that."

"Could we turn the lights on? This place is sort of... creepy." Isabelle had been quiet for the last while but now looked around the space with nervous curiosity.

Albert scoffed, shaking his head and opening his mouth to say something stupid. Instead, he seemed to think about it, closing his eyes and considering a response. "They cut the power to most of Paradise Valley. Nobody was paying for it, so after Macedon Tours pulled most of our funding they didn't really bother keeping the lights on. The only place that has it is the salmon hatchery since that's technically government property that we upgraded."

"You said Paradise Valley had power!" Marge turned to look at him, a hot streak of anger flaring up in her eyes.

"I said it sort of had power. The hatchery has plenty to spare. We can camp out in there, happy as clams."

"When you suggested Paradise Valley, I figured we'd be in log cabins, not a goddamn fish farm!" Marge started pacing angrily. "What the hell Albert?!"

Alex rubbed the back of his head sheepishly. "Look, Marge, it's not the best but... it's better than Squamish, right?"

"That's comparing a trash pile to a burning and underwater trash pile. It's a dumb comparison and doesn't make sense." Marge walked to the window, watching the acid rainfall with darkened severity. "Well shit. I guess we're here now. Sitting in another abandoned ruin full of nothing. But hey, look, at least it's a welcome center. Bet this place will make us feel really welcome. And hey, look! This place has some chairs! That makes everything A-Okay!"

Albert scoots over to a ragged couch, sitting on it and closing his eyes as his impact sends up a plume of dust. "Wow, we went from one dark abandoned tourist trap to another. But now we have *chairs?* Margey, baby, I never should have doubted you."

"Cut the shit Albert, you're the one that dropped the ball." Marge sighed, leaning against the glass. "Hey Alex, will the acid rain melt these windows?"

"I... no, I don't think so. It doesn't seem that bad. It just irritates, it doesn't... melt. Yet."

"Wow, you're a real goddamn morale boost, you know that?" Marge peered through the window, trying to spot the wheelbarrow through the darkness of the storm. "I know for damn sure that it's going to screw up all the shit we left in the wheelbarrow. Why the hell did you drop it?"

"I was running from the rain!"

"Yeah, well if it only 'irritates' then run back out there and get it! That's too much shit to just lose."

"Marge, we can't go back outside..." Isabelle looked up from where she had sat next to Albert, checking to make sure the rain hadn't gotten past his bandages. "It's too dangerous. Alex is right, we don't know what any of this means. We're just guessing. That rain could be way worse than we know."

"Thanks, Isa. Oh wait, no thanks, I didn't ask. When we run out of food, you're the first one we'll eat." Marge stomped off away from the window, grabbing the light and using it to peer behind counters and into back rooms.

She spent a while trapezing around the place, familiarizing herself with every corner and making sure it was empty. Alex watched her work, sitting back and flipping through the travel guide he had found in the shop yesterday. It was the same kind as the ones scattered around them in little displays, although those were much dustier and decrepit. It was all about Paradise Valley and the 'amazing attractions' within. He flipped through pages of campgrounds, nature trails and rustic cabins. There were advertisements for 'Paradise Nuts', unique and home-grown varieties of Hazelnuts, Pecans and Walnuts. There was a big full-page picture of the 'Salmon Hatchery of the Future'. He eyed the list of modern technologies that were meant to tout the Sudden Valley hatchery as a great leap forward. Glacier-fed waters. Auto-cycling tanks. Adaptive breeding compilations. It was impressive, technical and utter nonsense to him. He knew because he had been a part of designing the page. He had been a part of designing the entire travel guide. It was fun at the time, seeing all the things everyone had done to make Paradise Valley work. Albert's logistical prowess, Marge's administrative support. Isabelle's constant vigilance in making sure everything ran smoothly.

Of course, back then it wasn't just them. Alex used to be part of the PR department. Now he was the PR guy. Marge used to just work for the man in charge. Now she was in charge. The people they had around them were stripped away, first by corporate cutbacks and then by nuclear hellfire.

He realized why he was doing this. Survival. Why his speech had worked back then, after the end. Why they stayed together. It wasn't because of function, or necessity. Squamish probably would have been a better place to be in the end.

It was because they were all they had. The insurmountable darkness of looking back at what they'd lost had left them looking towards each other. It wasn't a friendship, not really. It was a dependency. Necessity. The last vestiges of that world that had just collapsed. Something old to cling to.

Or at least, that's what he figured.

He closed the travel guide, quietly looking over the back of the thing. All it had was a cartoonish map of Paradise Valley decorated with dramatic overrepresentations of each attraction. Still, that could be useful. He pocketed the brochure.

Again, they stayed in the darkness, this time without even the possibility of going outside. The storm raged on for hours, leaving Marge to pace, Alex to read and Albert to stew. Only Isabelle wandered, flickering between the each of them like a concerned hummingbird. Approaching Marge was like approaching a chained up dog, she would spit and snarl at her with her words. Approaching Alex, he knew that he was being distant. Isabelle tried to pierce his veil with words and questions, but the patter of the raindrops was like static in his head, drowning her out and leaving him alone in his philosophical misery. Eventually, she would give up, settling back down to talk quietly with Albert.

Right before Alex's eyes, the storm eventually faded away. The clouds receded back towards the mountains, pursued by the sun shining its rays through the former gloom. Soon enough, the sky shone blue for the first time since the fall of the bombs, threatened only by the swirling clouds of the mountain peaks. In silence, they all left the welcome centre. Puddles lined the road, each viscous and black as oil.

"We should go back for the wheelbarrow..." Isabelle glanced down the road towards the wheelbarrow, visible now, naked and alone on the road. She took a step towards it, pausing to look at the other three. Marge rolled her eyes, nodding and waving her off without ceremony. She leaned on Albert's wheelbarrow, basically ignoring his struggles as he tried to get comfortable inside it. Alex looked between the two, then started walking towards the other wheelbarrow. Isabelle followed him quickly.

It turned out to be mostly fruitless. Where there used to be bags of boxes and cans, now it was mostly just a wet mush. Alex reached into the disgusting brown mass, pulling out a single can and ignoring the tingling on his skin. The tag on the outside of the can was a little worn, both from the rain and it's acidic properties, but otherwise, it didn't seem too bad. He looked it over carefully, trying to see if there was any more noticeable damage. From what he could tell, it seemed fine. There were no breaches and 'JP's Baked Beans' weren't pouring out en masse. He dumped the wheelbarrow onto the ground, heaping the mess of cardboard pulp and cans onto the wet pavement. The water pooled into pre-existing puddles, settling darkly like pockmarks on the road. He rummaged around in the pile, joined quickly by Isabelle. Without a word, they dug through the mess, poking and grabbing at whatever looked salvageable. A few bags and cans were undisturbed, but most of the food was ruined and scattered through the pile, producing an unpleasant slimy sensation when their hands brushed past the miserably soggy remains.

They put what they found back into the wheelbarrow, after making sure that it was empty and that their loot was safe. Isabelle took the handles of the thing, heaving it and starting to walk back down the road. The wind brushed her hair, blowing again from the south. Alex felt it too, glancing at the southern skies with unease. The day was clear and the winds warmer, but he couldn't shake a sense that something was wrong. Something more. Like the shockwaves left after the bomb, something was reverberating in his skull. Like a small angry woodpecker, there was a faint and desperate cry to run and scream.

Instead, he just shrugged his shoulders, pulling his jacket a little looser off of him and following Isabelle back to the other two.

8: SHADOWS

Deeper into Paradise Valley, the forests grew sparser. Signs for campgrounds, trails and kitschy little attractions started to pop up alongside the road. Occasionally a distant bird would chirp, disrupting the otherwise nearly silent sounds of the road. Most of the time, it was just their footsteps and the wind in the trees, something that made the occasional shrill cry of a crow all the more disconcerting.

Even more disconcerting were the distant hulks of abandoned buildings. Macedon Tours had done their best to cover up the people who'd been run over to get Paradise Valley going, but the fake warning signs of off-path dangers and conveniently placed clumps of trees wouldn't fool a discerning eye. Abandoned homes hid behind these paltry concealments, watching like ghosts from their quiet disrepair.

Marge seemed to be hit by their presence a little harder. At first, she would point them out, scoffing at their presence like an offended dignitary. But the further they went into Paradise Valley, the more the shadows seemed to get to her. Every unconvincing sign and grove only seemed to draw her eye, and she mumbled and groaned unhappily at their presence. Alex was curious but chose not to press her. Instead, he just walked between the forgotten woods like a ghost, smelling the pine sap and flinching at the distant calls of the crows as they disturbed the ghastly silence.

In time, they reached Paradise Valley's 'thoroughfare'. Originally it was just a couple of nondescript roads running parallel to a train track. But with a little rerouting of roads and rail-lines, Macedon Tours had turned a strip of dirt and gravel into an attraction. The roads were paved and joined together, forming a circuit around a tree-lined train track, which had been converted for the most part into a museum. A railway station was built, roughed up and promptly established as being rustic, spinning tales of prospectors travelling here in olden days to seek their fortune in the mines of the nearby mountains. Alex eyed it's falsely rusted swinging sign as the four of them followed the thoroughfare to the hatchery.

"Who had the idea to build a tourist trap in an eco-park?" Albert glanced at Isabelle as the hatchery came into view around the bend of the road, sitting at its end before the asphalt looped it's way back around the tracks. "Probably the same idiot who decided we should spend so much on a fish farm, right?"

"It was Mr. Donahue dude. Both times." Alex paused in front of the sign outside the chain-link fence that fronted the hatchery, reading its phony taglines and promises of 'self-guided fishy family fun!'. He shook his head muttering to himself. "What were we thinking…"

Marge strode up to the chain-link gate, shaking it lightly and peering through it at the hatchery. Unlike the other places they'd passed, which had a looming sense of being unkept or swept under the rug, the hatchery operated openly and functionally. Behind the much larger and tackier advertisement, a simple green signpost let visitors know that the Tenderfoot Creek Hatchery was operated by the B.C. Ministry of Environment.

Isabelle read it curiously as Marge tried to open the gate to no avail. "So this is why it doesn't look abandoned?" She looked over at Marge, who was still struggling to pull the gate open. "It's not run by us?"

Marge gave up on trying to open the gate, wiping her hands off and placing them on her hips, looking at the gate with a scowl. "You nailed it. This place is functional because we didn't screw with it too bad. Macedon Tours breaks everything it touches, remember? Now help me get this thing open..."

Albert leaned up out of his wheelbarrow, looking at the base of the gate. "Hey Margey, I don't think that'll work. Now, I'm no genius, but I'm pretty sure that if the gate's locked, that means you won't be able to get it open."

Alex crouched down next to where Albert had pointed, nodding. "He's right. It looks like it's locked down here. They put a stake in the floor and a lock around it."

Marge sighed, shaking her head. "What kind of a world do we live in where Albert makes sense, Alex states the obvious, and the government is still screwing us after it blew up?" She sighs theatrically, leaning on the fence. "Oh right, this one!"
There was a subtle creak from the fence, causing Alex to look at Marge curiously. He noticed the way the chain-link seemed to lean in a little from her weight, creating a small gap between the gate and the fence. He walked over to her, carefully testing if his own weight would make the hole larger. It did.

He gestured at the gap, whistling to get everyone's attention. "Looks like there's a hole here. I think we might be able to fit through it."

Marge shook her head, pointing at the top of the fence without even bothering to look. "We can just go over. Probably simpler than trying to figure out how the hell we can get Albert's fat ass through there."

"Sure, but at least my 'fat ass' won't get cut up on that barbed wire." Albert snickered to himself, causing Marge to do a double-take upwards. Alex and Isabelle did as well, noticing the razor-sharp wire that decorated the top of the fence.

Marge uttered a silent curse, shaking her head. "Why the hell would they put barbed wire on a *fish hatchery?* Out of all the inane bullshit to guard..."

As Marge swore and Albert cackled delightedly at her misfortune, Isabelle came over to Alex to help him push the gate in. With enough effort, soon enough Alex was able to make a hole big enough for her to slip into. It was a bit of a tight squeeze, and her jacket got caught on one of the screws that held the thing together, causing her to have to fiddle around with it a moment before emerging on the asphalt parking lot. From there, she pulled on the fence from the inside to keep the gap open, letting Alex slide through.

Isabelle let go of the fence for a moment, rubbing her hands. She almost spoke up to mention that they were inside, but Alex shushed her before she could. "Wait a second. See how long it takes them."

They stood there quietly for almost a full minute, arms crossed and smiles smug, waiting for either of the other two to notice. Albert did first, noticing them and snickering even more. Marge yelled about the stupidity of Paradise Valley as a whole for another few minutes, before finally falling quiet and looking past the fence.

"How the hell did…" She glanced at the spot between the gate and the fence, then shook her head. "Oh. The hole. Right. Goddamnit, just help me open it."

The three propped the hole open, while Albert lounged there lazily, with a smug look in his eye. "I would Margey, but you see, I'm confined to this poor wheelbarrow. So I'm afraid you'll have to do this without me!"

"Hey Albert, toss those cans to me, will you?" Marge smirked at him with a cocky wink, still holding the gap open. Albert waited quietly for a moment, smirk dropping off his face quickly. He groaned, reaching over and grabbing some cans from the other wheelbarrow, starting to pass them through the gap. Marge looked on triumphantly. "Shows you for running your mouth asshole."

Once the wheelbarrow was emptied, Alex and Isabelle Albert duck past the fence and into the parking lot, tipping the wheelbarrow into a ditch next to the road as they went. Marge slipped in after him, glaring at the wheelbarrow as Albert leaned heavily against the fence. "Did you really have to do that?"

Albert chuckled, wincing. "I'm a petulant man-child, get used to it."

There was a collective breath released by the group, each turning to look towards the front of the hatchery.

The façade of the building was painted an uninteresting green, more akin to the colour of lime than to that of the forest. A simple metal door fronted the structure flanked on two sides by windows and marked by a small sign above that read 'Office.' Alex opened it without ceremony, leading the others into the vestibule that separated them from the rest of the building. Another door lead to the warm air inside, it's traversal filling their nostrils with the smells of carpet and metal. Alex reached around the wall next to them, finding a lightswitch and flicking it on to illuminate the room. The overhead tubes flickered on, revealing the inside with that insidious irritable buzz.

A couple of desks and chairs sat against the wall of the cramped space, stacked on top by personal effects and last year's cutting edge computers. The space was otherwise empty but mostly tidy. Clearly, it had only been about a week or two since someone checked in on the place. Automation had to have oversight every now and then.

"Creepy. Reminds me of our office." Isabelle sat at one of the chairs, peeking under the desk to find the computer's power button. The screen came to life, booting up and displaying the Macedon Tours logo, a stylized sun over a purple background. The machine prompted a password, which made Isabelle turn to the others and shrug.

"Try 'Greatness'. That was the default password for all our computers." Alex leaned on the desk, looking at the screen curiously.

Isabelle typed in the password and smiled when the screen changed to a loading icon. Marge sighed, facepalming. "I can't believe how pretentious that is. And unsafe. 'Greatness?'. Shit, they put barbed wire on the fence but didn't even bother to lock the door."

"That's the corporate lifestyle, Marge..." Isabelle clicked through several icons, each listing off seemingly random numbers that Albert looked at with notable interest. "It's airtight but also..."

"Also sucks, blah blah, blah, whatcha seeing there Albert?" Marge looked at the numbers too, sporting a look of confusion to mirror Albert's focus.

Albert gently took the keyboard from Isabelle, typing a few things and watching the numbers change as he did so. It all went over Alex's head, but Albert seemed to be getting something out of changing a 1 to a 5. He spoke with a sense of wonder, for once not tinged by humour or sarcasm.

"This is the control centre. Well, digital control centre. It runs everything in the hatchery, like temperature and cleaning. Food. Waste disposal. All of it. It's a whole isolated system. Proprietary software and whatever the hell else." Albert opened several tabs, showing graphs and illustrations. "Look, here's the production stats. This little line represents how many fish the place has at any time."

Marge looked closely at the graph, which seemed to trend constantly upwards before dropping suddenly and starting again. She tapped the screen at one of those points. "What are these?"

Albert typed a couple things into the computer, looking for something. "Oh, that's when the fish turn carnivorous and start eating each other in a cannibalistic frenzy."

"Albert, be serious or I'll shoot your other arm." Marge squeezed said arm to make a point.

Albert winced, shaking her off gently. "Ow, fine. Damn. You

could just say please Margey." He shook his head, sighing dramatically. "They're releases. Once it hits a certain quota, the farm will flush it's stock tanks and let excess salmon loose into the Cheakamus River. This is a hatchery. It's technically designed to repopulate, not harvest."

"Why? And can we turn it off?"

While Albert explained the finer points of fish-farming to Marge, Alex took another look around the room. Closer observation revealed another door in the corner, which he went over to. Isabelle watched him go, staying with the other two as they began arguing about the wisdom of releasing fish.

Alex peeked through the door as he cracked it open, revealing an equally drab and bare hallway. The carpet disappeared at the doorway, suddenly converted into a sad shade of linoleum. Alex could hear the buzz of machinery now, echoing down the hall from a fire door that occupied the opposite end of the space. A couple more doors branched off from the hall, giving notice to an otherwise depressingly plain space.

He peeked into the rooms as he passed them, looking through the cracks of the door at a depressing supply closet and even more depressing breakroom. At the end of the hall, he pushed the last door open, the buzzing of machines now more audible than ever.

Through the door and down a pair of concrete steps, the space opened up dramatically. It looked like a cross between a factory and a swimming pool, with rows of machines lining the walls around pools and currents of water. The gabled roof was crisscrossed with skylights, shining the afternoon sun down into the open space. Alex stepped over to one of the pools, peering inside. What seemed like hundreds of small fish swam around inside, darting around with an aimless gaze. He followed the pool further along, reaching a point where a waterfall split the thing in two. Beyond this, bigger fish swam and struggled, meeting in synchrony with a disconcerting mass of tails and scales.

Alex found it fascinating, circling the hatchery's pools along concrete pathways that intersected between them. He put his hands in his pockets, just watching the fish swim for a while and resisting the needlessly silly urge to toss them bread.

He looked up to notice Marge watching him from the doorway, arms crossed with an amused scowl on her face. He almost jumped out of instinct, trying to find some sort of excuse in his head for just standing there. Instead, Marge walked over and stood next to him. "Albert and I hashed out the details. Figured out what we're going to do with the place. Idiot finally seems to be good for something."

Alex nodded, glancing at her quietly with a sidelong look. "He's actually a pretty smart dude. More than you'd think. He's just… got a unique way of expressing it."

"Yeah." Marge shook her head. "You can say that again."

"He's got a unique way of expressing it."

Marge looked at him for a moment, then started laughing dryly. There was a release of pressure there, like something that had been dammed inside her and just broke free. It was a good laugh.

"Yeah. Sure, tell me that next time he gets himself shot." It was the same sort of dryly discontented comment that she usually made, but the smile she had and the laughter that still hung in the air seemed to pull the edge off of it.

"I will." Alex smiled quietly to himself. He liked it when Marge seemed happy. It was rare before the bomb fell, but now he realized this was the first time since that day that she hadn't been openly angry or discontent. It was… passive.

"So, we made it here Alex. As much as the 'smart dude' is still an asshole for suggesting the place, we do have food and water here. Indefinitely, so I'm told." Marge crouched down to look at the fish more closely, running her fingers through her hair. "Ever hear of Maslow's Hierarchy of Needs? It's an economic theory about human desire or some crap. It's like a pyramid, with all the important shit at the bottom. This place means we have the base of it covered. Which means we're safe, for now. As long as no more assholes show up to shoot us, I think we'll be fine here."

"For how long?" It came out sounding more hostile than Alex had intended, but Marge just shrugged it off.

"I don't know. In case you haven't noticed, we're running on survival mode here. We've got the basic needs met, so I wash my hands of the responsibility. All I know is, the world has changed quite a shit bit, and I think it's not about to turn back to sunshine and rainbows." Marge sighed, standing up again and crossing her arms.

"We'll need to deal with the aftermath. I... don't have that many friends, but... everyone else is dead. Like... damn, everyone." It hit Alex like a freight train, even if he almost saw it coming in a way. He knew that 6 billion people were dead or dying somewhere out there, and the 2 billion people left over were not close behind. Their struggle to keep moving and get to a safe harbour had brought down his perspective. Thinking about that was just too monumental a task to take on when your own direct survival was on the line. Doing so now almost made their own hardship seem trivial.

"Yeah. Yeah... we're all going to have to realize that pretty soon. Again, that's why it's important to be here. It's shelter, right? Better we make than realization here instead of somewhere everyone else is realizing it."

"So that's why you've been so... determined?"

"Bitchy Alex. The word is bitchy. In a word, yes. Nobody else seemed to realize just how bad this is. It's denial. Soon enough, it's going to break." Marge's face hardened throughout the conversation, returning to her previous scowl. "I'm going t- I mean, we're going to have to put out a lot of fires Alex."

Alex was lost in thought again, this time of Armageddon and smoke to the south. Of the hellscape that surely covered the planet. His name snapped him out of it, and he took a moment to process what she'd said.

"We?"

"Yeah. Like I said, I'm rescinding my position as leader. Emergency powers are caput. But that doesn't mean we get to relax. Isabelle isn't going to be able to take it and Albert's going to crawl farther into his hellhole of humour to put up with it, so I need you to stay with me on this."

Alex pondered it a moment. He realized then that there were two things he could focus on. The here and now, or the then. He could choose to keep his cool, look towards the task at hand. Zero in on the present and try to zone out the world before. Or, he could lose himself to what had happened, what he'd done. The end of the world, the incineration of society. The blood on his own hands and the hands of others. The darker parts of his mind. Even considering the choice made him plummet, sinking into that sinister place where the lurking of shadows sneered at his hope and determination.

What brought him out of it was Marge's hand, outstretched and beckoning. Like an animal clawing its way out of a hole, he fought through the despair to take her hand. The world around him brightened, drawing back to the present and clarity. He squeezed her hand, nodding and banishing the past into the depths of his subconscious.

"I'm with you, Marge. We've got this."

Marge nodded, letting go of his hand and looking back at the fish, eyes betraying her own struggle with what lay within. "Here's hoping."

9: HATCHING

While Marge returned to the office, Alex took another look around the hatchery floor. After a little more inspection of the fish and machines, Alex made his way through another door at the opposite end of the floor that lead into what he assumed was the touristy part of the place. Where the rest of the building had a sort of clinical life to it, here out back there was nothing but dusty silence. It was like the welcome centre, defunct and dusty in a way that even the dirty windows couldn't illuminate properly. Abandoned signs and expectations from the tour were strewn about, put back here and left to sit once the hatchery stopped being an investment worth keeping. He flicked the lights on here as well, trying to illuminate the darker corners of the building. Another door lead out into the parking lot, this one properly locked. A third door led to the other side of the building, where visitors could interact with guides among the piping and gradient lighting of a needlessly elaborate utility system. The fourth and final door led to the two restrooms, simple single toilet affairs that seemed to be the only part of the place maintained on this half of the property. Alex took a seat on one of the benches around the edges of the room, taking in the dusty signs and illustrations that detailed the intricacies of salmon lifespans. He read them with disinterest, more to fill space than to focus, waiting until the light of the setting sun shone through the dusted windows to signal his return to the group.

He found Isabelle and Marge in the breakroom, talking quietly and privately. It was the sort of thing he would have seen before Marge's promotion, just the two of them alone with their words and thoughts. He leaned on the door, listening in curiously.

"I just want us to make the best decisions Marge... I don't want you to think it's against you or anything... I'm just worried. Sorry." Isabelle rubbed her neck, not yet noticing Alex.

"I went a little crazy Isa. I know I ran over you a little on the way up here, I just need you to trust me, ok? It's worked so far, right?"

"Right. Just... sorry. Again. I'll support your decisions when you need me to."

"That's all I ask." Marge patted her back, noticing Alex and rolling her eyes at him. "It's our decisions. As a group. Really, you're just supporting what's best here."

Alex stepped back out of the room, fighting a sense of unease. Marge was being dishonest, and the strained smile on her face more closely resembled her look when she was leading a conference, not putting her best foot forward. It was a grifter's smile, not a genuine one. He tried to fight the unease, continuing down the hall where he found Albert still glued to the computer. He was eating a can of beans distractedly, resting one hand on the computer mouse and the other digging around the cold tin. His injured arm was undergoing a parodic imitation of physical therapy, twisting around to dig out the dregs of the baked bean deliciousness.

"That's disgusting dude..." Alex shook his head, smirking a little at the pure air of sloppiness Albert was putting off. "Can't you wait?"

Albert glanced at him, shaking his head and gesturing at the screen. "For what? The beans or this? Because in either case, it's a no. I'm just so golly gosh darn hungry, and the fish are just so golly gosh darn interesting."

He flicked a bean at Alex, smirking disconcertingly. Alex wiped off his face where he was hit, walking over to look at the screen. It was still just a bunch of numbers and letters to him, but Albert seemed genuinely intrigued by what was on screen.

"So…" Alex tried to think of something to say to no avail, daunted by the sheer data in front of him.

"Amazed by my technical skills I see. I'm damn good, aren't I?"

Alex blinked. "You're sure… putting numbers in places. Definitely."

Albert snickered, shoving more beans in his mouth and gesturing at different parts of the screen. "All of these are something that the system manages. Like, these three numbers here? That's how much food the fish are getting. And these ones are temperature."

"It's really amazing how you know all this… did you work on the system or something?"

"Nope. Just a peek or two and that's all. I just find numbers fascinating. The sort of things that runs this place are the same sort of things that you'd need to manage to get things built. You know, demand and shit. How much they need to eat, what factors they need to get their job done, how close they are to fertility, that sort of bullcrap. Fish are just wet construction workers if you think about it."

"…what?" Alex didn't really see the comparison, but Albert was evidently pleased by his ability to make an analogy. He leaned back in his chair, putting his feet on the desk and trying to put his hands behind his head before wincing when he remembered one of his arms was grievously injured.

"Ow. Look, Alex, maybe it's time you realize I'm actually an evil genius, and that nuclear armageddon is just a step in my plan for world domination. The fish I raise here will one day rule the world, and that's the Albert guarantee." Albert deadpanned a moment before both men started laughing uproariously. It wasn't particularly funny, but just like before with Marge, this sort of laughter seemed to bring the pressure off of Alex's shoulders. It was a welcome relief, and one that he appreciated Albert for delivering.

Alex sat down in the chair next to him, imitating Albert's position and reclination in the chair. He whistled innocently, putting his hands behind his head and nodding at Albert. That made Albert scoff, shaking his head and snickering. "Show-off."

They laid there for a few minutes, sitting in their chairs and just watching the numbers on the screen. Every now and then they would alternate, switching ever so slightly between tiny variables. It was the automation at work, and something about it was strangely hypnotic.

Alex got lost in thought again, concentrating on nothing but the numbers flashing before him.

"Hey, Alex?" Albert looked over at him, causing Alex to corral his focus back to reality and to him. "Do you have any family dude?"

Alex thought for a moment, then shook his head. "None that I'm close too. My parents have been gone for years, and I don't have any… you know, brothers or sisters. Why?"

Albert let out a breath, shrugging. "I have a brother. We haven't talked in a few years, but he lived in New York so…"

"So he was probably…"

"Yeah. He definitely was." Albert scratched his neck, looking at the computer screen once more. But in there, behind the usual tinge of jolliness and sparks of wit, there was a hollowness. Like a jack-o'-lantern smiling jovially, flames dancing on the wall like a spotlight, but only able to flash so gleefully because someone had put a hole in his head and an emptiness in his heart. "I don't want to think about what it would be like if he got out. If he survived. I want to hope and all, but it's better to just think about him going out immediately."

Alex watched him quietly, saying nothing about the tear he saw slowly fall down Albert's face. He tried to think back to what he and Marge had agreed on, about the here and now. Words that would draw Albert out of his memories and back to reality. But he couldn't, so he just sat there with an empty and idiotic stare, unable to comfort his friend.

"It'd be really unbelievably stupid if he didn't... one day I'd get a message from across the continent somehow. A big ass parchment carried by a falcon or something. I'd set off on a dashing adventure across the continent, battling mutant beasts and romancing the fine ladies of distant lands. It'd be one romantic shitshow, all across America."

Something to say popped into Alex's head, stupid, sudden and completely lacking in taste. "Aren't I the only bromance you need?"

Albert blinked at him a moment, then burst out laughing once more. Alex followed suit, feeling like an idiot but laughing at the absurdity all the same. By the time they were finished, they were out of breath. The laughter now wasn't a release, but rather a mockery of just how strange the situation had gotten.

Albert finally settled down, shaking his head and wiping his eyes. "Ah damn man, that was good. About as funny as a nail in the head, but good anyway. You're right though, I think you've got it covered. For now."

There was an emphasis in the way he said 'For now.' that sparked a curiosity in Alex. "What do you mean 'For now.' You're not going to actually try to find your..."

"What? No, no, nothing like that. I mean real romance. The kisses and shit. The good emotionally hearty meat of a shared touch."

"Did you just say 'Emotionally hearty meat of a shared touch'? The hell?"

Albert smacked his arm, scoffing with a quiet embarrassment. "It's better than anything you could have said. I mean... something real. With someone we meet out here. Or Isa."

He ducked his head after that. It was a strange sight to see Albert embarrassed, stranger still to see him do it with such meekness.

Alex clocked on to what he was saying. "Isa? You mean, our Isa? The woman you've heckled for the entire time you've known her?"

"Yes... look, she's pretty cool dude. All smart and caring and shit. I've been spending some time with her, and she's actually started thinking my jokes are funny."

Alex shook his head with disbelief, a shit-eating smile on his face. "You're such a child dude. Such a child."

"Well, guess what, I'm cool. She's cool. Deal with it dude." Albert crossed his arms, wincing slightly but still managing to deliver his signature smirk.

"Well, good luck with that. I hope she manages to see that you're a funny guy."

"Well, no shit I'm a funny guy." Albert snorted, offended by the implication. "I just hope she sees I'm more than that."

"Again, good luck with that." Alex shook his head, looking off at an empty wall and starting to stray back towards daydreaming.

Albert however, had other plans. "I should be saying that to you with Margey."

The words snapped him back out of his soon to be stupor, making Alex straighten his chair, putting his feet back on the floor. "What?"

Albert followed Alex's lead, planting his chair firmly back on the floor and turning to Alex. "Oh come on, it's obvious. There's so much tension there, what with her alternating between needing you and yelling at you. It's so dramatic, I feel like I shouldn't leave you two alone anymore."

"That's... that's not it at all. She doesn't flip-flop like that on me."

"You mean she doesn't flip-flop on you *yet*." Albert quirked an eyebrow, winking.

"You're disgusting. I don't think of her like that, it's just... she's my friend and she also needs help."

Albert imitated riding a horse, making clapping sounds with his hands. "Ah yes, it is I, Sir Alex the White Knight, here to help any and all females in need!"

"You're an asshole. Really, it's not like that."

Albert's eye twinkled knowingly as he laid back in his chair, nodding his head. "Sure, keep telling yourself that."

Alex shook his head, looking back at the computer screen with interest. "What a weird conversation."

Albert nodded, kicking lightly at the table as Alex reached towards the mouse. "Lots of flip-flopping, eh?"

Alex pulled his hand back, glaring at Albert as the latter snickered. He stood up, tempted to throw the balance off on Albert's chair as he passed by. Instead, he just flicked him on the forehead, heading back onto the fish farm floor to be alone with his thoughts.

Alex watched through the skylights as night came with a chilling of the winds and a twinkling of the stars. Marge had claimed the break room as her own, shattering the glass of the vending machine inside and falling asleep with her hand in a pack of cookies. This left the other three to try to find a comfortable and relatively clean seat in the abandoned section of the hatchery. While Albert and Isabelle settled down for the night, Alex handed out the blankets that they'd added to the backpack. They all drifted off to sleep eventually, undisturbed by the chill in the wind that would brush upon the building in the midst of the night.

10: CABINS

The next day, the clouds returned with a chill on the wind. Alex stepped out of the front office in the early morning, watching his breath curl in the air like a shallow mockery of the swirling clouds that surrounded the mountains around them. He was the first to wake up, something that left him woefully unprepared for what to do. In the last couple of days since the bomb, there had always been a reason to wake up. Something urgent to do or contemplate. But now, all he could do was put his hands in his pockets and wait.

The door opened behind him, making him turn his head to meet the gaze of whoever was approaching. Marge walked out to him, looking at the clouds like he had. She shook her head, mockingly amazed. "I don't see how you can just stare at nothing so long like that. They're just clouds."

Alex shrugs, peering through the cover of the high-up gloom, trying to see the peaks beyond the veil. "Mesmerizing, right?"

Marge scoffs, shaking her head and following his gaze. "I was going to say boring. What do you see in them?"

Alex scratches his head, shrugging and gesturing vaguely. "Anything. That's what clouds are about, right? Seeing... you know, whatever."

Marge makes a little *'pshh'* noise, shaking her head and nudging him. "If this is living in the present, maybe I prefer the PTSD. For you, anyway."

"Is it PTSD?" Alex looked over at her, quirking an eyebrow. It was a heavy word to throw around, and she seemed to realize it.

"No? Maybe? I'm as much a psychologist as you are a nuclear expert, so screw it. Let's say it isn't. I was joking anyway." Her face was flushed with the cold and she brought her hands up to her mouth to blow into them. "Mostly joking. You do need to find something better to focus on for right now."

"Like what? What's your way of focusing on the present?"

Marge blinked, gesturing towards the rest of the valley. "Exploring. Finding ways to stay alive. You know, with jobs and necessities and shit. Trying to turn the one place with operable central heating into somewhere people can live. We need more food, blankets, furniture, whatever the hell else. Comfort and shit. That's what I think about."

Alex suppressed a chuckle, nodding along. "You're not wrong. But my legs ache like hell from yesterday... and I thought you were done with being a leader." He rolled his shoulders, trying to relieve some of the tension that was building up in his muscles. "I thought you were going to kick back and let go of the reigns... right?"

Marge sighed, leaning back on her hands to crack her back. "Yeah, I was supposed to. But sleeping on a shitty sofa and being unable to sleep for hours because I made the mistake of eating sugar before bed... well, I realized we're totally goddamned boned unless we bring in some classic creature comforts. I swear, my back is already out of wack from sleeping in that damn giftshop, but somehow that sofa is worse. I figure it's better to nip this at the bud right now instead of waiting for a few days and letting it screw up something proper."

"So... you're the leader on getting us more stuff? And you're doing it so that we can solve *your* back problems?"

"No, no, hey, don't go throwing around the damn L word. I'm the organizer. The kick in the ass you need to get working. Trust me, after a night or two, I won't be the only one hurting. You'll see."

Alex turned his back to her, watching the fog on the mountain once more. "Sounds like a leader to me…"

Marge whacked him gently on the shoulder, smiling. "Hey, we already have Albert, you don't need to be a smartass too."

Alex snorted, turning back towards her. "Fine. So what's your plan for getting… 'creature comforts'? What are you suggesting?"

"There's plenty of things still scattered in the valley. Cabins, campgrounds, all that shit." She crossed her arms, shrugging and heading back inside. "It's not looting if we're stealing from a multi-national billion-dollar corporation that got incinerated by atomic hellfire. Try finding that exception in the shitty corporate rulebook."

"I'm not sure Isa will see it that way." Alex walked after her, following her through the door and into the warmer air of the office. "She's very sensitive. We've talked about this."

Marge sat in the chair in front of the control PC, now turned off and shut down, spinning around to face him dramatically in her seat. "Well, technically we paid for the whole place, so I'm sure she'll find it in her heart to forgive us." She snickered quietly, putting her hands behind her head. "And if she doesn't, I guess she can get the couch."

Alex didn't respond, watching Marge lean back in her chair with a contented sigh. Subtly, almost involuntarily, he started thinking of possibilities. Of what he needed. Of what they could find with some exploring. Almost subconsciously a shopping list started forming. Lamps to see by without the insufferable overhead light. Books to read in the long days ahead. Paintings and posters to decorate the drab life-sucking walls. He reached in his pocket, pulling out the travel guide from Cheekye. He set it down on the desk next to Marge, causing her to turn and look at it curiously. She picked it up, specifically looking at the map on the back.

"What's this?" She turned it over in her hands a few times before laying it out, spreading the map across the free space of the desk. "Where'd you get this? Actually, screw it, I don't care. Do you have a pen?"

Albert reached over to the desk, pulling the drawers open. After a few drawers of boring papers and unused office supplies, he found a box of pens which he handed over to Marge without comment. She started drawing routes and circling spots on the map, laying out a hasty master plan.

"Here, I'll draw what route we take, you head off and grab Isa. She's going to help us loot."

"That's assuming she wants to. Or even if I want to…"

Marge rolled her eyes, marking off another location to inspect on the map. "You brought the map out, you signed on. No takebacks. Just grab her and get her to help us loot damn it."

"I don't think we should use that word." Alex closed the drawers, standing upright and walking back towards the hallway. "It… puts a bad spin on what we're doing."

"Eh, screw it. Call it a 'friendship excursion' if you want, just get her over here, ok? I'd make it just the two of us if I could, but we all remember what happened last time we left her alone with Albert." Marge didn't look up from her map drawing, leaning down onto the desk. "And Albert alone is less of a danger. Well, less of a danger to himself. He's still a goddamn asshole."

"You should try talking to him." Alex heads through the door, pulling it closed behind him after one more comment. "You might be surprised."

He shut the door before he could hear her scoff and rebuttal, hiding from the viperish retort with the click of a handle. He set off down the hall again, peeking into each room along the way and seeing nothing. The utility closet was still full of dust and cleaning supplies, which came in dire need by the next room, where glass was still sprinkled on the floor near the vending machine. He stood a moment, watching the glass sparkle under the light of the buzzing and flickering tubes above. He wondered if it was worth cleaning up, and even more so if it would even be noticed. With a sigh, he went back to the closet, pulling out a broom and dustpan to clean up the mess. It was probably more trouble than it was worth to clean the glass, but he felt it was proper decorum to fix it. Plus, he didn't want to risk anyone stepping on it and cutting themselves.

He dumped the glass in the trashcan that occupied the corner of the room, pausing for a moment to wonder what they would do with the garbage. Food waste would start piling up soon, and so would plenty of other things like the glass. Alex doubted the garbage truck came out here much, and even then he doubted they would keep up service after the apocalypse. He stared at the can for a moment, wondering, before shaking his head and heading back into the hall.

After returning the cleaning supplies to the closet, he set out to look for Alex and Isabelle. They weren't on the fish farm floor, nor were they in the tourist section. He was worried now, looking into the restrooms after considerably knocking. He almost went into panic mode before noticing the sound of voices approaching through the closed door of the 'utility room'. He stepped back from the door, crossing his arms and smiling at Albert and Isa as they walked through the door. Their flirtatious laughs and smiles dropped when they noticed him, faces flushing red with embarrassment.

"Oh uh, hey Alex... we were just... checking out the pipe system" Isa stammered, trying to find a proper excuse for their obvious distraction.

"She means making out." Albert snickered, causing Isa to smack him and step away. "What? It's true!"

Isabelle glared at him, storming off, face as red as a tomato. Albert watched her go, smiling smugly to himself. Alex shook his head, also watching her go. He felt like he should say something, but Isabelle had slammed the door behind her before he could think up anything.

Albert turned to him, grinning. "See? What did I tell you, there's some ass-cracking chemistry there. She's totally into me."

Alex scoffed, shaking his head and resisting the urge to also smack him. "Not for much longer if you treat her like that…"

Albert waved dismissively, leaning on a wall and trying to adjust himself in a way that makes him look cool, while also not putting too much weight or stress on his injury. "Oh, it'll be fine. Ladies love me, she'll be back for more soon."

Alex was dumbstruck, rubbing his eyes and putting his hands on his hips. "You really are just an egotistical ass, huh?"

"What?"

"What?"

Albert looked at him for a long minute with a neutral smile and an even stare. He seemed to reach a realization, grinning once more and standing up straight, shooting finger guns at Alex in what he personally believed was a misguided attempt to look hip. "See, the thing is Alex, all it is at all is confidence. I know she'll come back, so she'll come back. I'm just that magnetic baby."

"I think that's called being an Egomaniac."

"What, me? Nahhhhhhhh." Albert winked, glancing back at the door to the farm floor. "So, what did you need from me? Butt stuff is off the table."

"Actually, I came here to grab Isa. Me and Marge decided that we should explore around the valley, see if we can find anything useful."

Albert stroked his chin, running his fingers along the stubble that protruded there. It reminded Alex of his own woefully inadequate and unimpressive facial hair. "First of all, I think you mean 'Marge and I'. Second of all, I think you mean. 'Marge decided'. You managed to not only capture how bad your grammar is but also failed to capture how we're all subservient pawns to Margey."

Alex felt offended, not only by the fact that he'd given Albert such easy ammunition but also by the very correct implication that Marge was the one calling the shots despite her continued refusal to be the leader. "It was a group decision between her and I."

"Yeah, that's about as true as the idea that me and Isa were checking the pipes. But hey, you believe what you want to believe. I'm going to go take a piss."

With that, he sidestepped Alex and headed into the bathroom, whistling some invasive tune as he did so. Alex watched him go, once again finding himself alone in a dusty and decrepit room. It occurred to him that maybe he should start leaving rooms first, just for effect.

***

Alex found Isa beside one of the pools, looking into the water at the young salmon swimming. He silently came up next to her, letting her know he was there with a hushed greeting. They looked at the wiggling careless fish for a moment, before he found the need to speak up. "He's sorry you know. Really... he's just not particularly good at drawing lines."

Isa brushed the hair out of her face, wiping her eyes. "I know. That's part of why..." She trailed off, struggling to find the words. She glanced at Alex, shrugged and hoped that it was enough to say what she was trying to say. He didn't think so, but it felt wrong to interject. "Anyways. He's an idiot. But like you said, there's also a little... more, to him. Something interesting. It makes me want to talk to him and stuff. Kiss him even. But like... he'll do that for a while, be all smart and caring, but as soon as something challenges that, he's right back to being... Albert. Have you noticed that?"

Alex nodded. "Yeah. It's like there's two of him. Maybe he has an evil twin."

Isabelle snorted, shaking her head and leaning back from the pools' side. "I hope not. That would be awkward."

"Well, I don't think you'll need to worry. He has a brother, but he's..." He trailed off, realizing that the road he was about to tread could be dangerous. Isabelle furrowed her brow, eyes focusing like the timer on a bomb. Alex had to defuse it before realization struck and the weight of apocalypse fell. "... not a twin. So... yeah."

Isabelle looked at him for a few more seconds. It was a flimsy excuse, and sweat began to bead on his neck when he realized he might have just directed Isabelle's attention to the exact place it shouldn't be. Luckily for him, she seemed more confused than inquisitive and more sane than mortally worried for her family. It felt like he'd dodged a bullet there.

"Ok... what did you want to talk about? Aside from that idiot?" Isabelle frowned down at the fish, shaking her head to clear it from the cobwebs of Albert.

"Marge wants us to help her go out and... have a friendship excursion"

"A what?"

"I... I can't think of a better name. It's what she suggested. She wants to go out and see what we can find in the valley."

Isabelle crossed her arms, turning to face him. "You mean loot. She wants us to loot."

Alex shrugged awkwardly, rubbing his hands together and nodding. "It's not really looting. Nobody lives here anymore, and we paid for all the stuff that is here..."

"People still rent out the cabins in summertime Alex. They're the reason we even bothered to keep them open. It's their stuff in there, it's their property we're robbing."

The door to the office hallway opened, interrupting Isabelle's flash of anger. Marge poked her head through it, narrowing her eyes at the two of them. "Hey! Are we going or not? Stop making out and let's get to work. Cooperative, non-hierarchical work!"

Isabelle blushed at the mention of making out, glancing over at the door behind which Albert lazed, crossing her arms and clearing her throat. "I'm not coming. It's wrong, however you try to… spin it"

"Really had to think about that last one, eh?" Marge shrugs, grinning sadistically. "Guess you'll just have to go without a bed. Or blankets. Or toiletries. Or toilet paper! Wow, you'll really be taking this whole 'out of civilization' thing to heart huh?" Marge chuckled, beckoning Alex over, which he did almost instinctively.

Isabelle blanched, thinking for a moment, standing still and scowling at them as they headed back to the office. Alex shifted uncomfortably, looking at Marge. "I don't think she's coming. You made her mad."

Marge waved him away carelessly. "Isa's anger is like watching a puppy try to kill a bug. More cute than scary, and totally ineffective. She'll stew a bit, then by the time she realizes that her pride is worth less than a functional mattress, she'll cave. I give it until we're at the train station before she comes crawling back."

As it turned out, it didn't even take that long. Alex had barely finished pulling the wheelbarrow out of the ditch before Isa squirmed through the fence to stand next to Marge. She tried to fit in without being awkward about it, but Alex caught the triumphant smile that graced Marge's face as the three started walking back down the road.

Soon enough the smile was wiped off by the cold gusts of wind. This cold snap was harsh, and their jackets were meant for the lingering cold of winter, not the sudden and irreversible vengeance of it's dying breath. They clung tightly to their meagre cover, trying to stay warm as the chilling breeze whistled through the trees like a ghostly howl. Alex wrinkled his nose at the smell of his own sweat, accumulated after days of being active and unwashed. Quietly he made a mental note to grab some emergency clothing from one of the cabins, alongside a more proper set of clothes for the weather, trying to ignore the freezing feeling in his hands as they gripped the wheelbarrow's handles and turned it off the road towards the first cluster of cabins.

From here on out, it became much harder to push the wheelbarrow. While the ground was mostly clear, it was soft from the recent rain, and his wheels would get caught in the mulch of dirt, moss and pine needles almost constantly. He struggled to the point of frustration, almost abandoning the contraption entirely. He pushed through more so out of not wanting to have to come back and grab it again than any other sort of determined strength.

Soon enough, they reached the cluster, three small and single floor log cabins that stood squat against the trees that surrounded them.

"Ok, so, do we take one each or search them all together?" Marge put her hands on her hips, blowing the breath out of her mouth with a small whistling sound.

"I think we should search them one by one..." Alex looked at the three almost identical constructions, trying to see which one attracted him most. He figured the one in the centre looked best, although he wasn't quite sure why.

"I think all together would be good. That way if there's anything inside..." Isa tried to pipe up, but Marge shushed her, shaking her head.

"I agree with Alex, so that's two to one. I'll take the one on the left, Alex you take the middle one and Isa you'll take the right, ok? Ok!"

She set off with a stride towards the cabin on the left, leaving

Isabelle gob stopped and Alex confused. "She said she'd stop that." Alex turned to Isa, concerned. "She said she'd stop acting like that."

Isabelle shook her head, adopting another familiar flash of a look Alex couldn't quite decipher. "It looks like she's not really who we thought she was, huh?" The look was replaced with what can only be described as a fuming rage. Isa stomped off to her cabin, almost kicking the door open with the force of her will. That left Alex alone, tiptoeing towards the cabin in the middle.

As much as the words 'log cabin' tend to bring up rustic images of handcrafted rooms and rustic interior design, the truth was less romantic. These 'cabins' were more akin to shacks, single-roomed affairs that barely stretched bigger than a studio apartment. Alex groaned when he saw the inside of the cabin, illuminated by the light filtering through the trees and window. The single bed looked heavy, and the shelves that adorned the walls were bare. He closed the door behind him, ducking into the musty space and started rifling through the cupboards and unnecessarily heavy chests.

He cleared the small wooden table in the corner, setting its contents on the bed and stepping back to survey the room. Everything he found that was worth noting, he put on the table. It turns out that the results were rather pitiful.

Laid out before him was a box of matches, a set of fleece pyjamas about three sizes too big and ridden with enough holes to make a convincing swiss cheese cosplay. He also found a couple cans of food, peaches to be exact. Their presence mystified him, but in the end, he figured it wasn't really a mystery worth wondering about. Almost as an instinct, he also grabbed the pair of candles he'd put on the bed, setting them with the rest of the stuff. He frowned at the meagre spread on the table, disappointed that he hadn't been able to find more. His eye caught sight of a basket of blankets at the foot of the bed, which he realized could probably help if the cold snap kept going. And the basket itself could help him carry the other stuff he'd found. He grabbed it from it's resting place, setting it down on the table. The blankets were rough and heavy, the sort designed to cradle heat at all costs, not comfort you gently and promise that the nightmares will go away.

They were arranged almost haphazardly, shoved in without much interest or care, making him shake his head as he pulled them out. As meagre as his offerings were, he'd have to put them back in with some tighter organization if he wanted to fit everything in. However, by the time he'd pulled out the second blanket, he noticed a bit of metal under the third, shining from the meagre rays of sunlight that moved through the cabin's gloom. Curiously, he reached in, glancing at the door and wrapping his hand around a cool piece of metal.

He pulled it out, holding up the object to the light. Quickly, his heart started beating faster, and his throat went dry.

The object was a gun.

11: LABOUR

Alex stepped out of the cabin with the basket, eyes wide and shoulders shaking from the wind. He'd left the gun on the table, choosing to ignore its presence entirely. It was a revolver, wholly different from the rifle he'd already used. But the feeling of its grip in his hand and his finger on the trigger had spooked him, bringing forth feelings and fears that made him decide it was better to leave and forget that it ever existed. He knew Marge would be pissed if she ever found out, but the memories it brought back of that night didn't serve the present. Regardless, he hadn't found any ammo for it, so he doubted that there would be much use for the gun anyways.

At least that's what he hoped.

He set the basket on the ground in front of him, cracking his back and wiping his mind of the gun's creeping imprint. Instead, he looked up to the cloudy sky above. The swirling shapes seemed darker than before, more menacing. Heavy and rough like the blankets from the cabin. They had more presence in the sky, teetering like they carried something with them.

Soon enough Isabelle and Marge stepped out, each carrying their loot nonchalantly. Marge groaned, dumping her assorted candles and cans onto the neatly sorted basket. Alex cringed as a couple of her objects rolled off and landed on the forest floor. Isabelle was more orderly, putting her acquired contents onto the ground in a line. Alex looked over it all. It was really just more of the same, blankets and candles alongside some cans and woefully inadequately sized clothing. It was a disappointing haul for sure.

Alex loaded the basket into the wheelbarrow, picking up Marge's items for her as she scoffed at a nearby tree trunk. Isabelle glared at her, fitting her own acquisitions inside the wheelbarrow, neatly filling the space. Alex grabbed the handle and started to push.

"Hey, wait." Isabelle glanced back at the cabins. "What about the beds? Wasn't that the point of coming out here?"

Alex sighed nodding. "Yes. Yes, it is. Ok... ok... how do we do this?"

Marge thought for a moment, still glaring at the tree. "I say, we just grab the mattresses. Maneuvering the frames out of there would be too much trouble, and there's no way we'd get all three of them back to the hatchery in one trip. Those assholes look heavy."

"What about the wheelbarrow? I still have to push it; I don't think I'll be able to carry the mattress and do that at the same time."

Marge rolled her eyes, walking over and squishing the contents down so that Alex could fit the end of the mattress in there. She raised her eyebrows at him, crossing her arms. He sighed, nodding and heading back into his designated cabin. He made sure not to look over at the table and its silver adornment, instead focusing on wrangling the mattress out the door. When he was out, the other two dropped their mattresses on the ground, carefully managing the sheets to not stick to the pine needles and sappy acorns below. Quickly they moved to help him mount the mattress onto the wheelbarrow, creating an uncomfortable but wholly manageable position from which to push the wheelbarrow.

What followed was a long and difficult plod back to the hatchery, where Alex struggled to balance the mattress and the other two could do little more than groan about it while carrying the weight of their own mattresses on their backs. The rain started up again, icy cold and terrible. While the other two were afforded cover by their charges, Alex was left exposed and shivering, hands almost freezing around the handles to the wheelbarrow as he shoved it back onto the road. From there, it was almost a full sprint to the hatchery, or at least as close as one could get to a full sprint with their cargo.

When they got there, they found the chain-link gate wide open, accompanied by Albert grinning in the doorway while spinning a key around his finger. By then, Alex was cold, wet and miserable, so all he wanted to do was find a warm spot to curl up and suffer.

He brushed past Albert, dumping the wheelbarrow and soaking mattress under the awning next to the door. As chatter and reprimanding erupted behind him from the commotion of Albert *daring* to open the gate, Alex found a spot next to a vent to sit and let the heat wash over him. He felt like crying. It wasn't from the gun he'd found, or from the way he saw relationships breaking among the group. Sometimes the greater challenges of life are minor compared to what someone was feeling just this moment.

And right now, Alex was cold, wet and exhausted.

***

He woke up later with a crick in his neck and confusion in his mind. He didn't remember falling asleep, but his clothes were more moist than wet, and a blanket was laid over him almost theatrically. Blearily he brought himself to his feet, looking around the room with confusion. It seems he was in the office, or at least that's what the faint glow of a pair of screensavers on the monitors indicated. Night was here and he'd slept the whole day away. Alex almost had to laugh at the absurdity of it. Quietly he fumbled around in the dark, looking for a light switch to illuminate his world again. When he did find the light switch, he squeezed his eyes shut and watched the blast of light permeate through his eyelids. Carefully he blinked his eyes open, looking around now properly.

Everything seemed as it was before. He looked out the windows, trying to see past the glare of the glass and out into the parking lot. The gate was closed again, and the wheelbarrow lay empty and turned over. The mattresses were nowhere to be seen, so he could only assume they'd been brought inside. Something was off about the whole scene. He couldn't tell if it was just the lingering sleepiness of his brain, the dim brilliance of the light on the glass or even just nothing at all. But he felt like there was something out there that he was missing, a piece of the puzzle that he'd lost. Perhaps even one he'd never seen. It was a creeping feeling that started to needle into him. Shaking his head to clear the uncertainty, he turned back towards the rest of the building past the closed door to the hallway. Whatever it was, it was less important than finding out what happened, or at the very least finding some food.

His stomach rumbled angrily, devoid of a whole day's worth of nutrients. Slowly he opened the door to the hallway, walking down it carefully, steps tracing loudly on the floor at a volume that felt like thunder. He worked his way into the breakroom, barely illuminated by the light of the office. Just inside the threshold, he bumped into something firm and soft on the floor, an unknown shape occupying the center of the room. Something groaned from on top of it, mumbling some dream ambled nonsense. He figured it must be Marge asleep on the mattress she'd claimed, a theory supported by the vague shapes and shadows cast by the meagre light.

He carefully felt his way around the mattress to get to his vending machine prize, careful not to move too suddenly and wake her up. His throat was as parched as his stomach was empty, so once he had grabbed a handful of chip bags and a fruit fritter, he readjusted his goals to look for a proper way to drink water that didn't constitute the rain. Perched on one of the machines that covered the hatchery floor he found a cup that at one point served to test the waters of the hatching pools. He decided to use it for himself, grabbing it and heading towards the bathroom to fill it up. He almost fell into one of the pools in the dark, his foot hit the cut-off point and almost sending him tumbling into the swirling mass of scales and flesh. Instead, he merely stumbled a little, straightening up and moving forward more slowly. He made it to the bathroom without further issue, passing through the abandoned section, with the snores and outlines of Isabelle and Albert marking the spots he should avoid. When he turned the bathroom light on it spilled out into the rest of the area, letting him know with some annoyance that Albert had taken his mattress. He shut the door behind him, putting his cup under the tap and filling it with water. He sat in silence under the buzzing light, quietly eating his stale fruit fritter and sipping at some metallically tart water. His reflection looked back at him, dirty and bedraggled. His hair was unkempt, his skin unhealthy. The dirt of the cabins and claptraps that they had explored almost seemed fused to him, diluted by the rain into a more permeating and permanent shade to his skin. It's as if the very pores of his skin had been clogged.

Alex had to fight the instinctual feeling he had to take pity on the figure in front of him. He looked like a homeless man and he realized with a less than flattering sense of self-awareness that he probably smelled like one too. It hadn't even been a week since the bombs dropped down on his world, but already he was turning to something more base and instinctual. The required grooming of an office job and the supplies that he used to have on hand to manage that grooming were gone, puffed into smoke and ash. It would be thrilling if it wasn't so depressing.

Once he finished his midnight snack, Alex tried to sleep on the row of seats he had occupied the night before. But he was cold and restless, so he ended up walking the halls for a few hours. It was strange how night changes a place. It makes corners sharper and angles fuzzy. It turns the shadows of the little lights we use into long and arching things, stretching a filter over our artificial world. Alex took some time in the dark, looking outside at the rain-streaked pavement with the lights off. He even turned the computers off, keeping his hand over the light-switch as he plunged himself into complete darkness. The stars did not shine through the ash-streaked sky, and the moon was only the faintest of imprints over the cloudy shroud. Alex closed his eyes, finding no difference between when they were open or closed. It was a panicked feeling, but one so senselessly euphoric. He could hear the raindrops, feel his breathing, taste the staleness of the air and smell the rank odour of his own body.

But when he opened his eyes and turned the lights back on, the world was back once more. The experience was... strange and he stood there for a while pondering it.

Footsteps snuck down the hall behind him, causing him to turn his head. Marge emerged through the doorway, looking at him sleepily. "What the hell Alex?"

Alex shrugged, blinking at her. "What? What's wrong?"

"It's..." she instinctively checked her watch, before realizing she didn't have a watch. "Really goddamn late. Why are you over here flicking the lights and creeping by my bed?"

"I couldn't sleep." He shrugged simply. "I was also hungry, and I don't know where you put all the food we have."

Marge scoffed at him, running her hands through her hair and sitting on the desk. "Well no shit. You collapsed like a flower under a heavy dew. The hell was that?"

Alex sat in the chair, still looking out at the parking lot. "You ever get that feeling?" Marge opened her mouth to make a comment, probably to the tune of pointing out the stupidity of that question, but chose to let him finish. "You know, the one where... it just sort of feels like something is damming up inside of you and if you don't scream or pass out, it'll kill you?"

"I get something like that every day of my goddamn life. Doesn't give you the excuse to be a wet blanket." Alex just shrugged, making Marge sigh and lean her back against the wall. "You know Isa's heading towards that right now. That feeling. She was all quiet and shit today. Really uncomfortable. I think her mind's going to those places we didn't want it to go."

"I don't think there's anything we can do about it." Alex shook his head, looking back at Marge. "It's… natural, for her to worry. If she ends up thinking that maybe it's better out there than in here, that maybe there's some hope she can cling to that maybe people she knew are alive… we can't try to take that away from her."

Marge laughed, a dry and apathetic laugh that seemed to suck some of the air out of the room with its presence. "We have to. If and when she remembers more than just survival, she's going to break. Isabelle… cares Alex. She cares about people around her and people she's never met. It's a good trait, sure, if this was a shitty ass desk job. But hey, guess what, the world went up in smoke. And Isabelle's just going to chase that shit until it suffocates her. Keeping it out of her mind until the time comes where she has no choice but to face the truth? *That* is how we survive."

Alex felt uncomfortable. Marge seemed to take the role of puppet master in stride, trying to hold the strings of the group from within. He could almost visualize it, small intangible strings reaching into each of their heads, pulled by the force of her will and the diffusion of her ideas. He shook his head, clearing the tendrils of ethereal string that he could almost feel curling around his brain. "You talk about it like it's just… a chessboard. Like you have to manage us under a set of specifications."

"Alex, do you remember what I did before I was in administration?"

"Statistics and data analysis, why?"

"My job was basically the same. You look at people, you see who they are and what drives them. Little tidbits of info. For example, Isabelle is fragile, and Albert is an idiot. You're curious and mildly…" She paused a moment, seemingly searching for a word to use. "…artistic. Point is, that shit helps. And sometimes I get the better of myself when shit goes wrong. That right there is why I was such a shitty manager at Macedon Tours but I'm basically Jesus out here."

"So it's like what Albert does. He looks at people and does what he thinks they need?" Alex was very uncomfortable now. Marge was sleepy and distracted, but the way she laid out her control scheme was so very clinical and cold.

She laughed again, this time with more humour than dry wit. "Albert is an incredibly good social observer. He's such a prick, but we keep him around because it's endearing. It's a whole other set of skills. A lot more personable. But screw it, it works. Even on the night that the bombs... you know."

"On that night... what?" Alex leaned towards Marge, who now seemed a little lost. Like her train of thought had derailed into a puff of smoke. "Was... did you actually *enjoy* yourself at dinner or was it still just... a spreadsheet."

Marge didn't respond. It seemed she'd taken a page out of his book and took upon herself a sudden interest in the benignly uninteresting while he spoke. Alex relented. He figured that maybe he didn't even want the answer.

"I'll... just go back to trying to sleep." He got up from the chair, heading back down the hall and into the abandoned section once more. His conversation with Marge echoed around his head. It made him doubtful. Of himself and his intentions. Of her intentions as well. Marge had always seemed to hate being the boss. It was something she'd worked for and grown to utterly despise. But now it seemed she was embracing the role from the sidelines. As he settled down in the darkness, thoughts and the snores of Albert and Isabelle bounced through his head, colliding with each other like cacophonous whispers in the empty part of his skull.

12: BACKUPS

In the couple of days that followed, the work was much the same. While Albert lazed around and opened gates, the other three scavenged the valley for what they could find. Food, books, clothing and furniture, all of it uprooted and dragged back to the hatchery. As they worked, the days grew colder and the frosts of each morning longer. In every expedition, they never managed to find proper clothing for the weather. Each of them had to hold a blanket around themselves and hope that the physical activity was enough to ward off the chill that creaked bones. For now, they limited themselves to the closest attractions the valley had to offer, mostly cabins and campgrounds.

They reconverted the pipe room into a storage room, using the empty space to store the supplies they deemed ultimately more important for the long-term. Or rather, what Marge deemed more important for the long run.

By the time of their fourth morning in the hatchery, Alex felt more at home, but also more concerned. The tension in the air was palpable. Marge remained distant, divvying up supplies and assignments like a taskmaster, while unequivocally denying that she had any authority at all. Isabelle suffered from mood swings, sometimes seeming irritable and angry while at other times being the same old friendly Isa. Albert lounged about, making the most of his injury and inability, two handicaps that nonetheless allowed him to torment the other three with his usual brand of humour.

The tension in the air was palpable. And even though by now

Alex slept on a proper bed, brushed his teeth with a proper toothbrush and didn't really want for food or water, he felt darkness coming down on the world. There was a storm brewing inside the hatchery, and he knew that it was inevitable that it would soon break out.

***

It was the dawn of the next day. The sun was a shrouded enigma behind the clouds, lost beyond the heavens. Alex sat by the windows of the abandoned section, which now served as essentially a dormitory for everyone but Marge. They had each considered moving into somewhere else, but the office was already essentially serving as a common area, and nowhere else was free from the ever-present hum of machinery. Alex glanced behind him at the other two, trying to gauge what they were feeling. They were sat on Albert's bed, embroiled in a friendly war of whispers, hands held together in the tentative way a pair of high school sweethearts would bond, ready to separate at the soonest sign of disruption or authority.

In the past few days, they'd grown closer. It was the small things that made Alex realize their investment. They would sit closer together and nod their heads as they passed each other in the hall. They would whisper secrets and brush their hair out of the way every time the other came into the room.

It was an almost mocking parallel to what Alex did with Marge, long-winded talks in the dead of night that seemed to more alienate than relate. That was the difference, Alex guessed, that left the other two mostly content.

Alex looked back up at the clouds and the distant ring of fire that was the sun behind them. The peaks cut into the swirling darkened mass like knives into felt, going to a place above the ground that was distant from what was on the earth below.

The truth was Alex had been up there once. On an overcast day only a few years ago, he had ascended to the top of Whistler Mountain. His gondola had driven up the sheer cliffs and green meadows of the mountainside, heading towards an indomitable wall of clouds that served as the lid of a coffin that laid over the valley below. He'd instinctively held his breath as the gondola entered the stifling embrace of the swirling mass, spending a precarious moment shrouded in the fog that dared not reach the top of the world.

And then… he was there. Below him, the clouds, above him nothing but the sheer blue sky and the shock of the golden sun. He almost had to laugh once he stepped off of the lift, enthralled by the vista. He reached the edge of the platform placed at the top, moving past mobs of tourists and fellow gawkers, entrapped in the drastic difference from the world below. The sun shone brightly on his back and the world before him almost seemed to stand still. It was an infinite sea of cloud, an uneven mass of fissures and peaks that echoed the mountains that stood above it. They sat there, snow-capped and distant, floating figures on an ocean that hung over the world below.

The feeling was simply put, pure. It was the heaven that lurked atop Olympus, the sort of experience that inspired men and women to change their world.

But when he was done, the descent came again. Back beneath that suffocating blanket. And the feeling was gone.

Alex blinked back to the present, stepping back from the window. His mind had gotten the better of him again. The past should have no purchase, that was the decree he and Marge had agreed on. But right now, in the quiet moments that occupied the empty spaces of activity, those memories were the only thing he had.

***

It was later in the day, after a breakfast of canned peaches and metallic water, that Alex saw Marge again. It was while he was trying to catch one of the salmon in the pools, using a net that he'd found in the utility closet. They had agreed a few days back, on their second expedition out to the valley, that they would need to figure out how to capture and cook a fish properly so they could eat it. As much as the prospect was unnerving and unlikable, the truth was that it would be inevitable. It was the main draw of moving here, after all, the infinite supply of salmon. Their supply of stolen and looted produce would only last so long, so getting used to eating a lot of fish was high on the list of priorities.

As such, Marge found him there by the pool, on his knees in front of the water with an empty net and a frustrated look on his face.

"Any luck Hemmingway?"

"Hemmingway?" Alex looked up from his spot, sitting back on his calves and letting the net rest next to him. "Why Hemmingway?"

Marge shrugged, sitting next to him. "He wrote 'The Old Man and The Sea'. It's about a guy catching a fish."

"You're... reading Hemmingway? How did you even get it?" Alex was sort of amazed. He'd never figured Marge for someone who read many books, let alone Hemmingway.

"I found it in one of the cabins and I was bored. So..." She spread her palms out. "Hemmingway it goddamn is. Do you read Hemmingway?"

"Well, no... but..."

"Then don't be so surprised. Sheesh. I do more than yell you know."

"You also scheme." He passed her a dirty look. It was subtle, but he was sure she saw it from the way her face twisted a little from the words.

"I don't scheme. I plot. Maybe a little manipulation. Shit, I'm just trying to keep us all alive." Marge looked down at the fish, chuckling dryly. "And at least I can catch a fish."

Alex shoved the net towards her, raising an eyebrow. "Sure... give it a try."

She scoffed at him, grabbing the net and using it to stand up. She dipped it into the pool, frowning as the concentrated mass of salmon slipped away from her net as soon as it dipped into the water. She shook her head, moving the net around without much success. Alex could tell it frustrated her. He figured it was a better idea to distract her and fill the air before the frustration manifested itself in an outburst.

"Isa and Albert seem to be getting closer. They've been hanging out a lot." Alex watched the fish continue to dodge the net, noticing their natural instinct to avoid the way the object disturbed the surface. What was even more obvious was how little Marge seemed to notice their patterns, only ever swinging the net through the water with clumsy and aggressive strokes, each of which never did anything more than push the masses away.

"Have they? I didn't notice." It was dripping with sarcasm, and Alex felt that the fish were getting through to her more than he was. "Alex, of course they are. Albert got shot and Isabelle is the only one out of us who knows any goddamn first aid. Of course she's going to hang out with him, she's a sucker for pity."

She dropped the net angrily, crossing her arms. "Just like these fish are suckers for avoiding my net. Feed us you pricks!"

She kicked the net into the pool, making Alex quickly grab it before it got caught in the flow and swept to pools unknown. "They're just fish, Marge…"

"Yeah. Just fish. Asshole fish." She shakes her head, stomping off. Albert watched her go, looking back down at the fish pensively. He grabbed the net and dunked it into the pool, letting the fish flow around it rather than pushing the issue himself. They avoided it at first, but soon after they swam with it like it was barely there. It was just moments before he felt something pull on the net, meaning it was just a few moments more before he had pulled a couple of fish out of the water and onto the poolside.

It was that moment, looking into the stagnant dead eyes of the still very-alive salmon that he realized this would be more of a process than he'd thought.

"Hey, Marge?" He looked over at her, watching her turn around to face him with her hands on her hips. "Do we have a knife?"

**

As it turns out, gutting a fish with no prior training or experience was a brutal affair. Since Alex caught the fish and Isabelle was generally squeamish towards the affairs of the dead, Albert got the job of preparing the fish to be cooked on a meagre hotplate that they'd found at one of the campgrounds. And since Albert was 'too injured' to work, that meant that the only other available option was Marge. The other three watched as she bemoaned her position, unsympathetically offering suggestions. Isabelle wasn't happy about it, Alex was just a tad disgusted and Albert had the sort of shit-eating grin that you would commonly see on a lunatic watching the pretty colours of red and silver. "I'm definitely not saying I enjoy this, but something about Margey elbow-deep in fish guts brings me a little giggly feeling."

Marge groaned, glaring daggers at Albert as she pulled out the last of the fish's insides. "If you don't shut the hell up, I'm gutting you next asshole." As Albert mimicked an intense parody of fear, Marge threw the fish guts on the floor, holding up the once proud butchered wreckage of a salmon. "Alright, I spent long enough looking at this thing. Let's cook the sucker."

They all gathered around the hotplate, setting the bits of salmon that Marge had clumsily divvied up on the hotplate. Carefully they watched it heat up the salmon, poking it over when it looked like the heat was cooking too much of one part and not enough of another. They were like cavemen, huddled around a fire as they took their first steps to figure out its wonders. And no doubt like those ancient humans, the food turned out almost inedible. They had no idea what to do to make the fish cook properly, and the heat of the hotplate produced an unevenly cooked mess. Each of them tried a bite and each of them spat it out almost instantly. Albert at least tried to pretend he enjoyed it a moment for a joke before the taste got to him and he had to spit it out in disgust. The second part produced a greater laugh.

So it was then, that the salmon hatchery became less of a boon than they might have believed. Alex figured that once the rest of the food ran out, the only thing they could do was to choke down the salmon anyway. Until then, they all agreed that avoiding it was by far the best option.

Something told Alex that it wouldn't that convenient for long.

13: DISTRACTIONS.

It had been a week since the bombs fell. Alex was wrapped in two layers of blankets and still freezing cold as he trapezed around the side of the building and watched his breath curl in the air. He could almost swear that he could see flurries of snow in the distant clouds above, white swirls of frost among the droplets of the falling rain, but as far as he knew it was just a trick of the eye. Ever since the clouds folded over after the clear sky, the temperature continued to drop. It was terrifying, not only for their lack of proper winter clothing to withstand it but also for the dark and dusky mood it sent down upon the world.

Isa and Marge had set off shortly beforehand, off on another scavenging run to try to find more food and especially more warm clothing. Albert had made one or another excuse about revising and rechecking the systems that left the hatchery running. That left Alex to make sure that the fence that surrounded the hatchery was secure and strong enough to deter any hungry predators driven by the cold snap and potential smell of fish. His imagination wandered to bears, cougars, bigfoot. All manner of wild animals and monsters that roamed between the shadows of the darkened pines. He shivered again, this time not from the cold.

He ran his hand along the fence, feeling his fingers slip over the cool metal of the perimeter. It wasn't particularly strong, designed more as a deterrent than an obstacle for any animal determined to force it's way inside. The mesh of the wire felt almost brittle under his touch, and his skin burned with the cold of the metal. He pulled his hand back, burying it in his pocket with a wince. The perimeter was as secure as they could make it, that was for certain. But was it as secure as they'd like?

He turned back towards the building, noticing the ladder that was adjoined to the flatter part of the building. He figured maybe it would be better to make a final sweeping check, using the vantage point to make sure there was nothing he'd missed. He put his hand on the first rung, recoiling as the sting of the cold metal struck his palm. He grimaced, looking back at the ladder and shaking his head. It was getting too cold outside to climb, he'd need gloves if he wanted to get on the roof.

Alex ducked back into the building through the side door that lead into their improvised dorm room, shutting it behind him to lock out the chill. Albert was laying on his bed, reading a book in a single hand and generally lazing about. The enduring laziness that he'd partaken in ever since being shot was an obstacle the rest of the group had to learn to compensate for. All in all, since coming to the hatchery Albert had limited himself to the management of the farm itself, and nothing else. Alex knew that there was resentment. Mostly from Marge and partially from himself. It did sting to watch Albert laze around with a wrench in one hand and 'The Dazzling Diary of one Ruebeck Stoveholm' in the other.

"So… I guess you finished your work??" Alex glared at Albert as he sat on his own bed, wringing out the blanket he had wrapped around him and swapping it for another. He set the wet one out on the windowsill, pulling his week old and wet socks off.

"Yeah, and with time to spare. I'm a real maestro when it comes to pressing buttons with numbers on them." Albert snickered to himself, setting down the book to talk to Alex.

Alex put his socks next to the air vent, rubbing his hands together next to it. "Is… is that all it is? Just pressing numbers? Why are you the only one doing it then?"

"Because I'm a lazy ass who exaggerates how little work I do. It's not just pressing buttons. It's also flicking switches."

That got a chuckle from Alex, who laid back on his bed with tired bones and a sudden seeping lack of energy. "Really though. I know you've been shot and all, but it wouldn't hurt to help out a little more around here."

Albert sat up, gesturing at his wound. "You sound like Margey. This hurts you know. Like hell. I need to keep resting with an upright attitude if I want to make it through this." He laid back down, wincing theatrically.

"You are such a drama queen dude." Alex stared at the ceiling cringing at the words coming out of his mouth. "You could try. Maybe teach me how to flip those switches and press those buttons. Work together?"

Albert only made a 'pshh' sound, waving his hand dismissively. "Shit dude, that would make me obsolete. And the way Margey is running things, that probably means I'd be kicked out to die of hypothermia or something. She's cold dude, real cold."

"It's not like that…"

"What, you don't think so? I'm sure she's just a fountain of puppies and fudge in your eyes, eh?"

Alex shot him a warning look, annoyed at the implications. "She works hard dude. She's just trying to get us all through this alive. It's… it's normal, for her to be a little harsh."

Albert waited a moment for the silence to settle, before shaking his head and sitting up. "Spoken like a true bottom. Look, dude, the problem isn't that she's a raging bitch, that part is well known. The problem is that she's just going, going, going. Have you noticed that it's been a whole week since the world went to shit, and I'm the only one who ever relaxes? Margey was fine being a type-A ass when our lives where on the line, but she's running you two like robots. Soon enough you're going to break down." Albert pushed himself off the bed and to his feet. "Luckily, I have just the solution."

Without another word, he left onto the farm floor, giving Alex nothing to consider but his own thoughts. At least for a few seconds. Albert peeked back in once the door shut behind him. "That was badass-talk for 'come over here and let me show you my amazing plan' jackass."

Alex blinked, then got to his feet and walked after him.

***

Albert turned around to face him once they were on the farm's main floor. He was illuminated by the faint specialized lighting designed to keep the trout healthy and nothing more but the faint and distant rays of the shrouded sun. Alex would call it dramatic, almost like the final scene of a thriller, where two mortal enemies stand at either end of a precipice, ready for the duel that would decide the fate of the universe.

Or at least, it would have been if Albert wasn't holding a deflated football.

"Where'd you get that?" Alex had his hands in his pockets, wiggling them around in the empty space to keep them warm in the colder cavernous space of the farm.

"Isa found it on one of your little expeditions. Gave it to me as a gift to keep myself entertained while you all went and did the hard labour our great leader demands. So, I'm going to pass along that gift, by playing catch with you."

"Playing catch?" Alex had to suppress the urge to laugh. It was a ridiculous idea, like a mortuary that specialized in bright pink coffins. Stupid levity in a time of darkness. And yet, he couldn't help but feel like Albert was onto something. "That's your big plan?"

"Hell yeah, that's my big plan. Badass, huh?" Albert grinned in his unsettling way, but Alex could tell he was hinging on the idea more than he let on. "Now, can we do this or do I need to explain the plan here?"

"Look, Albert I…"

"Ok, here it is. I'm going to throw this ball at you, and you're going to catch it and throw it back. We do it back and forward until someone gets hit in the face or we get bored, capiche?" Albert had an intensity in his gaze that left Alex a tad intimidated. It wasn't the sort of look Albert usually gave him, and he had an uneasy feeling that he was being volunteered to play catch if he liked it or not.

"Ok, yeah... fine. Let's play catch."

Albert whooped, pumping his arm before groaning in pain. "Ow, ow, that was the one with the bullet wound, definitely the one with the bullet wound."

Alex facepalmed, rubbing his temple. "You're an idiot."

"Hell yeah I am, now let's toss the pigskin!" Albert lobbed the ball at Alex rather clumsily, limited by his lack of motion in the other arm. Alex nearly had to dive for the ball but managed to lunge forward quick enough to grab it before it fell. He brought it up to his chest and thought for a moment on if he should throw it or not.

The implications of it were unknown, the effects it would have on his environment were unpredictable. If Marge was here, she would be yelling at them to stop and find something useful to do. But in the end... wasn't that the point?

The ball left his hand almost without him noticing. Albert caught it with a grin, whooping and throwing it back. The excitement of it was infectious. Soon enough, Alex too was laughing and whooping, throwing the ball back and forth between them like friends were oft to do. It was a singularly strange and out of place experience in this new post-apocalyptic world. But, Alex realized, it was also the first time he'd felt happy since the end of the world.

But as with all good things, it had to come to a quick and decisive end.

"Hey!" The voice pierced the room like the shriek of a banshee, driving a wedge through the air of the room like a cleaver. Both men looked towards its source, the football falling unceremoniously towards the ground. A soaking wet and very angry looking Marge occupied the doorway to the hall, shivering and glaring with cold fire. "What the hell are you two doing? You didn't let us in! There could be anything out there, and we're piled with shit! What, do you want to sell us to the goddamn wolves? The hell were you doing?"

In an instant, the room had changed. The levity that had existed so briefly in this world had vaporized into a puff of smoke in a moment. Alex was dragged out of the warm place that was this idyllic game between friends and back into the cold dark truth of the hatchery.

Albert meanwhile, seemed determined to fight for his fantasy. "It was just a game of catch Margey, relax. It's not like it's the end of the world."

Marge strode into the room, glaring daggers at both of them and looking very much like she wanted to crush something. "No Albert you moron, that was last week. And this isn't a damn game where you can just laze around and play ball. This is a real goddamn apocalypse, and if you're not going to help out, then at least don't distract Alex. Speaking of Alex, you goddamn moron, go open the gate for Isa."

"You... didn't do that? You just left her out there?" Alex was coming back down to earth now, and it irked him somewhere towards the back of his mind that Marge had prioritized yelling at them instead of actually solving her issues.

"Yeah yeah, cry about it later. I need to solve Albert's lazy ass out, right now. Chop chop!" She flourished behind her, cocking her head strongly to order Alex through the door.

Unfortunately, he complied. It felt like he had lead weights welded to his shoes, each step towards the door taking hours. There were things he wanted to say and excuses he wanted to make. But he knew that they would fall upon deaf or powerless ears. So he just walked. Eventually, he got there, ducking through the door with two pairs of eyes piercing deep into his soul, one filled with anger and disbelief, the other filled with regret and determination.

14: EVALUATION.

The storm was growing stronger.

This was true in two ways. On the one hand, the weather was getting worse. Days without sun were regular for the season, but the black stain of the bombs had seeped into the atmosphere and driven a darker bargain for the climate. While it had been drizzling this morning, the rain now drew down like pellets, liquid hail in its intensity. He languished through puddles towards the gate, hand wrapped tight around the key to the fence's lock. Bending down to shakily unlock the gate, he realized the second way a storm was brewing, and it was just on the other side of the fence.

He looked up, towards Isabelle on the other side of the gate, shivering and chattering in the cold, holding meagre shelter under a thin woollen blanket. Marge abandoning her here to chew out Albert felt simultaneously counter-productive and depressingly apt for their current situation. As soon as he pulled the bolt out of the ground, Isabelle threw the gate open and dashed towards the doorway, ducking under the awning like a shivering kitten hiding from lightning. That left Alex to pull the half-flooded wheelbarrow back towards the hatchery, dragging it clumsily through the puddles and pitfalls of the parking lot.

He very nearly tipped it over as he leaned back against the side of the building, feeling the water soak through his skin and into his bones. In an almost shocking suddenness, he felt a pang of embarrassment and hoped nobody was around to see just how pathetic the pair of them looked.

"S-so…" Isabelle chattered through her ricocheting teeth. "Did

Marge ever get to yell at Albert? Be-e-because that was clearly more important to her..."

Alex nodded, pulling the contents of the wheelbarrow into his arms, which once again were disappointingly just blankets and cans. He kicked the door open, ushering Isabelle into the warmer space that was the office, pushing the door shut behind him until he was sure he heard a click. Now the first storm was locked outside, and all he had to face was the one brewing inside.

Isabelle sheltered herself next to an air vent throwing off the soaked blanket that shrouded her and tried to hug the grate in the wall.

"You're feeling it too?"

Isabelle nodded, trying hard to stop her teeth from producing a sound that Alex could almost swear had a passing likeness to maracas. "Marge is s-such a hypocrite. Sh-she spent years trying to become th-the boss, but when she f-finally got there, she hated it. A-and now that sh-she's still ordering us a-around even though she's p-pretending she's not in charge." Isabelle banged her head lightly against the wall, grimacing. "I-I just don't get it."

Alex gritted his teeth, grabbing one of the blankets that hadn't been soaked to the core, laying it over Isabelle's shoulders. "I guess this is just who she is. She's so scared of the title, but she wants the power."

Isabelle nodded shakily. "I-it's how she is. D-did you know she's the one who s-suggested Paradise Valley as a development? M-Mr. Donahue didn't like the idea at first, b-but she convinced him."

"Really? But… she hates this place. She's said as much."

"B-because she wants to distance herself from it Alex… i-it's shameful for her. Sh-she told me b-back when she got the job as boss."

Alex couldn't believe it. But then again, it did make a sort of twisted sense. The ridicule Marge hounded onto Paradise Valley had to come from somewhere. "But that's so... clinical."

"Of course it is." Isabelle was warming up now, sitting back from the vent and laying against the wall. "Marge is a really good manipulator Alex. I-I'm sure you can tell. You and her slipping off to talk all the time. I-I bet you two talked about us, right? About keeping us in line?" Isabelle shook her head. Alex felt a pang of guilt when he realized that not only did Isabelle know that he was conspiring with Marge, but also that she knew exactly what it was they'd spoken about.

"That was... how do you..."

Isabelle chuckled, but it was dreary and defeated sound. "I was her yes-man for years Alex... she used to have everyone's best interests at heart. She's just wrong, not evil. Paradise Valley could have been fantastic, b-but... it wasn't. She could have been a great leader if she'd just let go of the strings and taken the reigns. Back then I was ok with it because I thought all she needed was to settle into the role a little. I thought it was a moment for... I don't know, growth. I was rooting for her."

"And you wanted to help her..."

Isabelle nodded, wiping her eyes. The water on her face made it hard to tell if she was crying or not, but the movement alone tempted Alex to hug her and tell her everything was alright. Instead, he just patted her shoulder. "That's what you want to do most, right? Help?"

"I do.... I really do. I don't think that what's happened means we can be bad people. We're not... savages. Marge is trying to bring us down, but that's not who we are."

"Maybe it's who she is..." Alex was struggling now, thoughts tumbling madly through the spin cycle of his mind.

"It's not. It's not who I am, and it's not who you are. Albert..." She smiled a little to herself. "Albert maybe a little."

Alex made a 'pshh' noise, shaking his head and smiling. "I'm sure he'd take that as a compliment."

Isabelle nodded, grabbing the desk and shakily pulling herself to her feet. "Yeah. I meant it as one."

They stood there a moment, smiling and thinking about Albert. Alex broke the silence once he remembered the man's current predicament. "We should probably go rescue him from Marge. I don't think she'll let him off easy."

Isabelle gasped, nodding quietly and leading the way down the hall. They found the fish farm lit up by the lights that stretched across the ceiling. Marge was standing between the pools, tossing the ball up and down, glancing at the two as they entered the room. "Hey there. You two done lamenting a little water in your boots?"

Alex glanced around the empty space, half expecting to see Albert chopped up and shoved in a trashcan. "What happened to Albert?"

Marge shrugged, gesturing behind her. "He's busy organizing our supplies. Maybe you two could help him out, eh? Isa, where's all the shit we nabbed?"

Isabelle looked towards Alex, who looked back down the hall. He had a vague memory of setting the cans and blankets down on one of the desks. He sighed. "Back in the office, on the desk."

Marge crossed her arms, shaking her head. "Well, go get them then."

Alex took a step towards her, trying to think of something to say. "Marge, I…" He paused. He couldn't figure out what to say, how to relate his own thoughts to what the other three had told him. There was a synthesis of thought in there, hidden by the maelstrom of worry and confusion. Isabelle put a hand on his shoulder, almost seeming like she wanted to pull him back. Marge just looked at him blankly, arms crossed.

"Yeah? You what Alex?"

Alex took a step back, slumping in place. "I'll go get the stuff."

Marge sighed, shaking her head and smiling softly. "Good. That's good. Hey Isa, a quick word?"

Alex turned back into the hallway, clicking the door shut behind him. Nobody had told him that the end of the world would involve so much political bullshit. He had a temptation to run away, flee down the hall and into the darkness of the day, arms waving over his head and screaming towards the clouds.

But he didn't. Instead, he just plodded down the hall and grabbed the supplies like a good worker bee, feeling the metaphorical collar on his neck settle ever so slightly tighter around his throat.

***

The rest of the day was silent at the hatchery. Albert was confined to the storage room, struggling for hours to sort their supplies in a way that passed Marge's inspection. Isabelle was assigned to 'keep an eye on the fish', a job everyone else recognized was just a way to keep her out of Marge's way. Marge meanwhile was fashioning an umbrella out of unused blankets and scrapped wood. Alex had to help her, in a way that didn't much differ from holding a flashlight over the engine of a car while the mechanic got it to work.

The end result was a haphazard collection of fleece and polyester, unwieldy and barely wide enough to fit one person. Alex had a striking suspicion of who that person might be.

Marge had scheduled one more scavenging run for the day. She and Alex set out within an hour, Marge holding the umbrella and Alex dragging the wheelbarrow. Isabelle had been given the order to wait for them once she was done with the fish, something she resented with a frown and a knowing glance at Alex.

"We should be going to those cabins we looted when we first got here. Me and Isa found some shit under the floorboards of some of the other ones, so who knows what we'll find under those."

Alex shifted uncomfortably, trying to stay close to Marge to stay under the umbrella and out of the driving rain. "The first ones? The three?"

Marge nodded slowly. "Yeah, those three. What other ones would I mean?"

"I don't know..." His voice betrayed the unease he had. Going to those cabins meant seeing the gun again and seeing that cold ruthless metal again would dredge up the refuse of memory that he'd buried from that night in Cheekye. "They're just unsettling... is all. Musty and dark."

Marge scoffed, shaking her head. "That's everything out here Alex. It's an abandoned nature park, the hell did you expect? There's a reason it's called a 'getaway'. It's not like you're going to find a fully stocked Tim Hortons out here."

"I know... I know... it's still unsettling. I don't like it." His heart started pounding in his chest and his throat dried up. He opened his mouth for a moment to let in the rain, spitting it out once the acid taste struck his tongue. Even if the rain didn't burn anymore, the taste of apocalypse still hung in the clouds. It was a reminder about the state of the world.

Passively, Alex wondered how many people were still alive out there. A billion? Half a billion? 8 billion people lived before the bombs dropped, and now it could be as low as 1/10 of that. Nine in ten people gone, like specks of dust on a wind of flame.

"Hey Alex, how does Isabelle seem to you?"

Marge's voice dragged him back to the present, out of the dark fantasies of statistical annihilation. He blinked, wiping the rain out of his eyes. "She's... not happy."

"Yeah no shit. I mean do you think she's thinking the no-no thoughts?"

"No-no thoughts? Marge, she's... well, she's not fine, but she's... she's coping. I don't think she's ok, but she says that's more because of how we're treating her than how... all of this went down."

"Oh right, and you believed that?" Marge shook her head, thwapping him on the head lightly with her umbrella. "Alex, she's projecting herself onto you, moron. Of course all the turmoil's about the goddamn nuke, she just can't deal with it. That's why she's been so uppity lately. She'll snap, I'm sure of it."

"How... how do you know Marge? She's saying it's because of you. Because of how you're running things. It's... really stressful."

Marge barked out a laugh, shaking her head. "I'm sure it's a slightly bitchy boss and not the end of the world. That's *definitely* the problem Alex. Good detective work." She kept laughing to herself as she turned off the road and towards the cabins while Alex followed uncomfortably.

The outlines of the cabins emerged in the woods, creaking softly as the wind blew in between the cracks. Alex stopped the wheelbarrow outside of the door, letting the wheels sink into the muddy ground. He let out a breath, looking towards the cabins with poorly disguised hesitation. "So, we should... go into one at a time, right?"

Marge didn't notice or didn't care, coming to a halt next to him. "Yeah, that's right. I'll take the one I took last time; you take yours and then we both split the last one. Deal?"

Alex nodded, hesitantly stepping towards his assigned cabin. "Deal..."

***

Marge walked into the dark space of the cabin, illuminated only a little by the light outside the window. She set the umbrella against the doorframe, navigating the space mostly by memory. The floor was slick with water that had leaked in from the roof, and her heart sank when she realized that anything they found would be soggy or ruined. Regardless, she went to the corner and got her fingers around one of the floorboards. With a creak and small shower of rotted wood, the nail that had been embedded into the floor to keep the board down flew free, landing behind her.

The hole left in the floor was dark, leaving the imprint of a void within the corner of the floor. Hesitantly, she poked down inside it, feeling around. Her fingers ran through wet dirt and woodchips, landing on nothing of importance and leaving her more disgusted than satisfied. She groaned, standing up and heading towards Alex's cabin.

She stepped into the doorframe of the cabin, leaning on the side. She noticed Alex immediately, standing in the centre of the room and staring at the empty table that sat against one of the walls.

"Hey, Alex, chop-chop. Is something wrong?"

Alex turned to look at her, face as white as a sheet in the gloom of the storm's light.

"It's gone…"

15: GHOSTS

The gun was gone. Alex's mind raced, searching for an explanation. It didn't make any sense. He knew for a fact that he'd left it right there. He could almost see the imprint it left on the table, an incorporeal mark of presence that screamed at him that something was missing. Nobody could have grabbed it, they would have said something. He stood there quietly in the darkness of the shack, staring at Marge with astonished fear.

"Alex. What the hell is wrong with you? Did you find anything or not?"

Slowly he shook his head, blinking in astonishment. "No. There's... there's nothing here. It's empty."

Marge looked at him like he was crazy, which in all fairness wasn't the farthest off from the truth. "You're an idiot. Come on, let's go look at the last cabin." She turned away from him, heading back out into the rain and towards Isabelle's claimed cabin. Alex tried to follow after her, teetering for a moment as his feet felt glued to the floor. He finally fought his way into motion, stepping out into the rain and pulling the door shut behind him with force.

Something was very, *very* wrong with the missing gun, and it chilled the blood in his veins to think of what it could be.

The third cabin was just as dark and musty as the other two. By the time Alex stepped through its door, Marge was already at the far wall, fiddling with the floorboard to pull it free. This one was putting up more of a fight, a prospect that seemed to excite Marge. "Hey, come help me with this! This bit is newer."

Alex tried to shake the cobwebs of the second cabin out of his head, crouching down with her. "Newer?"

Marge nodded, tracing her finger across the space between the boards. "What did I say? Look, these ones are less rotted than the ones around them. That means someone put these in more recently than the other ones."

"How long ago?"

"How the hell would I know? A few months or something. Definitely after Paradise Valley sunk us, that's for sure. Stop gaping and help me get it loose!"

Alex nodded, reaching down to help Marge pry the board loose from the floor. It came off with a surge of momentum that almost sent Alex tumbling onto his back and onto the floor. He regained his composure, setting the plank down next to them and peering into the hole with Marge. She reached into the darkness, grasping something cold and heavy that reflected the light of the windows faintly. Pulling it out, she placed a long iron box onto the floor, grinning at it like a pirate who'd just found buried treasure.

"What is it?" Alex looked over her shoulder at the thing. It was a little rusted and dirty but otherwise seemed solid. It conjured images of those little boxes that fishermen would carry around to hold their lures. Tackle crates, or something like that.

Marge fiddled with the latch on the front, trying to pry it loose and open the top up. "Probably something good." With a creak of metal and an audible impression in the air, Marge opened the box and scattered some dust into the musty air.

"What the hell..." She reached into the box, pulling out photos and scraps of cloth with disgust. She picked the box up, turning it over and shaking it with intensity and causing bits of dirt and old pine needles to fall out and scatter across the floor. "This is just crap! What the hell?"

She threw the box at the wall, causing a dim thunk as it hit the wooden siding. "Who the hell does this?"

She stood up, charging out of the cabin angrily. Alex meanwhile was absorbed with the mementos that had fallen out. Half a dozen pieces of multi-coloured cloth scattered around a pair of photographs. He picked up the first, looking it over with interest. It was a polaroid of a small group of men, dressed up in fishermen's gear and holding the trophies of their day by the river: Three different salmon, all accompanied by hooks in their jaws and smiles on the faces that held them. Alex didn't recognize any of them, but their faces stuck in his mind. He wondered where they were now. Were they alive? If they were, where? How? Each of them had a story they could tell, but Alex had the sinking feeling that most of them weren't alive to tell it.

He silently pocketed the photo, taking a look at the other one. This one was blurrier, more smudged around the edges in the process of printing. The setup seemed much the same. Several men with fish and gear. A woman stood in front of the rest, grinning ear to ear and holding a rather large salmon. Something about her seemed familiar, but it was a recognition that Alex couldn't place.

He folded up the photo, putting it with the other and stepping out the door. Marge was waiting for him under the umbrella, standing next to a now upturned wheelbarrow.

Silently, he straightened it up, starting to push his way back to the hatchery. He didn't need to ask why Marge had turned it over. She was fuming, adding an anger to the air that brought the mood down almost as much as the pouring rain.

The slog home to the hatchery was a cold, wet and miserable affair. Alex found himself delving back into the metaphysical realm of his mind, somewhere the rain didn't fall and the cold didn't strike. Much.

In doing so, he realized something.

Home.

He thought of the hatchery as home. Not a shelter, or even a hideout. A home. Somewhere he could be comfortable, kick back and relax. When he thought of home, he didn't think of his apartment, presumably because it had been atomized, but rather of a squat little fish farm at the edge of human settlement between the cold mountains of British Columbia. It was something that made him laugh. Drive the cold away a little. He had a home here, and in a way, a family. A dysfunctional, bitter and ruthlessly divisive family, but a family, nonetheless.

He just hoped that it could last whatever was coming.

***

Back at the hatchery, night came with an apex of cold. Alex sat on his bed, staring out the window and at the frost collecting on its edges. It was as cold as winter, and the weather didn't seem to want to let up. He cringed at the thought of endless days of driving rain and unending chills. The winters of Vancouver may be some of the mildest in BC, but they were still wet and rainy affairs that zapped the soul and left you wondering when the sun would ever shine again.

Alex didn't know if he could take the weight of it again. Spring had only just recently arrived, the promise of another season of chills and driving rains was almost as off-putting as life in the post-apocalypse.

Almost.

When the sun set beyond the shroud above and dipped below the horizon, the camping lights came on. Albert and Isabelle cuddled up on his bed, whispering things to each other in hushed and giggling tones. The setup reminded him of boarding school, of desk lamps casting shadows over cheaply made beds and tired people as the sun came and went beyond their care.

He couldn't hear what they were saying from here, but it had all the trappings of a high school romance. Quiet words exchanged in the dead of night, terrified of being caught by their superiors but thrilled even more by the risk.

Alex reached over to turn off his light, flicking it's glow out of existence and darkening the shadows of the room cast by the other light. Slowly and quietly he ventured into sleep, barely noticing the conversation turn from content, bubbly tones to the darker and heavier sounds of plotting.

***

Morning came like a freight train, slamming into Alex with the sort of shock that electrifies your nerves and shoots your eyes open. The sort of wake-up that the busy can only dream of, taking you in moments from sleep to alertness. There was no yawn, no rubbing of the eyes. There was only the moment that Alex became aware of the world, staring at the ceiling with a sense of unearned panic and a blip of confusion.

He sat up in bed, rubbing his forehead and looking around to try to identify what exactly it was that merited him the dignity of a quick awakening. He reached out with his senses, looking, listening even smelling the world around him to find out what was off.

The first thing he noticed, was the silence. The distant hum of machines permeated the air as always, but the semi-constant sound of raindrops on the windows and roof was mercifully gone. The second thing he noticed was the light. The windows were fogged over, caught behind a web of moisture and frost that denied anything but the smallest semblance of understanding to what was behind its translucent façade. But the light that shone through the misty veil was bright, and the colours that lurked past its barrier showed the brighter blue of a clear sky than it did the clouded shroud that he had come to expect.

The third thing he noticed, was that he was alone.

Quietly, as if not to disturb the unearthly silence that permeated the air, he pulled himself out of bed and onto his feet.

Staggering, he pulled his jacket on to ward off the cold that still penetrated through the electrified heating, moving towards the fish farm and towards where he hoped the rest would be waiting.

The inside of the farm was filled with more noise than the dorm, but that was only thanks to the lack of insulation from the hum of the machines. It was dark in here, specialized lighting and little dials across the machines being the only source of illumination. Alex was surprised. He didn't realize the skylights could be closed off, but looking up at the gabled ceiling, the little holes that had allowed the sun's rays to reach them had been shut, and the very tops of the space were shrouded in darkness.

Now into the hallway, he started to feel an unease. There had been no sign of anyone else along his route, and that was half of the hatchery covered. He peeked into Marge's room quietly, relieved when he saw that she was snoring away under the soft light of the vending machine, a piece of paper clutched in her hand like an angry CEO getting a report he didn't like. Her sleep was far from restful, it seemed. Quietly he shut the door again, perplexed. He peeked into the utility closet, a quick visual sweep confirming that they weren't there.

By now, Alex had started to worry that maybe something worse had happened. Worse than the bombs. Aliens and murderers. Kidnappers that came in the dead of night and stole the other two away. It was nonsense, the land of fiction and fantasy, but Alex wasn't exactly renowned for keeping his thinking grounded.

That's why when he found them sitting in the office with their backs to the wall and clutching blankets wrapped up neatly full of supplies, he was more relieved than he was concerned or outraged.

The feeling didn't last long.

"Albert? Isa? What the hell are you guys…"

At the sound of his voice, the two of them snapped to attention, pulling themselves out of whatever stupor had left them there. He could read the look of guilt on their faces the instant he saw them, it was the look that the teenage sweethearts had when they were being caught. Which in turn, Alex realized, made him the catcher.

Isabelle spoke first, stumbling over her words and trying fruitlessly to kick the balled up blanket behind her. The sound of her foot hitting the bag produced a metallic tink, and the clattering of cans against each other did nothing to assuage the guilt on her face. "Alex! Hey, we were just... we were thinking of..."

Albert sighed, shaking his head. "Come on Isa, don't dig deeper into this hole. That's my job." He didn't get any laughs. Both of them just stared at him blankly, waiting for him to offer up some sort of excuse. He cleared his throat. "We were booking it."

Isabelle smacked him, looking back towards Alex with guilt-ridden eyes. "Albert! I thought we agreed to..."

"Make excuses, blah blah blah. The cat's out of the can filled bag Isa. Not like we could even pull it off anyway." Albert shrugged his shoulders. "No point in hiding it from Alex at least."

Alex just blinked, shocked. *This* is what they were planning? To run off in the middle of the night on a hormone-fueled whinge of freedom?

Maybe Marge was right about them breaking.

"You were going to leave? Are you guys... are you nuts?" Alex wasn't a particularly angry sort of person. At most he tended to feel mild disdain. But this drove a dagger into his heart, plunging ice-cold steel into his body and filling it with a hot fire. In a moment, he was about to explode. Albert's nonchalant un-deferring look didn't help at all, and Alex almost swore that he felt his fists balled up in anger to punch his stupid face. It was only Isa's grief and guilt-stricken face that pulled him back to reality, out of the hot-headed rage that he was about to break into. He searched for words that wouldn't hurt, words that wouldn't betray how wounded and abandoned he felt that they would just leave.

All he found was: "Why?"

Isabelle stammered, looking to Albert then back at Alex. "We... we... we can't take it under Marge. I-I told you, Alex, she's going nuts. I'm scared she's going to snap."

That shocked him. Snapped? Marge? Out of all of them, she had her shit together the most. She'd burned through the restless and unfocused anger, hadn't she? All that drive she had now, the determination to survive, that was what was keeping them going! His mind scrambled together these thoughts and more. Put up a bulwark of defence, of counter-arguments, of reprimands. But while internally he built a case against running away, his mouth moved in a way he didn't expect.

"Why didn't you tell me?"

The question surprised everyone, none so more than Alex. He could see the minds working, the gears clicking behind the faces of flesh and bone. It mirrored the same biological whirring that dominated his thoughts.

"To be honest dude..." Albert winced, rubbing his neck. "You're too close to Margey. We wanted to get away for real here, like... I don't know, freaking Tahiti or something."

Isabelle whispered to herself. "Or L.A..."

Albert nodded, patting her shoulder. "Or L.A. The point is, Margey's presentation of "The Great Dictator." isn't funny anymore, and we were going to go nuts if we staid in here with her any longer."

Alex shook his head, images spinning through his head on a whirlwind. L.A, Tahiti, the infinite bomb ravaged wasteland that both must be. It was hard to grasp. To quantify. The sheer scope of their ambition, to cross half a world in search of peace from Marge, was astonishing. "So, if that's what this was all about, why haven't you left? Why haven't you just left us to die so you can go off and... and..." His voice was rising now, the anger coming back. Why Tahiti? Why L.A? Did they have somewhere better to be? A family there that served them a more nuclear bond than this scavenged family of a fish hatchery? It was a maddening prospect, that maybe in the end Marge was right and there was nothing left of the single pure-hearted ambition of the world. Just fear and chaos and an idiotic searching for what was little more than nuclear ash.

"No way to manage our food, no way to heal our wounds... you'd leave me with her. How much of our food did you steal?! How much of our world would you cut away?" Tears were in his eyes, and Alex could feel the cracks inside him breaking. The boxed memories of the man he'd killed, the sealed off thoughts on the dead that covered the globe. Billions of people reduced to ash and corpses. The worries about the winds, about the rain, about the cold. How long would it take for the fallout to settle and for the radiation to burn off their skin? How long would it take for the suffocating clouds to return and finally smother the life down below?

His breathing quickened, his body curling into a ball. Everything he'd offset for survival, for fortitude, it was all coming apart. He was gone now, farther into the hole that his own mind had been trying to destroy, so far gone now that the light at the top was just a distant haze in a blackened sky.

He felt, distantly, arms wrap around him, comforts of blankets and warmed air washed over him. Isabelle had succumbed to her guilt, trying desperately to amend for this panic with hushed words and inconsequential reassurances, huddled next to his curled up form in a comedically macabre imitation of a mother comforting her child after the night terrors sieged them deep in their sleep.

Albert watched it all in stunned silence.

Alex could have been there for 5 minutes or 5 hours. For all he knew, it had been a week. By the time he'd crawled out of the hole, the world looked much the same. The efforts he made to shut it back up inside the box and the bottom of his brain had been successful. The tears still streaked down his face, and the pain was still there. But Alex was also here, at least for now, ready to confront the present.

"So… why didn't you leave?"

Isabelle pulled herself away from him, sitting on her feet and shaking her head. Albert just pointed at the fogged-over windows.

Alex struggled to his feet, bringing his hand up against the glass and wiping the condensation clear. His eyes widened as his mind reeled, shocked and confused at what he was seeing.

Out there, across the parking lot, into the trees and all the way up to highest peaks, was a shining frozen expanse of snow.

16: SEAS

It was like he was standing up there on the mountain again. A blanket of glistening white spread over the world, coating the ground and trees with a shimmering, frozen veil. The clouds had sparked away, dumping their contents in the night and freezing the earth in one swift motion.

Alex could barely fathom it. It was just so incomprehensible. He expected rain, sleet, hail. A miserable spring filled with cold and unenthusiasm. Instead, he was faced with a return to winter. A winter that was harder and more intense than anything he'd seen in Vancouver. There was as much snow covering the world like a tapestry as there ever was for a whole month back down south. Grasping and searching, he tried to find a word to describe the sheer implausibility of it all.

Nuclear Winter.

He stepped back from the window, blinking away the shock that lingered from the vista. It was such a terrifyingly confusing thought, facing the reality of Albert and Isabelle's betrayal was a simpler prospect. "That's… that's why."

Albert snickered to himself, nodding. "As much as I'd like to say it was for the power of friendship or some shit, the freezing cold was the bigger obstacle."

Isabelle punched him in the arm, glaring angrily. "Shut up!"

Alex could tell Isabelle was looking out for him somehow, but he was too mentally exhausted from the morning's events to process how exactly that was. He'd woken up about 15 minutes ago, but already it felt like hours.

"Alex... we didn't want to hurt you like that." Isabelle was pleading, trying to make up for Albert's total lack of tact. "We just couldn't take it anymore. We had to try... and I'm so, so, so sorry that we didn't tell you, or... look, will you please forgive us?" Isabelle was making the most convincing case Alex had ever seen of someone having 'puppy dog eyes'. Alex also happened to feel the most convincing case of heart-break that he had ever felt as well.

"I... I don't know Isa. This... this is hard to face. I'm not ready for that. At all. Hell. I don't know if I ever can, just not... now. Not now."

Isabelle nodded her head mournfully, closing her eyes. "I get it. I'm still *so* sorry Alex..." She hung her head, letting silence wash over the room, if just for a moment.

"Well, what do we do now?" Alex looked at the two of them, then at the bags, then back at the snowfall outside. "What the hell do we do now?"

Albert snickered, shaking his head and gesturing vaguely. "Well, nothing. We're snowed in without any winter gear, so unless Margey actually has a secret stash of parkas and ski masks, we're stuck here until the snow melts. Speaking of Margey, another thing we do is never tell her what happened here."

Isabelle and Alex nodded, understanding the absolute shitstorm that would emerge if Marge ever got wind of how close the two of them were to deserting. Something that stung Alex a little more when he realized that they were planning to leave him all alone to feel the brunt of her wrath.

"Never tell me what now?"

The temperature of the room seemed to plummet in an instant, and Alex's veins turned to ice. He could see on the faces of the other two that something terrible had happened. He turned around to face the source of the voice, a yawning, bed-headed Marge with sleep in her eyes and a crumpled piece of paper in her hand.

***

The room froze, staying still in the moment that she entered for what felt like a full minute. Alex could hear his heartbeat, a sound that was almost drowned out by the heartbeats of Isabelle and Albert. As much as he knew now, and as complicit as he was about to be if Marge discovered the treachery, he was only an accomplice. Isabelle and Albert were the prospective culprits, and the hell would be paid onto them if Marge found out what they had planned.

It was a tense situation.

Isabelle broke the silence, finally finding a simple excuse that probably should have been their first instinct regardless. "It snowed last night."

Marge yawned, shaking her head and looking blearily at the window. "Yeah right, that's something you'd be able to hide from me. Pshh..."

But then her eyes focused. Her vision narrowed. Her breathing accelerated. And before they even knew it, Marge had her face pressed up against the glass in panic, looking out at the field of frozen ice in much the same way Alex had. "No, no, no, no. That... that can't be right! It's mid-spring! We're mid-global warming! This shit isn't supposed to be happening!"

As guilty as it probably made her feel, Isabelle shoved the makeshift bags of supplies under the desk, moving the chair to cover them mostly in shadow. Albert stood between her and Marge, pretending to look out with her at the frozen world outside, while in reality just blocking the sightline between Marge and Isabelle. Not that it was necessary.

"We don't have coats! We don't have any way to move! We're goddamn stranded!" Marge ran her fingers through her hair, brushing past the grease and dust to almost pull her roots out. "What in the ever-loving hell?! Why? Why this? Why now?!"

She punched the wall angrily, storming off back into the rest of the building, shoving past Alex maliciously.

Once the door had shut behind her and the distant sound of something metallic hitting a wall had reverberated through the building, Albert let out a sigh of relief, stepping out of Isabelle's way as she slumped heavily into a chair.

Alex opened the door, peeking down the hall in silence.

"Alex." He turned to face Albert, who had his hand on Isabelle's shoulder as he spoke. "You need to distract her for us dude. We got all this crap here when she was asleep, but if she sees us carrying it all back to the storage room, you can wear our skin instead of jackets."

Isabelle narrowed her eyes, looking at Albert with disgust. "What? Albert, Jesus!" She shook her head, looking back to Alex. "Don't listen to him. Well… do listen to him because we need the help but… not the skin jackets part. That's just disgusting."

Alex looked at the two of them, then at the blanket backpacks, then at the snow. The truth was, a small part of him did want them to be found out. For Marge to call them out on their selfishness and their unjust abandonment, to make them suffer the same sort of pain that he had suffered in realization.

But that wasn't him. At least he didn't think so. He wasn't cruel like that, and he didn't sell out friends like that. So as much as Marge may have wanted to know and as much as Albert and Isa stabbed him in the back, he wouldn't stoop to their level. He refused to.

"I'll go talk to her. You… you two be quiet, ok?"

Isabelle nodded quickly, taking his hand and shaking it eagerly. "Thank you, thank you so much. You don't know how much you just saved us." She turned back to Albert, grinning uncertainly and kissing him quickly. He smiled, giving Alex a thumbs up and turning to help her manage the supplies.

It made Alex feel a little bit warmer inside, insomuch as someone could under current circumstances. He opened the door to the hallway, walking down the linoleum floor towards Marge's room. He considered knocking a moment, hand hesitating over the door's façade as he asked himself if this was really a good idea. In the end, he elected to just push his way into the room, closing the door behind him and turning on the light, bringing awareness to the otherwise darkened room.

What he expected to find was a raging beast, a caged animal that would bark and snarl at him to leave, to further distance herself from the trappings of others. Instead what he found was more like what you'd expect to find in a young child's room after a particularly poor showing at a spelling bee. The trashcan that had previously sat in the corner of the room was upturned and strewn over the floor, it's contents scattered across the ratty carpet. Marge was curled up on her bed, hiding beneath the blankets with uneven shakes ravaging her body.

Alex had *no* clue what to do now. Hesitantly he stepped towards the bed, reaching out a hand to touch her somewhere, let her know he was there in a comforting way. She rolled over underneath the blankets, enough to make him recoil backwards in fear. He shook his head, trying to break free of the constraints his mind was setting on him. She wasn't a raging monster, woe to snap at any moment. She was his friend, and she needed Alex's help right now.

Gently, ever so gently he sat down at the end of the bed. His weight shifted the balance of the bed a little, clueing her in to his presence and making her lie very still. He felt a sudden sense of pure ridiculousness. Here he was, a 27-year-old man sitting at the end of a bed in a salmon hatchery, walking on eggshells around a woman his age like she was a petulant child. The sheer incomprehensiveness of the situation almost made him laugh out loud, but the following sob from Marge was enough to wipe the humour from his face.

"Marge?" He reached towards her, hesitating for a moment before placing a hand on the outline of her shoulder. She made a sudden spasming shrugging motion that made him pull his hand away. "Marge, it's me. It's Alex. I... we're worried about you. You just... ran off."

Marge didn't reply, steadying herself and curling further into a ball under the blankets. Alex looked around, watching Albert and Isabelle dart by in the hallway, bags over their shoulders. What that meant, essentially, was that Alex was free to go. But he didn't.

"Marge, things... things are really bad, ok? I know they're really bad. But you can't... no, that's not right... Marge, I know you're scared. We're all scared. I-I don't want to be stuck in here either. But... but goddamnit, we are..." Alex put his elbows on his knees, gripping his head. This speech wasn't coming out right at all. Instead of pulling Marge out of her state, he found himself being dragged into hers. "We're screwed, aren't we? I mean, there's no way out. We don't have jackets... we don't... damn it!"

Alex slipped into that dark place again, the world of betrayal and insurmountable obstacles. Slipping down the slide and into the darkness of the hole below.

That triggered something in Marge. Underneath the blankets, she pulled herself into a sitting position, peeking out at him in the cracks between the blanket and the bed. What she saw was the very thing she just fell into. Weakness. Inability. But instead of her usual ponderings of how to turn it to her advantage or benefit the rest of the group, she saw the very same thing Alex had seen and oh so poorly failed to put a stop to. A friend in need. Carefully, she extracted herself from the blanket and draped it over his shoulder.

They sat in deep silence a while, stuck by the hopelessness of their environment and each hoping to find a way to comfort the other. Alex fought to stay focused, to turn back towards Marge. To the closeness of conversation and the physical world and away from the freezing terror that laid outside the doors.

"Sorry about that." Marge's voice snapped to attention, like an anchor pulling taut, securing Alex to the here and now. "I should have been more professional about our situation."

"Professional?" Professional was the sound of intrusion. It was the sound of Marge bottling up this sudden surge of emotion and turning back to the puppet master. The words bounced inside Alex's head, the implications of its existence eking their way into his thoughts. "No, no, Marge that was... that was ok. You panicked. We all panicked."

Marge shook her head, clearing her throat and sitting up. "No, really. As much as I hate it, you dicks look up to me, so I need to be more composed."

Alex grabbed her hand, squeezing it. That shocked her, causing her to look down at his hand and then up at him. "What the hell are... Alex, what are you doing?"

"Don't think like that Marge. You don't... you don't have to pretend you're ok. We get it, alright? You don't have to yell... or run... or pretend you're ok, alright?"

"Shut up Alex, I'm not... I'm not pretending, I am ok. And I yell at you because you deserve it." She pulls her hand away from Alex's, shifting down the bed to distance herself from him. "I'm trying to apologize, damn."

Alex moved after her, feeling a little desperate. Maybe it was the weight of Albert and Isabelle's betrayal still weighing on him, the fundamental realization that they had a point or even just an unknown need, but Alex didn't want to let the Marge he thought was there slip back beneath the surface. "You don't have to! You don't have to... we all freaked out when we saw the snow, trust me."

Alex could swear he saw cracks forming somewhere in there. Marge emerging from this shroud of professionalism to reveal her true grief. It was such a brief sight he could have imagined it, but he was sure that Marge was trying to suppress her weakness.

She worked like that.

"Alex. Shut the hell up, alright? This is just another obstacle. We'll surpass it goddamnit, or we'll die trying."

Alex faltered. He reached over to her again, but she shied away from his touch, standing and glaring at him. "Marge, it's not about…"

She crossed her arms at him, eyes ablaze, like she was trying to burn away the part of her that was scared and confused. He wilted under that gaze, nodding his head and walking out of the room. She slammed the door shut behind him, shaking the walls with the 'oomph' of the impact.

***

Back in the dormitory, the rush of the day's events had created a fever in the air. The excitement of their illicit dealings had left Isabelle and Albert buzzing, alternating between intense alertness, riveting joy and squeamish shame. The same aura of silence that tended to follow Alex after a particularly hard day had enveloped him, pushing him into the corner to watch them flit about uneasily in the half-light of the frosted windows.

It must have been only 9 a.m.

There was still a whole day ahead of them. Expeditions that were planned, ideas that were put forth to be executed. Now that was gone too, shattered like a boulder in a quarry. Alex didn't know what to do. All he did know was that if he didn't do *something* to keep himself occupied or he'd have his third breakdown in about an hour.

So he grabbed a book. Or he stacked cans. Filled time. The other two quieted down eventually, alternating between miscellaneous activities like he did, and each other. Alex had to go down to the storage room after a while just to give them space. The soft lights and rows of cans atop blankets and buckets were an almost otherworldly sight. The light was too faint to continue reading 'The Dazzling Diary of one Ruebeck Stoveholm', so Alex preoccupied himself with stacking cans. Strangely, it reminded him of those alphabet blocks you would see on T.V or in movies. The sort of things that people had long moved past, but also the sort of things that kept their appeal to an adult.

Stacking cans in a faux imitation of urban planning wasn't exactly the most enthralling thing in the world, but the simple amusements were all Alex had anymore. The very televisions that he'd learned about the blocks from must have been fried in the blastwaves. The EMP that swept across the world cut out phones, computers, movies. Everything, essentially, that had defined mankind's advancement in the 21st century.

It was a chilling thought, 30 years of progress crushed by one man or woman somewhere in the world pressing a button. A big red button in some underground bunker, far from the consequences of their actions. A button that, when pressed, triggered warnings across the world of what was to follow. More buttons would be pressed in retaliation, strikes being ordered on unsuspecting people for whatever contrived reason had justified their existence in the first place. A cascade that spread across the world, extinguishing lives and cities in nuclear hellfire like a plague of brimstone cast to the core of the earth.

A simple press of a button.

And a Cascade that followed.

Even as these thoughts beat their drum somewhere inside Alex, his focus was on the cans. He built towers and streets, layered and levelled up and down like condos in a grand metallic city. Strangely, he felt accomplishment. Like the rudimentary stacking of metallic objects had actually produced something of value. It was the same sort of feeling a toddler would have gotten, the joy of building something from simple resources. And just like that toddler, Alex would knock it down and build a new one. There was power there, a fantasy that everyone had in some way or another.

Not just the ability to wreck things, but the knowledge to build them again.

There were wider implications at stake in this simple joy. Human instinct, ingenuity and belief were all set into motion for the purposes of analogy. But it all went over Alex's head.

For now, all he wanted was a small place he could build to ward off the dark.

***

Hours, several towers of cans and a little bit more of Alex's sanity later, the tin cities of beans and mangoes returned to their natural and organized state, reflecting faintly against the buzzing dim lights of the storage room. The metropolis Alex had built was gone, returned to the clinical and organized storage space that the group demanded. Quietly, he let them be and put his ear to the door. It was quiet there, which gave him the assumption that it was okay to leave now.

He clicked the door open, peering through and into the dorm. Albert and Isabelle were cuddled up under the blankets of his bed, holding each other closely. It was a sweet sight, the two of them holding each other intimately, comfortable with each other. It was something Alex felt confused about. Not jealous of course, that sort of feeling was impossible when you saw such a strangely compelling relationship. It was more of a distance. A gap between them and him that he no longer felt he could cross.

Softly, he made his way past them and onto the farm's floor, a strange and mourning feeling in his heart.

17: ISLANDS.

The snowfall had changed everything.

The group was already isolated, hours away from the closest human settlement, especially so since Chekeye had been scoured. Chances for interaction with the outside world would have already been limited, but the new coating of freezing snow essentially guaranteed that there wouldn't be any visitors to their little corner of this broken earth.

On the flip side, it meant that they couldn't leave it either. Not the valley, not the hatchery, not even outside the building. They were totally and indisputably cut off from everywhere else, and until the snow melted or they found some way to stay warm, it was as if they were on a spaceship, cruising through the cosmos on a frozen wind.

In the weeks that followed, everyone dealt with it differently. Alex read a lot of books and spent his days rearranging things in ways that he thought would increase their efficiency. All the spare furniture and blankets that they'd salvaged from the valley were put to use in elaborate separations and coverings. During the day, he'd split the fish farm into different sections, allocating a single chair to what he called 'the living room', and a nightstand to his conception of a 'dining room'. He was sure that to others it would seem insane. In fact, he accepted it mostly was. A single blanket spread over the floor and held down by a desk did not qualify as a 'study', but playing house with what he had was the best way to keep himself busy. In time, he was sure that there would be some benefit from the madness.

He was interrupted from time to time by Marge's ambitions.

While everyone else essentially resigned themselves to the isolation, Marge ploughed on determinedly towards whatever goal she had decided was the most crucial. It varied wildly from day to day, scattered across the spectrum of possibilities. One day it would be crafting makeshift coats, wherein she would pull the rug out from under Alex's 'study' and fashion a crappy cloak that, upon being tested, resulted in her huddling next to a warm vent for hours, chittering and chattering from the near-full exposure to the cold. Another day, it was an irrational fear that someone would break down the front door that lead her to disassemble one of Alex's few available chairs and haphazardly arrange its planks to hold as a defence against any intruders. It was definitely annoying, but Marge was in such a state that Alex didn't have the heart to deny her or to get yelled at for denying her.

But Marge wasn't his only issue. Albert and Isabelle took the time afforded to them to spend together. It was intoxicatingly sweet, seeing the way the once combative and hostile couple had found post-apocalyptic comfort with each other. It was less so sweet when you had to eat breakfast while watching them tongue wrestle. Alex had to move his bed into the storage room, as the couple demanded privacy, with kind words and subtle suggestions of course, but with the implication that they weren't exactly asking. There were fights, sure. Someone as naturally charismatic and abrasive as Albert is sure to have been a heartbreaker if it wasn't for his dedication to being a jester. With an absence of humour to go about, and a severely limited pool of options, Albert manifested the long-suppressed ladies' man within him, and the resulting passion, argumentation and constant pendulum of emotion ended up being a dizzyingly overwhelming crux that sent Alex running whenever it seemed close to manifesting. But, and this was the part that sent him spiralling into emotional confusion, even when their arguments over petty nothings got tough, at the end of the day they would still fall asleep together in each other's arms.

This unstable, even if straightforward social dynamic wasn't exactly the storm Alex was expecting. It was more of a slow burn, a pot filled with water and set upon a stove at the lowest setting. The water wouldn't boil immediately, far from it in fact. But slowly the bubbles would rise, and it would boil over.

Or maybe he just wasn't as good at social observation as he thought.

What he could observe, through the frosted windows and the foggy glass, was that the snow was not letting up. The clouds had come back right on schedule, and every morning it seemed that the shimmering sheet of ice climbed higher. It was blocking parts of the windows now, an outright hill on top of which rested the impenetrable truth of their confinement.

18: ROOTS.

It was an uninteresting day when their confinement was forced to end. Marge was continuing her frenzied projects, striking down Alex's attempts at home-making. It was getting to the point of frustration, but Marge seemed convinced that she was on the edge of a breakthrough in whatever mad scheme was currently on her mind. Alex sat with her in the office as she haphazardly strung together pieces of wood and cloth, absent-mindedly looking out the window at the way the snow nearly reached the boughs of the bottoms of the trees. He thought he heard a rumbling somewhere out there, but he dismissed it passively as figments of his mind. But slowly, as Marge held up her strange creation, it started getting louder.

"Alex! Look at this shit, it's badass!"

Alex drew his attention away from the mounting noise, looking back towards Marge to behold her creation. In her hands, held up proudly like a toddler with a finger painting, was a loose woollen sweater, aggressively stapled to several boards that protruded along the arms and torso. On top of those boards, a blanket was also stapled to the sweater, constructing a second layer and firmly convincing Alex that Marge was losing it. "What... is that? A sweater?"

"Even better. Even goddamn better! It's a sweater, with armour! And it has a blanket around it, which makes it even warmer. With this shit, we'll be able to go outside whenever we want, and we won't get cold, or attacked by bears or some shit! I am a goddamn genius!"

The crazed look in her eyes was enough to freak Alex out, and he turned to face her fully. "Marge... maybe you should lie down. You're getting a little..."

He trailed off, looking back towards the window. He could swear that the noise was louder now, playing through his hears like the gutting sounds of an engine roaring over an otherwise empty field of snow and trees. It was something to worry about, maybe even panic about. But he couldn't focus on his growing dread because Marge was grabbing him by the shoulders. "Genius! I'm going genius Alex! I'm not just going to wait for some bullshit nonsense to plop down an easy escape into our laps, I'm going to take the goddamn initiative! I'm sick and tired of you wasting all of our shit on useless nonsense!"

Alex took a moment to appreciate the irony of those words for a moment, looking back towards the window and out into the frozen wasteland. Something seemed to be moving out there, far down the road. It just looked like a yellow blur from this distance, but one that seemed to be getting closer. He stepped towards the window, wiping away the fog that was forming on the glass from the cold. What he saw made his eyes widen, his heart quicken and his head spin.

"Alex, turn around and talk to me goddamnit! This isn't a joke, this is a serious invention and it can change the whole way we do things. We can go outside Alex! Outside!"

Alex turned towards Marge, letting her see the excited panic in his eyes. "Marge, look out the window!"

Marge scoffed, setting her invention down and walking over to the window. "Oh sure, I'll just look out the window. It's more goddamn snow! Shit, I know that asshole. Thanks for the..."
Marge trailed off when she spotted what Alex had seen. A moving, rumbling yellow dot that was getting closer and closer down the road.

It was a man on a snowmobile, and he was coming this way.

"Alex... go grab the gun."

***

Alex ran back into the hatchery as he'd never run before. It was a mixture of panic and excitement, of fear and anticipation. Someone was coming. Someone new, someone from somewhere else. Someone from human society, or whatever was left of it. It was worrying, intimidating and all manner of other things. But above all, it was new, a break in this godforsaken routine of madness that had subsumed their lives for the last few weeks. Past the machinery and splashing fish of the farm's floor and straight through the protests of Isabelle and Albert in the middle of something dire, Alex found himself in the storage room. He started digging through blankets and mostly empty cans to find the spot they'd stashed the rifle.

He found it, still tied to the backpack, there beneath the rest of their supplies. Previously, he'd purposely turned it against the wall, hiding it from his sight for whenever he forrayed in the shadows of his room. He put one hand around it, but the memories of using it seemed to break through at the mere feel of its wooden stock. He shivered, not from the cold but from the way just touching it sent him back to the darkness. He jolted his hand back, instead pulling his arm through the pack's strap and jamming it onto his back. It was empty, so the weight threw him off a little, almost causing him to fall over in a scattering of cans, but he managed to catch himself in time. Running again, he burst through the door into the dorm once more, startling a much more clothed couple that had been standing in wait for him.

"What the hell dude? Is there a half-off sale at the 'Interrupting Dickhead' store? We were in the middle of something!" Albert had his arm around Isabelle protectively, the two of them frowning dramatically like annoyed parents.

"Someone's coming...." Alex took a breath of air. Weeks of essentially nothing had left his legs hurting and his lungs struggling after just a short dash. "Someone on a snowmobile... coming to the front."

He started running again, not stopping to answer any questions but leaving the doors open behind him because he knew they would want them answered anyways.

Running back into the office, he burst through the door just as the snowmobile pulled up outside the gate, dropping the pack on the floor so Marge could bend down and pick up the gun, brandishing it unsteadily. Albert and Isabelle walked in after him, peering out the windows at the figure on the other side of the gate.

It was a man, that much was clear from just his frame. He was clad head to toe in winter wear, wearing at least 2 layers of cold gear and sporting a ski mask that covered his face and goggles that covered his eyes. He peered at the hatchery, the reflective material giving no credence to what sort of gaze lay underneath. He shook the gate to the parking lot, but the snow had gotten high enough that trying to wrestle it free would be a waste of time, even if it wasn't locked. Instead, he went to the back storage of the snowmobile, pulling out a tarp of some sort. He threw it over the top of the gate, making sure it was firmly over the barbed wire before he climbed up it and across, into the soft landing of snow in the parking lot. After a moment where he struggled free of the small hole he had produced upon landing, the man straightened up and cracked his back, advancing towards the hatchery.

Inside, everything was silent. Marge had shushed everyone towards the back wall, holding the rifle in an iron grip and levelling it towards the window. The visitor's frosted footprints left imprints in the snow as he circled around the front of the building. He peered into the first window, seeing nothing but an empty office. He tried the door, but it had been locked from the inside. He jammed it a couple times, trying to force it open, but it didn't happen. The door held tight, and he grunted annoyedly, a muffled sound that nonetheless seemed to echo through the quiet space inside. He put his face up against the glass of the final window, peering through to see what Alex would have guessed was the last thing he might have expected.

Marge levelled the rifle at the visitor, the polished wood accenting the barrel of the gun that was shakingly squared towards the centre of his forehead. There was a muffled yell and a scattering of snow as the man stumbled backwards in surprise, landing in the drift of frost and alternating between the two instincts he had of putting his hands up in surrender and stopping his fall. The former won out, and the resulting image was that of a man half-submerged in a pile of snow, with his hands in the air and a head covered in little clumps of white. Marge advanced to the door, opening it slightly inwards, allowing in a small smattering of snow and a much more intense chill of wind through and into the office. Alex shivered as he watched Marge level the rifle through the crack of the door, grimacing as the shock of the icy wind collided with her face.

"What the hell do you want asshole? Why the hell are you here?"

Slowly the visitor tried to pull himself out of the hole he'd fallen into. To pacify Marge, who was at this point still essentially waving a gun in his face, he had to do so while keeping his hands in the air, creating an effect that looked like a puppet being suspended by an invisible string, with the puppetmaster's hand striking up a frantic motion in the legs as he tried to walk out of the freezing prison he'd inadvertently created.

"Hey, hey, hey, calm down. Please, just calm down. I'm not here to attack you, alright?"

Marge tried to dramatically brandish it towards him, pulling the bolt back to show it was loaded. In reality, it was more of a fiddling motion, producing the intended effect of ejecting a bullet only after Marge's freezing fingers had failed a few times. Alex had no idea how many bullets were in the gun and had a brief moment of panic when he realized that they didn't have any spare ammo.

In the meantime, the man winced at the sound of the bullet clattering to the floor, pausing for a moment before continuing his escapist scramble. "Jesus! I'm not here to hurt you! I just said that, Christ! Don't shoot me!"

Marge peeked the door open a little wider, letting the visitor see her face as it flushed from the cold wind that now blew freely into the office. "Give me a reason! What the hell else am I supposed to do when some asshole rolls up on my lawn with a goddamn jet ski on wheels?"

"I wanted to help! When you were at the fire... wait, have you never seen a snowmobile?" The visitor put his hands down a moment, baffled. Even past the goggles and mask, Alex could tell the idea of not recognizing a snowmobile was odd to him.

Marge, slammed the side of the gun against the door annoyedly, producing a hollow sound that seemed to echo outwards. "I don't give a shit if I've seen your hillbilly bullshit or not, I'm the one with the damn gun! What fire?"

The visitor's hands shot back up, remembering his situation and coming to the realization that the woman at the other end of the barrel wasn't the sanest or calmest. "Shit! The fire at my apartment building! One of you stopped to help me out, made me keep going. That was you, right? One of you? I heard you mention that you were heading up here, I just wanted to check on you, Christ..."

Marge kept her gun trained squarely on the visitor, but her glance fell on Alex, and it was mad. "Alex, did your idiotic surge of patriotic vigour let the entire shitting town of Squamish know we're here?"

The visitor had finally pulled himself out of the snow by now and was standing stock still on top of the snowfall, hands moving to rest behind his head. "Actually, I think it was you who actually mentioned this hatchery..."

"Shut up asshole." Marge lowered the gun, just a little bit. "So what if I did? A passing comment from a travelling circus of idiots doesn't justify driving your ass all the way up here for nothing. So what the hell is your game?"

The man seemed to lose focus a moment. Like he was reading a script, but the words had just run off and there was nothing on the other side of the page. He ended up just shrugging in response. "Can I come inside to talk?"

Marge had been resting the gun a bit, letting it trail downwards, but at that, she pulled it right back up again at the mere suggestion that the man move closer. "Hell no! I'm not letting you inside, what the hell?"

It was then that Isabelle, who had previously been hanging back with Albert in quiet observation, made the decision to dart forwards and put her hand on Marge's gun, pushing it downwards. Marge resisted, trying to shove her away, but Isa held firm, keeping the weapon pointed at the ground. "Marge, this isn't time to turn people away, ok? He hasn't threatened us... he could help us."

"We don't need the help, Isa!" Marge shouldered her away, standing back. "We're doing fine on our own. Some asshole with a jet-ski and a goddamn balaclava can't just waltz into our home, and we're sure as hell not going to lay out the red carpet."

"It's a snowmobile, not a jetski. And if we don't let him in, then who *are* we going to let in? Because I'm not going to live my life with just the three of you for the next 70 years."

"Bold of you to assume we'll live that long, especially if we let in the goddamn riff-raff. He's not coming in and that's final." She turned back to the door, shouting an expletive at the man and making a hand gesture with the finger that wasn't on the trigger.

"You don't get to decide that, we'll have a vote." Isabelle crossed her arms, turning to look at Albert and Alex. Albert nodded, while Alex shrugged. Isabelle glared at him a moment as Marge turned around to stare at her.

"A vote? A goddamn vote? What is this, student council? There isn't a vote."

"Why not? Nobody is in charge, remember? We all have an even say. So, we'll have a vote. Everyone who thinks we should let him in, raise your hand."

Albert and Isabelle's hands both went up immediately, which left Alex with the unenviable position of being the decider. He knew Marge would only bend to a full opposition, so this vote would be the one that mattered. And as always, he knew that it could tear him apart.

The threat was definite. The man was an unknown, it could be anyone beneath that mask. And as much as he claimed to be the man Alex had helped, they couldn't know until he took it off inside. It was just as likely that he was spitballing, spotting patterns and drawing conclusions all in an attempt to get inside their home and fillet them like the fish they had inside.

Or, he could be an ambassador of whatever society was left out there. He could represent their chance to make contact with the world again, speak to what was left of humanity. He could be a bridge over their river of isolation.

The truth was, he figured either option would be more interesting than slowly going insane inside of a mostly abandoned fish farm. So Alex raised his hand, averting his eyes from the betrayal that he knew would haunt Marge's eyes.

19: COMMUNICATION.

The visitor slipped through the door and into the office. Marge had stormed off, shoving the gun into Isabelle's hands and swearing that she'd regret it. Isabelle had peeked out the door and invited the man in, watching as he stumbled his way through the snow and nearly tripped on his way into the building. He had stumbled into the foyer, scattering snow across the ground as he pulled the door shut behind him. Now, after passing the gun to Albert, Isabelle looked past the goggles and ski-mask, towards the man underneath, and extended a greeting.

"Hi…"

The visitor choked back a laugh. Alex knew he must have heard at least some of the dispute, and he must have known that there was a lot more to the group than a simple greeting would communicate. Carefully, he pulled off his goggles, slipping them into the pocket of his jacket and blinking at the influx of light. His eyes were a muted green, reflecting the ceiling lights in a shimmering sort of way. He then grabbed the top of his mask, gripping it tightly and pulling it off with a warping of fabric and a sudden smell of B.O.

The man underneath did in fact bear a striking resemblance to the man Alex had encouraged by the fire. His face was dirtier and his hair more unkempt, but it was difficult to deny that they were one and the same. The man breathed a sigh of relief now that he was free from the stifling environment inside the mask, glancing behind him to make sure the door was closed.

Once he knew for sure that the cold was locked out, at least for now, he turned and looked at the rest of them with a deep exhale of air.

"Thanks. I guess..."

Alex looked cautiously between Albert and Isabelle, both of whom were looking at the visitor expectantly.

"Well, I guess I should, you know, introduce myself huh?" He rotated his shoulder a little uncomfortably, seemingly not enthused at being the centre of attention. "Well, my name is Ethan and I live down in Squamish, so... yeah."

Nobody else said anything. Alex realized it might have been more than a little creepy, but Marge's words had put them more than a little bit on edge. They wanted him to make the first move.

"Ok look. Your friend was right, I'm not here just to check on you. I wish it was, it makes me feel like less of an asshole. I really do appreciate you helping me out. It gave me the hope I needed. If you hadn't stopped, I would have given up. Probably lost a lot more in that fire. I swear, I would have come up here to thank you anyway, eventually. I didn't come here *just* because I wanted something."

He paused, which left an absent word hanging in the air. It was on everyone's minds, but it was only Albert, fingers still gripping and ungripping the stock of the gun, that was willing to say it. "But?"

"But... well, shit I do want something. I need something actually." His eyes crossed over one of the chairs, and he gestured towards it. "Can... can I take a seat?"

Albert narrowed his eyes suspiciously at him, but Isabelle nodded her head.

"Sure. Sorry, we're being a little cold." Isabelle shook her head and tried to smile reassuringly. "I'm Isabelle, this is Alex and the guy with the gun is my boyfriend, Albert." In Marge's absence, she was stepping up to take the role of quasi-leader of the group. It was a seamless shift in dynamic, and one that interested Alex almost as much as the inevitable interview that was about to take place. Ethan carefully sat down in the chair, wincing and holding his side as he did so. He evidently noticed the inquisitive gazes, shrugging and gesturing vaguely.

"I had a run-in with an idiot and a crowbar. It's really not something to be concerned about. We have a doctor back home. Well, a doctor in training but he can.. whatever." He took a breath, seemingly spitballing on what to say. "Okay. Okay, look. I'd love to talk to you more and all but... Squamish is in pieces. I mean, literally, pieces. All of downtown got flooded, lots of apartments burned down like mine, and the streets are filled with Vancouverites who don't have a home. Shit, I don't have home... I've been staying with some people up in the suburbs and..."

He grimaced, waving his hands in front of his face. "Not important. Just, it's a big crapshoot right now, and we need help."

Albert snickered, which earned him a glare from Alex and Isabelle. He relented a moment, turning sombre and clearing his throat. "Look, dude, as shitty as that sounds we're just three and a half people with a decade-old gun and some fish."

"That's exactly it. I don't think we can save Squamish. It's... well, it's basically hell. The mayor got stabbed in the streets and I think I saw a mountie shaking down a twelve-year-old yesterday. It's all kinds of screwed up. But, here's the thing, the thing I think you can help with I mean. We're shit out of food." He put his hands to his face, breathing a sound into his gloves. "Like, so shit out of food people are raiding each other for cereal boxes. Most of our groceries got flooded by the wave, and the rest got taken over by the Vancouverites. So we're basically just living on what we already had. Pantries, fridges, even berries if we're particularly desperate."

"And you want to throw fish into the mix." It dawned on Alex just what Ethan was asking for. Salmon. Access to a near-infinite supply of meat. "That's... smart, actually."

Ethan smiled sheepishly, rubbing the back of his head nervously. "Thanks. I don't need a lot, just enough to keep my people going for a while. They've taken me in after..."

"The Cascade?" Alex blinked, surprised by the words that came out of his mouth. He wasn't even sure why he'd said it. But just like the apocalypse itself, everything had cascaded and ricocheted into action, creating a crescendo that resulted in this new world they lived in now. Alex could think of worse things to call the end of the world.

"Is that what you're calling... it? The Cascade? Is that good?" Ethan seemed to consider the name, as did Albert and Isabelle. Alex thought of trying to explain himself, but sufficed with just a shrug and a nod, allowing Ethan to continue his plea. "Anyways, look. I owe them a lot, and I can't stand to see them struggle like this. I just need some fish for them, only a little. I don't have much, but..."

"We'll give it to you." Isabelle turned to look at Albert, who nodded. Alex nodded as well, in agreement. "Marge won't be happy, but we won't let you starve, ok? I don't know how much we can give you, but I promise it'll be what we can spare."

"Give it? Just... away?" Ethan shook his head, blinking in surprise. "No, I can't let you do that. I'll trade you, shit, even pay for it. I don't think you'll be needing money anytime soon, but even still. I can't just let you do so much for us without getting something as a thank you."

The door to the hallway opened behind the group, drawing eyes and ears towards the figure standing in the doorway.

"Winter clothes, fuel, and a snow-jetski." Marge strutted into the room, brushing past the other three to stand in front of Ethan, hands on her hips and a fire in her eyes. "That's what we'll trade you for. You make a down payment on all that, we'll start supplying the goods. As much fish as we can squeeze out of this place."

Ethan swallowed nervously, seemingly not expecting the crazy woman with the gun to start negotiating. Isabelle tried to protest Marge's sudden coup of the conversation but got shushed before she could deliver her complaint.

"Well I'm... I'm sure we can give you *some* of that. We don't exactly have that much fuel... and we only have another snowmobile so..."

"Get it, or you don't get any fish. It's that simple. Those are the terms, for now. Once you've stuffed yourself full of enough goddamn salmon to make a vegan cry, we'll see about future payments."

Isabelle wasn't going to be held back anymore, stepping forward to complain. "Marge! This isn't right, that's not how we negotiate!"

Marge turned to Isabelle, a sympathetically sinister smile on her face. "Isabelle, if you want to be stuck in here for 40 goddamn years, be my guest. But you just let a complete stranger into our house, and I'm going to take goddamn advantage of that, ok? Ok good. So, are those terms ok with you Jetski?"

Ethan coughed uncomfortably. The moment a negotiation came into play, Marge had clocked up her businesswoman skills to 100%, and the effects were noticeable. He was nervous, submissive, and felt he *had* to make a deal. It was the sort of thing that she had picked up on in her career. The sort of methods that made Macedon Tours so effective elsewhere.

"That's okay. I mean, that's great actually. Thank you. I don't know if they'll agree back home but, well, I don't think we have much choice."

Marge stepped back, sitting in one of the rolling chairs and leaning back dramatically. "Sounds perfect. I'm glad I didn't have to shoot you, Ethan. Come back here next week with all our shit and you'll get your fish."

Ethan was visibly more on edge now, putting his guard back up. He realized that he'd caved a little too much under Marge's demands, and now he faced the prospect of trying to sell this deal to his group. Alex recognized it, he'd seen it on some of the faces of the people who'd sold their homes for Paradise Valley to be built. It wasn't the regret of a bad deal, nor was it the satisfaction of a well-executed swindle. It was an uneasy sort of giddiness, the kind of feeling you got when you win 10$ on a lottery ticket. Sure, it's more money than you spent, but you also need to go home and justify just why you wasted your milk money on an insignificant shot to be a millionaire.

***

Isabelle basically dragged Marge out of there afterwards, Albert quickly in tow, leaving Alex alone with Ethan and the gun. It was a startling realization that, if Ethan was in fact here to kill them all, then this would be the perfect opportunity. The only person standing between him and the singular weapon in the building was a man with limited physical strength and a deathly fear of holding guns.

But instead of jumping at Alex and putting the rifle to his defenceless skull, Ethan stood up with a sigh. He glanced towards the door, then towards Alex. "Is she always so... aggressive?"

Alex shook his head, shrugging with his palms outstretched helplessly. "She's in a weird spot right now. We're all sort of on edge. She used to be our boss, so she's sort of just... defaulting to that. She's not technically in charge, and she swears she doesn't want to be, but whenever something big happens..."

"She pounces." Ethan nodded, rubbing his side and wincing. "My sister's like that. She wasn't my boss, obviously, but she really liked being in charge. Leadership scared the hell out of her though. Still does really, but she's stepped up a lot since..." Ethan trailed off, gesturing vaguely.

"The Cascade?" Alex still felt a little unusual calling it that. Sure, he'd coined the term, but saying the words still felt like trying to move an uncomfortable object through his mouth. "Is she… you know?"

"Alive? Yeah. She's been staying with me since my parents died a couple years back. I think the trauma of that whole deal really helped her cope with all this. She's still a little shit, but now she's a little shit who can give speeches and comforting words. I'm proud of her."

"Sounds cool." Alex shrugged. He didn't really know what to say. He didn't have any siblings and his parents? Well, it was better not to dwell on it.

"Yeah, it is." Ethan shook his head a little, smiling to himself. "Anyways, I should get going. I promised I'd be back in time for supper. I sort of assumed I'd be bringing home the fish today, so I hope they've actually made something else, just in case."

"Sorry…"

Ethan waved him off, shaking his head and pulling out his mask and goggles. "No, no, I get it. You have to survive, just like the rest of us. You can make it up to me by having a bunch of it ready by the time I get back here."

"We will. I promise. One week, right?"

Ethan pulled on his mask and tightened the goggles around his head. He held up a finger. "One week." Alex could hear him suppress a laugh, moving to the window to watch him get back on his snowmobile and ride off, shooting up a small plume of snow behind him as the throaty rumble of his vehicle filled the air once more.

20: OPERATION

Back in the hatchery, in what was once a break room for the occasional utility agent that roamed these halls, Marge and Isabelle engaged in a verbal debate. The windowless room bounced their words around like a wrecking ball, colliding with each corner in a cacophony of sound. Albert's occasional interjections of wit and annoyance only seemed to raise the tempo, especially with how critical he was of Marge.

It was an uneven fight.

The result was like the screeching of harpies, and Alex was loathe to try to intervene, standing just outside the doorway as another crash of verbal lightning collided with the room.

"What the hell were you thinking?! 'We'll give it to you'?! Why the hell would you ever say that, we need so much shit!" Marge was leaning against the wall, failing to downplay her anger in a mostly nonchalant pose that seethed with a tense rage.

"We also need to not be jerks, Marge! Those people needed our help, and you have no right to... to... barter away their ability to survive!" Isabelle was pacing around Albert, glaring at Marge with an intensity that made Alex more than a little uncomfortable.

"Well, I'm sorry that I care about surviving and not about the goddamn moral high ground. You need to get some priorities Isa, shit!"

"You..." Isabelle lunged at Marge, a move more fueled by anger than reason. Alex and Albert quickly jumped in to hold her back, making Marge recoil a moment in shock. She blinked a couple times, then started laughing as Isabelle's stare bore a hole through her heart with its intensity.

"Whoah Isa, I thought you were all about peace and hippy love? Where's this coming from?" She kept snickering to herself, seemingly enjoying the way Isabelle raged. She was still running on the corporate cylinders, and she had the same sort of look on her face that Alex figured oil tycoons had when they got the rights to a native reservation. Needfully unsympathetic, needlessly gleeful and overtly satisfied that they had come out on top.

Alex pulled Isabelle out of the room, having to battle her all the way. Albert helped, but not particularly well. It was clear that he was holding himself back as well, and only Alex's presence had stopped him from joining Isabelle in that lunge. Once Isabelle was safely out in the hallway, he turned back into the office and slammed the door shut behind him. The tempo reached the limit then, with the shouting almost shaking the walls. Alex was too distracted to listen in, instead focusing on Isabelle, who had put her back against the wall and slid to the floor, crying.

"What happened to us Alex? What happened to her?!"

Alex wasn't ready to confront the question. Marge had turned on a dime once more. At this point, Alex wasn't even sure who the real Marge was. Was it the determined lunatic who drove them all to push endlessly towards this hatchery and this shelter? Was it the quiet and manipulative snake who downplayed herself just so she could move the pieces around her better? Was it the ruthless businesswoman who took it a step further, diminishing her partners and competition until she could get what she wanted?

Or, and this is the one Alex feared the most, was she the quiet and happy woman who he caught a peek of during the darkest night before the Cascade's dawn?

In the end, he hoped it was at least one of those. Because those were versions of Marge that he could grasp. Expressions of taste and emotion that made some sort of sense to him. As much as he may hate the type of person she could be, at least it was a person he could *get*. It's so much simpler to just call her angry, or uncaring, or even just a flat out bitch.

But people were more complicated than that, and Alex knew that in all likelihood, she was somewhere in the gray area. Somewhere between each box, where the rules blended together and the complication of the human spirit came into play.

He could deal with a banshee. He couldn't deal with a person.

***

While Alex slipped off into the pondering state of mind he tended to find himself in, Isabelle picked herself up and dusted herself off. She had overreacted, and she knew it. The derision that Marge had shown towards the idea of being kind, that just broke something inside of her. Before, Marge was a tragic hero, someone who'd struggled under the weight of the world and now had no idea what to do when the world disappeared and the weight stayed the same. All that time slaving away to put her on top of the world, spinning that ball around and around like a beachball so that Marge would end up on top. What was that now? Ashes, smoke and radioactive hell. But Isabelle was getting an idea of what it would have looked like anyway.

It was her voice, again, that brought Alex back from his own ponderings on the topic. "Something... something has to change Alex. It could be her, it could be us... but we can't keep going like this, right? I mean, it's impossible!"

Alex took a breath, nodding as Marge's bedroom went suddenly silent. The two of them glanced towards the door, waiting for an explanation. A reaction. Something to explain the sudden, suffocating and inescapable silence. They got it when an explosion of noise conceded with the door opening and Marge storming out. She marched straight past them, ignoring them in a fit of enraged focus, slamming the door behind her as she entered the farm's floor. A red welt was seen on her face, and there were faint tears in her eyes.

Shocked, Alex and Isabelle both turned towards Albert, who was standing in the doorway to the bedroom.

"Albert? Al, did you... did you slap her?" Isabelle was floored by the implication of the strike. Alex could see already that Albert regretted it. He didn't know if there had been warnings or if Marge had realized that she pushed him too far, but the red handprint on her face and the fuming sheepish look Albert had on his was enough for Alex to build a theory.

He could picture it from here, the argument mounting, tensions flaring and Marge cracking enough to threaten something important to Albert. Labour, abandonment, maybe even just a hurtful memory. And by then, Albert was so tired of the argument, even the smallest provocation took down his nonchalant and indiscriminate barriers to trigger something reflexive and painful.

"You slapped her. You... slapped her." Isabelle blinked, shocked, horrified and amazed. It was such a flagrant, out of character action for him, the sort of nasty rumour that would be perpetrated by someone who didn't know the man.

"Isa, she threatened you. She said she would throw you out into the cold until your toes fell off. She...she goddamn threatened you, and I wasn't going to stand for it."

"So you slapped her?!" Isabelle was once again in a frenzy. It was the last thing anyone would have expected from Albert, least of all her. She stormed off after Marge, following her onto the farm floor.

Albert just stood there, watching her go and shaking her head. Alex turned to him, gesturing towards her. "What are you doing? You need to go after her."

"Her, or Marge? Because I really screwed up with both of them just now."

"Isa! You... Marge's pride might be wounded, but Isa needs to know you didn't mean it!"

Albert shook his head, sighing. "She's not that fragile dude. Look, I know her. She won't talk to me until she's decided to forgive me herself. Shit, maybe you could talk to her, but she's really righteous. I'm in the doghouse, and these walls are sound-proofed as far as she's concerned."

"Dude..."

"Alex, trust me. I've screwed up plenty of times in my life. Maybe it's just because I'm a sarcastic asshole, but 'sincere apology' isn't really in my playbook. She'd shut me the hell down if I tried. So instead of dwelling on that, let's figure out how the hell we're going to distribute the bullets in that gun so we can all off ourselves evenly. Marge would get jealous if any of us got a little bit more lead in our mouths than her.

Alex was horrified, something Albert realized but didn't seem to care about. "What the hell dude? That's not even... like, in the orbit of funny."

"Yeah, yeah, maybe the emotional turmoil of slapping my pseudo-boss and scaring of my pseudo-girlfriend have left me a little off my game. I'm a funny asshole, not the goddamn Joker." Albert let out a breath of air, shutting his eyes for a moment and letting the cold air of the room flow about uninterrupted for a moment. "So, I say, we let this whole thing cool down, get that delivery of fish ready for the nice man in the balaclava, and try to avoid getting murdered in our sleep by the vengeful women."

"That's... wrong. Sexist and wrong."

"So you admit those are two separate things?"

"What?" Alex realized that Albert was trying to turn around the situation on him. And like a fool, he'd already taken the bait.

"Exactly. Alex: Woman Hater."

"I hate you." Alex shook his head, heading to the farm floor.

"And men too! Men Hater." Albert followed, and the air got a little bit warmer. The memory of the fight wasn't going away anytime soon, but even after his most serious moments, Albert had a way of turning the world back to levity.

As annoying as that may be.

***

The fallout of the fight ended up filling the air inside the hatchery just as the fallout of the Cascade filled the skies above it. There was an unspoken, regimented agreement that everyone would work to fulfill the trade requirements. Everyone avoided each other, the only person Alex had done more than share a curt 'hello' with was Albert, but somehow the group worked in wordless synchrony. Alex would net the fish, setting them aside on a table in the moody lights of the farm's floor, and the next time he would enter the fish had been gutted and cut up, ready for storage. That came in the form of repurposing what was once Alex's bedroom, turning the needlessly complicated utility into what was essentially a freezer. He and Albert had agreed on that part, and an unhappy nod from Marge let them know that the idea was good in her eyes.

The unfortunate side effect of the change, however, was that he was once again back in the dormitory, and had to listen to the drama unfold around Albert and Isabelle's relationship.

The details of it eluded him, all he really got past was the fundamental truth that she was more than a little concerned by him and his behaviour. Over the days, they slowly got over their issues. It was like watching a wound scab over. On the first day, it's bloody and raw, something not to be touched lest it get infected. The next day, it was clotted and the bleeding had stopped, but there was still a ways to go. Slowly, throughout the week, the wound healed itself, leaving a scar that they would laugh about one day and tell their grandkids a fancified story about.

If they ever had grandkids.

And if those grandkids didn't suffer too many genetic defects from the inevitable radiation that would settle inside their bodies.

It wasn't a particularly promising future, all in all.

But still, Alex appreciated what the mend did to the atmosphere. Marge still remained on the outskirts of the group, doing her duties quietly and without comment. But the heart of the endeavour was back, and the atmosphere felt a little clearer once Isabelle was back on speaking terms with Albert.

21: BARTER

Ethan returned a week later, heralded by the rumbling of a pair of engines as he tore down the long white stretch of road that had been buried in the snowfall of before. Alex had taken that as his cue, and now waited with the others, holding two buckets full of chopped fish and snow. Two more were on the ground, ready to be carried when needed. The roaring engines were the only sound, each of the group standing as far apart from each other as possible in the small space. Even Alex and Isabelle were avoiding staying near each other, the former's hands wrapped nervously around the rifle. This was a precarious situation since the results of this meeting would determine just how they interacted with the outside world. In an ideal situation, they could just do the trade, exchange some pleasantries and be on their way, future engagements and interchange freshly negotiated and peacefully agreed upon. But, life wasn't that simple. Nor was it an ideal situation.

Ethan pulled up to the gate, trailed closely by another snowmobile. They both parked in the snow out front, Ethan grabbing the tarp to ease their climb into the hatchery while the other looked at the hatchery with hands on their hips.

It was a woman, as much as the snow gear concealed her identity, her frame and figure made it clear enough that she was female. She seemed unimpressed, inspecting the hatchery behind the reflective tint of the goggles, much in the same way that Ethan had last week. Alex realized that she must be the sister that he'd mentioned. She had an air of sass around her that seemed to reach past the faceless appearance of the winter gear. His suspicions were confirmed when Ethan stumbled as he climbed over the fence, and the woman laughed at him instead of helping. It was the mischievous sibling relationship that always got dramatized in books and movies. The sort that tended to leave Alex a little emptier inside when he realized that it was something he would never have.

It struck Albert too, but in a much harder way. He tried to hide it, but the devil-may-care attitude he once loved to purport had fallen away, and there was a pain behind his eyes that reflected the distant desolation of his brother in New York. It made Alex realize that maybe it was better to never have that it was to have and then lose.

Once Ethan had dragged himself out of the snow, he and his sister trudged towards the hatchery, carrying bundled packages that had been crudely put together out of wrapping paper. He knocked on the door while his sister peered in through the windows, causing Alex to suppress a shiver when her hidden eyes passed over him. Masks and ski goggles were a creepy mix, regardless of however much you knew of that person's good intentions.

A scattering of snow fell into the doorway as Isabelle pulled it open for the pair. The two slid into the room, setting their bundles down on one of the desks at the back wall. Ethan pulled off his mask and goggles, setting them next to the packages and smiling a little nervously. "Hey guys! I see you uh… you've got the fish."

Marge scoffed at him with hostility. Alex wanted to shoot her a look, but with tensions as they were, all that stood to do was ruin the deal that was about to go down.

Ethan didn't seem to mind, gesturing at the still fully masked woman who had accompanied him. "This is uh… this is my sister, Amanda." Alex felt a little spark of ego when he realized that he'd guessed right. Ethan continued. "She agreed to drive up here with me so we could get you guys the other snowmobile."

"Reluctantly." Her voice was muffled by the ski mask, but

Amanda didn't sound impressed. "Ethan, I thought you said these guys were intimidating."

"Amanda! Hey! Don't be rude. We're guests here."

Amanda scoffed at him. "You can't tell me what to do." She pulled her goggles off at least, eyes wandering over the crowd. "So, you're Ethans whole secret? You know he's been blah blah blahing for weeks about you guys. He hasn't shut up about it."

Isabelle smiled comfortingly, trying to take the lead of the situation before Marge could scowl her way into talking. "Well, we're very flattered but we're not anything special. We're just some people with some fish who want to help you guys out."

Amanda scoffed, stepping forward to grab one of the buckets and hoist it onto her arm. "You don't have to talk like that with me, I'm 17 not stupid." She rolled her eyes, starting to carry it back out to the snowmobiles.

Ethan shrugged sheepishly, shaking his head. "Sorry about her. She's not happy with the deal we made. She... hates fish. I don't think she's really realized just how bad things are. So... sorry." Carefully, he grabbed another bucket and headed out after her. Evidently, Amanda had heard him, because as they walked away Alex spotted her making a rude hand gesture towards Ethan. He had to suppress a chuckle. She was definitely full of angst.

Marge rolled her eyes, turning towards Isabelle. "Ooo, she's not happy with the deal. Someone throw a goddamn riot." It was a thinly veiled criticism of Isabelle, and she didn't seem happy about it.

Alex set down the buckets he was carrying, moving over to inspect the packages. As clumsily wrapped as they were, he appreciated the gesture. He imagined some kindly older folk putting together a gift like they were Santa Claus in mid-November. He carefully opened up a corner of the first one, revealing the polyester exterior of a winter jacket. He pulled the rest of the wrapping paper off, managing to extract three jackets of varying size and design. They were a little rumpled and a little compressed from being jammed into the wrapping, but he smoothed them out and set them aside with careful unpracticed precision.

The door opened again, sending another chill into the room as Ethan and Amanda strode back into the building. He could feel Amanda's eyes boring into his back judgmentally, not even needing to turn and look to know that she was mentally chastising him for opening the packages before they even left. The energy she put off made him shrink a little, feeling like a grave robber who went after the buried jewelry before the body had even gone cold.

There was a small clinking sound as the two guests picked up the rest of the buckets. They were still on edge, the tension of the hatchery seeming to seep into the air and make its way into their lungs. Ethan had stopped trying to break the ice, realizing he was perhaps trying to use a sun lamp on a glacier. And Amanda? Well, Amanda seemed to be providing some of the angst in the air herself.

"Hey, Alex?" Ethan gestured at him, holding the bucket over the elbow. "Could you throw that on so I can show you how the snowmobile works?"

"What?" Alex snapped out of his meteorological analysis, hand over the packaging of the second bundle.

"The snowmobile. It... well, it's not the easiest thing to manage. Have you ridden one before?"

"No... let me just..." Alex quickly opened up the second package, pulling out a pair of snow pants. Quickly, he pulled them over his worn and extremely dirty jeans, slipping the jacket on afterwards. The third and final package contained miscellaneous accessories, such as gloves and toques. He quickly pulled these on, realizing too late that he'd put on two left gloves. He realized he was about as haphazardly dressed as he could possibly be, but Ethan and Amanda were already at the gate by that point. He set off after them, pausing at the door to look at his friends.

Marge was too busy concentrating on the clothing to care, Isabelle gave him a little wave and Albert nodded his head. "Careful dude. They might still throw us for a loop."

Alex nodded carefully, trying to smile reassuringly. "I think I'll be ok. I... well, I want to trust them." With that, he opened the door to the outside world, feeling the chill wash over his face.

***

Stepping out into the muddled sunlight of the eternal cloudy day, Alex took his first steps onto the snow of the outside world. It had been so long since he'd deigned the outside with his presence, even the muted gray tones of the sky above rolled over with an intensity that made him wince and blink to clear his eyes of their light. It was freezing outside, and his breath turned to steam, curling into the air in front of him. It was such a foreign experience, to feel the snow underneath his boots and the sting of the cold air on his face, but all the while knowing that the majority of his body heat was not at risk, entrapped in the warm embrace of the jacket's interior. It had been what, almost a month since he'd seen the outside walls? Since the breeze had been more than just a ghost working its way through the doors and windows? The feeling was foreign to him now.

He plodded over the snow, careful to not let himself sink too far down into the cold embrace. He made his way over the tarp, careful to avoid the strips of wire that tried to pierce their way through the tarp's slippery embrace. Ethan and Amanda watched him, having pulled their masks and goggles back on in preparation for the ride. He worked his way towards them once he was on the other side of the fence, cheeks flushed red from the cold of the day.

"Hey guys. So uh... which one is mine?" Alex looked between the two snowmobiles, trying to appraise the group's newest acquisition. Ethan gestured towards the faded green paint job on the second snowmobile. Alex frowned. The model was clearly older than Ethan's own bright yellow vehicle, but he guessed that it wasn't something that could be helped. He bent over to inspect it, looking over the body of the vehicle with an unexperienced air of appraisal.

Ethan bent down next to him, pointing at the engine. "Here's the engine, Ed gave it a tune-up back at home, so it should run well for a while. This here's the heater block, you have to turn that on yourself so it doesn't freeze up." Ethan motioned Alex to look towards the back of the snowmobile, which was hitched to a small sled with a couple of gas cans on top of it. "Here's the fuel we promised. That should last you... eh, a week or two. Depends on how much you use it."

Alex listened to his explanation carefully, trying to remember all the important details. It was like that auto-mechanics class he'd taken in college, trying to remember so many small but significant parts that all summed up made a vehicle worth driving. It did raise a question though.

"How is this still working?"

Ethan turned his head, stopping himself mid-explanation. "Huh?"

Alex gestured at the vehicles, shrugging. "The snowmobiles. How... how do they work? Our car broke down when the Cascade happened."

"Oh... well, shit. I don't know? Maybe it has something to do with how the electronics are integrated? Remember, a few years ago when the government passed that bill that made everyone install electric engines in their cars? To fight global warming and shit? They didn't do that with these things, so maybe whatever EMP got created by the bombs didn't impact it the same way. I do know that the seat warmer is screwed. Which... well, make sure your seat isn't frozen over."

Ethan launched back into his explanation, which Alex seriously did try to listen to. It was difficult, but he genuinely gave it his best shot. By the end, he'd sort of grasped what parts were meant to rotate, what parts were meant to hum and what parts were meant to whir. Now all that was left was figuring out how to drive it.

22: INEVITABILITY

Snow kicked up behind them in a soft arc as Alex and Ethan rode through the frost-bound forest. Amanda followed behind them at a slower pace, more there to monitor than interject. Alex was at the wheel, driving the machine between the trunks and poking ferns of the forest floor, wrestling with the controls to keep the pace under control. The snowmobile wasn't properly designed for two people, so it felt even more so like trying to balance a bucking bronco than the simple act of seesawing.

Ethan had called him a natural. Alex felt like a maniac He'd learned to drive at the age of 16, and even if he'd never gotten his license renewed after it first expired, he still felt like he could drive a car if it really came down to it.

But a snowmobile was an entirely different beast. It crossed the line of experience long past what Alex was comfortable with. So as much as it must have been exhilarating to see the open snow ahead and understand that all of it was in reach, Alex focused on the trees more so than the forest, mostly so he could traverse the latter without crashing into the former.

They made their way across Paradise Valley, venturing towards it's ends far beyond what the group had on foot. They crossed buried campgrounds, cozy shut up cabins and old train tracks that crisscrossed the centre of the valley. They even passed one of the old houses that used to be the singular structures of the valley, a sad and decrepit two-story affair that made Alex shiver for a reason that was not the cold. He could almost swear he saw the shadows of the past inhabitants swirl behind the windows of the place, a quiet reminder that all of this was built on the expulsion of others.

Alex parked next to the river, an almost entirely frozen over affair with a small and turbulent channel working its way through the middle of the ice. A more poetic mind would have pointed out the analogy of the situation, with a turbulent and ongoing effort making its way down the middle of a frozen expanse, but Alex was too preoccupied with the exhilaration and coursing adrenaline of his mad dash through the frosted forest to be mindful of casual symbolism.

Ethan disembarked from the snowmobile, while Alex mostly just tried not to fall off as he stumbled on unsteady legs. Ethan helped him stay upright, letting Alex lean against him as he got his bearings. Amanda pulled up next to the two, stepping off her own snowmobile.

"Ethan, are you sure it was him driving? I could have sworn I saw your most famous manoeuvre, 'Driving right into a snowbank and nearly flipping the thingy.' You've really taught him your style."

Ethan swatted at her playfully. "Or maybe you're just too busy focusing on everything but the road Miri. Alex had it handled, I barely had to teach him anything." They both looked over at Alex, who at this point was doubled over and looking a little green in the gills. "Well... I guess maybe I should have taught him about... you know inertia."

Alex nods, leaning back on the snowmobile, taking in breaths of the cold air and struggling to keep himself from throwing up. It was awkward, especially since the other two were just watching him unabashedly as he fought his breakfast of pudding and fish back down into his stomach.

Ethan waited until he had recovered a little to speak up, clearing his throat awkwardly. "Yeah... so... we're going to head back with all the fish. Do you think you can make your way back home by yourself?"

Alex nodded, waving them off while still feeling a little too queasy to talk. He could follow their tracks back to the hatchery, he was sure of it.

"Alright, Alex. We'll... be in touch. We'll come back up here to check on you in a few weeks."

Amanda had climbed into the driver's seat of her snowmobile, shaking her head. "He means that *he'll* be back up here to get more fish from you."

Ethan smacked her on the shoulder playfully "Hey, uncool. And that's my seat."

Amanda held firm, starting up the engine and revving it. "Under whose authority?"

"Under mine you little twerp... It's my mission, so I get to assign seats." Ethan gently sat himself down in the driver's seat, jostling her out of the way with a playful gentleness.

Amanda groaned, crossing her arms and scooting backwards onto the passenger hump. "That's bullshit and you know it. You just get to drive because I can't kick the shit out of you yet."

Ethan turned towards Alex, who just shrugged. "She's not wrong."

Ethan spluttered, revving the engine and starting to pull away. "Thanks man, I'm never going to hear the end of that." Amanda laughed at him, drowned out by the engine as it picked up and the two headed back into the forest, destined for home.

***

Alex took a few more minutes to recover, sitting back on the cold vinyl of the seat. Snow fell softly around him, accentuating its white drifts with the green and greys of the forested mountain slopes. It was peaceful, reminding Alex of one of those static images people used to animate, a lonely scene with a quiet snowfall raining on it peacefully. He could picture it now, a rustic cabin by the riverside, snow falling softly as the chimney released the gentle smoke of a roaring fire. It was like a holiday movie, furniture befitting the fir and spruce trees that surrounded them, with a great big bear rug set over the floor.

Maybe that was something to aspire to.

Snapping himself out of his idle fantasy, Alex started up the snowmobile, taking a moment to let it reheat before treading his way back into the forest. The trail was easy enough to follow, winding around a few times through the trees. He moved at a much slower pace, no longer fueled by Ethan's encouragement or the adrenaline and testosterone-fueled need to succeed. It was scenic, and he followed the trail exactly, ignoring places where it went back over itself in loops, and when he spotted recognizable landmarks that he could use for navigation. Instead, he took the longer route, appreciating the natural beauty that at once had been the backyard of the local inhabitants. He paused when he saw that same house again, noticing the red snowmobile half-buried under the snow next to the decrepit shed. He felt silly when he realized that they could have used it instead of trading, assuming they could get it out. He felt even sillier when he realized that if it was parked there, that must mean there were more abandoned vehicles around the valley, forgotten vestiges of the valley's residential past.

He roared his engine again, revving a little too quickly and jumping up onto a snowbank. He didn't like that house, or the feelings it gave him, so he chose to move just a little bit faster than he probably should have. He just couldn't shake the eerie feeling it gave him like it had ghosts with piercing eyes that would bear down on him if he stayed around too long. The languid pace evaporated like the frost that had preceded the snowfall.

He finally pulled up outside the hatchery's front gate, trying to execute a parking job that would allow an easy departure. The tarp was still laid over the fence, and Alex wasn't sure if it was a gift from the two visitors, Ethan being forgetful or even just for convenience's sake. He shut off the engine of the snowmobile, dismounting and taking a final look over the snowy landscape. He then climbed over the tarp, pulling it over with him so that there would be no way for anyone else to enter.

Shoving the tarp into a ball, he carried it under his arm like an astronaut with their helmet, ducking down into the doorway of the hatchery and the warm air inside.

The office was empty, with the wrapping of the clothing scattered around the floor and chairs. The items themselves where nowhere to be found, assumedly brought back into storage for later use. He shook his head. It really was like Christmas, with each recipient running off in each direction with their shiny gifts, ignoring the mess they left in their wake. Alex almost had to laugh, pulling off his jacket and toque, setting them on a chair and cracking his back as the warm air inside the office fought the clinging cold from his bones.

As the warm air of the vents reheated his chilled insides, he cracked the door open to the hallway. Evidently, he interrupted an intimate scene as Isabelle pulled away from Albert where they had been making out against the wall with uncomfortable confidence.

"Alex! Hey, you're back!" She straightened her ratty hair, trying to look less ruffled and caught in the act. It was a patently useless attempt, and Alex felt a little queasier that she had even tried to pretend that he hadn't walked in on the two of them making out. "How was the… snowmobile ride?"

Alex cleared his throat, uncomfortable with the way Isabelle was embarrassed and Albert was so proud. Their twin smiles of sheepishness and smugness were an unnerving contrast to the rampant beauty outside. It was strange, the way a single ride through the trees could redefine the way someone sees sights that they had previously become familiar with.

"It was ok. I think I've figured out the controls by now, so… yeah. I can drive us around so we can keep scavenging. Maybe go down to Squamish if we wanted to."

Albert shook his head. "About that... Marge wants us to have a meeting. Something about dealing with things."

"Dealing with things? What does that mean?"

Albert shrugged, putting his palms outwards. "I don't know dude. I just know she locked herself in the main floor after you left and she's been rearranging things in there. I can basically smell the melodrama. And like, 5 minutes ago she said to knock when you got here."

Alex furrowed his brow, looking at the door. "So... why haven't you knocked?"

"What, so she can grab my hand and shank me? Shit dude, you're the only one who hasn't *totally* pissed her off. I'm letting you do the honours of getting shredded first."

Alex sighed, striding forward and knocking on the door. This did not bode well. "Marge? Are you in there?"

Her voice echoed from the cavernous ceilings of the room, muffled through the door. "Come in!"

Alex glanced at Albert, then at Isabelle, who both shrugged. Gently, he pushed the door open.

***

The farm's floor was illuminated dramatically. Lights were turned on in strategic patterns that seemed to exemplify severity, casting shadows across the floor in strange ways. Alex wasn't convinced that Marge hadn't spent the entire time he'd been away planning this, flicking the lights on and off into a sufficiently melodramatic setting for whatever she had planned.

The woman herself was standing at the end of the farm, flanked on both sides by the pools of salmon, swirling mysteriously in the shadows of the tank's edge. "All right assholes, let's get this meeting started." Her gaze was steely and determined, and it looked more like she was facing off against a bear instead of her own friends.

Albert looked at Alex and Isabelle, noting their silence with a shrug and stepping forward past Alex. It was a little timid, he knew that there were unrained consequences for his actions. "Ok Margey, you've got us all spooked here. Can you tell us what you're doing here? Or did you give the fish a taste for human blood so you could use them to execute us?" He chuckled a little at his own joke, trying to ease some of the very intentional tension in the air.

"Oh Albert, why couldn't your unfunny wit die like the rest of the world?" That gave the rest of the group pause, reeling back a moment to react to what she just said. It was a vicious comeback and one that brought them so strikingly back to their post-apocalyptic present. The welt on her face had faded, but clearly the memory of the slap had barbed her tongue.

"Now, I'm done screwing around. We've been locked in here like it's 2020 for what, a month? That's way too long to have all these goddamn issues stewing and goddamnit if I'm going to let that keep us down. This trade deal of ours has just opened up a real bitch of an opportunity. We just spent, I don't know, weeks faffing around like shit children. And I'm sick of it. We're useless, abusive and isolated assholes, but by goddamn Odin or whoever the hell else is still watching us on this goddamn planet, we are going to fix it."

She paused a moment, letting the words sink into the weak crowd. Alex felt belittled, like his long-gone mother had come back from the grave to chastise him for hogging the salmon.

"We are going to run this damn hatchery like it's our only lifeline to live because I swear to you it is. We've been treating it like some infinite source of whatever the hell, and that's got to stop. We're going to turn this place from a hatchery into a base. This isn't a summer camp anymore. We need to stop treating this like whatever the hell we have is ok. It's not. We are going to go insane if we keep going like this. Shit, I'm sure we already have based on *some people's* reactions."

She paused again to glare at Albert, who sheepishly looked at the floor. Marge was humbling Albert, and it was an incredible show to watch.

"It's not just the snow, ok? It's us. We're a dysfunctional mess. I know you guys all hate me. I'm a bitch, and I wouldn't be surprised if you'd use a whole shitload of words that are worse than that in private. But I'm out here trying to survive, while you all canoodle and stare at thin air. You'd give away all our shit because of a damn sob story. Think a little! So here's the deal. I'll stop pretending I'm not in charge because clearly, some asshole has to be. I'll stop yelling at you as much. But in return, I need some goddamn commitment, ok? I need you all to dedicate yourselves to survive because if you don't, you're not going to. This hatchery, it sucks alright? It's easily one of the shittiest, darkest and most depressing places I've ever been, and that includes that hellhole we used to call our office! But it's our home now. We need to turn it into the post-apocalyptic fortress it needs to be. Am I clear?"

The room was dead silent for a moment. It seemed the buzzing of the lights had stopped, the splashing of the fish had faded away and all that was left was the four of them breathing. Alex looked between Albert and Isabelle silently, hoping one of them would say something. But what? That Marge was crazy? That the sudden possibility of escape had broken her? That she was speaking nonsense? Or conversely, that she was right? That they had essentially been spending weeks stumbling around in the dark? That this opportunity they'd been granted was more of a blessing than they could have imagined? It was a decision to rationalize.

Albert decided first. "Fine. You know what Margey? Fine. I think you're a goddamn lunatic, but you're not wrong." He stepped over to her, reaching his uninjured hand out to shake hers firmly.

"I know tempers have flared, and that I've been an ass. But as long as you recognize that goes both ways, I'll try to tone it down."

He stood next to her, quietly looking at the rest.

Isabelle stepped forward next, nodding her head. "I... we've had some rough days Marge... some of the things you did... you can't do them anymore, ok? We can't break down like everyone else out there has. We're better than that, right? We... we need to be the Ethans of the world, not the crazy people with tire irons."

Marge hesitated a moment, before nodding. "We are. I really hope we are. But Isa, we're going to have to do some bad shit to survive. People are going to want to take this place one day. When all the cans run out and the berries get picked dry, we have something they won't. Food. Water that isn't, you know, goddamn radioactive. And most people won't just ask nicely like Ethan. There are some real big assholes out there Isa, and you need to accept that they'll be coming for us."

Isabelle hesitated, then stood next to Marge, nodding. That left Alex, with all three of them looking towards him across the pools of the farm.

He didn't know what to do. For Albert and Isabelle, the choice was easy. This was the Marge they knew. The boss, the professional. Someone who had ambition and drive. Someone willing to do what they needed to do. But it wasn't the Marge that Alex knew. What he wanted, more for her sake than anyone else's, was the Marge that shone through the cracks. The happy, funny woman who puts up the wall for the sake of others rather than herself. The woman who loathed to go out to dinner that night, but in the end shone through stronger than any other time he'd seen her at all. The woman who confided in him because she needed to, broke because she had to and fought because she wanted to. He wanted Marge to be the Marge of his mind. And he was terrified that stepping forward would lock her up, bury her beneath the Marge that she chose to showcase to the rest of the world. That enabling this version, this façade of the greater woman beneath her, it would bury who Alex wished she really was.

His feet felt glued to the ground, even as much as he wanted to move forward. He *wanted* to let go of the pre-Cascade vision he had of her. Adapt, survive, realign himself with this postnuclear world. But he couldn't do it.

Instead of stepping forward to meet the others, join them in their quest to assert themselves in this new world, he stepped backwards, into one of Marge's dramatically placed shadows. He couldn't, and wouldn't bear to lose the glimmer of hope he had for what was.

"Marge. Marge, I... I can't."

Isabelle and Albert cringed, looking at each other with trepidation. But Marge stared at Alex, the almost forgotten unknown gaze that people used to give him in her eyes. He never could quite decipher what that meant. It seemed to bore into his soul as she stepped forward, moving her hand upwards. Alex flinched back, worried that she was about to lash out, start shouting or breaking. Become the banshee that had driven them to this point in the first place. But instead, she reached out and offered him her hand.

"Alex?"

He opened his eyes, looking confusedly at Marge's outstretched hand. She smiled at him. It wasn't the warmer smile of that Cascade bound night, but it wasn't her business formal smile either. It was somewhere in between, with an almost motherly sort of aura. "Alex, this is how we survive."

She takes his hand gently, looking back at the other two. "This shit is going to suck. I hope I made that clear. But guys, this is who we have to be, okay? We don't need to be evil, and as I said, we won't. But shit people, the world ended. Clinging to that vestige is just wrong. We're not who we were. And that isn't some heroes' journey bullshit, that's just facts. We're different because we *have* to be different. And that's just life."

Alex bows his head, shaking it and using his free hand to wipe at his face. "I don't want to let go Marge. I don't... I'm scared. I like who I am. Who you are, when you're not doing this... this... business bullshit."

She snickers a little, smiling. "Well Alex, that's what we call getting stuck in the past. It's unfair that we're the ones who have to deal with the nuclear hellhole that we live in right now, but we can't just ignore the fact that our lives before the... screw it, Cascade, they were different."

She turned to Isabelle, nodding at her. "Isabelle was right, it's not me to be as much of a bitch as I have been. But... goddamn it, Alex, we can't be as soft as you guys were being. We're not different people, you know? Just evolved. Adapted. I'm still Marge, I'm just not going to let emotion dominate me." She squeezed his hand, a little flash of something passing through her eyes. "Because that's what we need to do to survive. We can't give an inch, but I realize now that doesn't mean we have to take one either, alright?"

Alex nodded slowly. Maybe that was... well, it was the inevitable truth. He'd fought so hard to avoid thinking about the past, about the desolation that lay behind him, but he'd never let the soot of the dead world before wash off of him.

Maybe he had to accept that the darkness of what he'd done was inevitable. Accept it, let it flow through him. But not dominate him. He could still be in charge. He couldn't fill in the hole, not in his lifetime anyway. But if he stopped pretending it wasn't there, perhaps it was possible to stop falling into its depths.

He gripped Marge's hand back, looking up and nodding. He stepped over with the rest of them, sitting in the small beams of light cast by the buzzing lamps above.

23: REPARATIONS

As much as any of them would like to swear that the meeting had ended all conflict and coalesced them into a single hive-mind of efficiency, the truth is never as glamorous.

The next couple of weeks were difficult. Everyone was putting in an effort to stay strong, confidently striding from one task to the next, greeting each other courteously and doing whatever job Marge had deemed necessary with efficiency. But everyone knew that in private the issues wouldn't fade away immediately. Albert and Marge still bickered, Isabelle had the occasional indignant retort and Alex had more than one moment where the bad things came to the forefront. As easy as it was to make the decision to become a post-nuclear badass, the romances of this sort never seemed to mention the inevitable pitfalls.

But the important thing, to Alex at least, was that they were giving it their best shot. Steeling yourself to a cold harsh world and forgetting the indignities of a dead one is about as easy as it sounds and striking that proper chord within the gloomy mess that was personality had each of them struggling. But it was the continued dedication to finding it that meant one day, perhaps not today and probably not tomorrow, Alex could find peace.

For now though, he crouched next to Albert as he dug around inside one of the big machines that rang around the farm's floor. The arrays and wires of lights behind the side panels of the machine barely seemed to make sense to Albert, even less so to Alex. It all just seemed to be a mess of worms and strobes. Evidently though, Albert saw something that had gone so far over

Alex's head, it was beyond the clouds. He sat back with a sigh, placing the panel back over the inside of the machine. Alex turned to him and waited expectantly. When he didn't offer an explanation, Alex had to clear his throat.

Albert rolled his eyes, standing up and rotating his now much more healed arm. "The problem isn't here. I think it might be somewhere along the pipeline. Because that shit's perfect."

Alex scratched his head, not understanding... well, anything. All he saw was the convoluted mechanics of wiring and the disappointed wit of a very unhappy man. "Ok... where's the problem? And what is the problem?"

Albert was unimpressed but tried to suppress his snickering. "We're not getting enough flow from the pipes that bring our water in. We have a whole underground system running here from the glaciers in the mountains. It's why we have fresh water and not glowing goop from whatever the hell settled in the waterways around here after the kaboom."

"But it's not coming in anymore?" Alex tried to envision it, a huge line of piping, running beneath the valley and fueling the hatchery with its liquid gold. It was weird, to think that such a naturally incorporated place was undercut by such an industrial idea. "Why, is it broken?"

"Shit, I hope not. It's still coming in, just not nearly as much as there should be. More likely it froze over or some shit. Which is definitely all we need." He rubs his forehead, gesturing at the pools full of fish. "It won't screw us over, yet. But we'd need to start recycling water, and that causes plagues. And if our fish get a plague, we're more dead than your chances with Marge."

"Hey!"

"I'm not taking that back. Shit boils down to this, we have to unfreeze those pipes, or we'll last a couple months before dying from fish cooties."

Alex shook his head, looking over towards the pool full of fish.

It was a little hard to quantify, the idea that simply recycling water would turn the writhing pools of food into a mass grave of disease.

Thematically appropriate, he supposed.

"So how do we do that? Can... we do that?"

Albert nodded, gently rubbing his shoulder. They had made the decision a few days past to lower the temperature inside, so they could go outside without suffering a major thermal shock. So, while it wasn't nearly as cold as the outside, everyone still tended to wear their jackets indoors and Albert loved to complain about his shoulder aching. Right now though, there was a more pressing matter.

"We can. But not here. We'd have to hike on over to the pump station and do... well, some bullshit I'm sure. I've never actually been there myself, but this isn't exactly unprecedented so... there must be something up there to fix this shit. Probably some sort of chemical that'll make the water taste like shit, but I prefer that to making a bucket line to the nuclear backwash that's filled the river."

"Do you need help dude?"

"Hell yeah, it's not like I could drive myself up there. Although..."

Alex chuckled as Marge emerged from the hallway, walking over to them with a smirk. "Albert, last time you tried to screw with a motor vehicle, the Cascade happened. Let Alex drive."

While Albert sighed and tried to think of a retort that was clever and polite, Alex narrowed his eyes suspiciously at her. "Were you just... sitting there? Listening?"

Marge waved his concerns off dismissively. "I was just heading to the bathroom when I heard you two plotting. I figured it was better to hear Albert's entire stu-" She caught herself, clearing her throat. "Albert's entire stupendous plan before I decided if it was a shitty idea or not."

Albert rolled his eyes, shaking his head. "Okay IRS, what was your verdict then?"

"It was all a good plan until you thought it was a good idea for you to drive up there by yourself. And it was the FBI who spied on people, not the IRS. The IRS just went after you if you screwed up financially."

"And how the hell do you know so much about that?" Albert was scrambling now, trying to recover his dignity from screwing up what he thought of as his one redeeming quality. "That's all American bullshit. How was I supposed to know?"

"It's called being multi-cultural. You should tr- damn it!" Marge was evidently having difficulty reigning in her own instinct to sting as well. It did warm Alex's heart a little to see both of them trying to commit to being less confrontational. "I went to school in the States. So I was more worried about the IRS than I was about the CRA, which is what you should use if you ever want to scathe back at me for educating you."

"Ah screw it…" Albert was defeated, which was a sight that Alex would never have believed just a couple of months ago. "Can we go or not?"

"Sure. You can use the jetskimobile tomorrow morning. Isa and I still need it to haul a couple of dressers we found out at the farther edges. Unless one of you wants to volunteer?"

Alex continues his silence, while Albert just shrugs.

"Lazy dickheads. If you didn't have work to do tomorrow, I'd make you go." She shrugs, heading off to complete her business.

Albert turned to Alex, looking annoyed. "Could you remind me why she gets to still be a bitch while I have to reign myself in like I'm crazy or some shit?"

"She… doesn't?" Alex watched her go through the door, eyes following the way it swung shut behind her. "She's trying, just like you are. Didn't you see how many times she stopped herself there? It's hard for her as well."

"Sure, but she gets more leeway." He rubs his dirty scalp, giving the door a dirty glance. "If it wasn't for that whole commitment bullshit, I'd be pretty mad."

"But you're not? Because we made a commitment?"

"It's not magic dude, but yeah. I'm a little *less* pissed. Still makes it bullshit." Albert kicks the machine a little. "Screw it I guess. Let's work on the fish."

Alex nodded, dipping over to the pool and getting to work on letting the fish swim themselves into the net he cast. It had become his job, and with good reason.

The tranquillity of dipping the net and waiting was a harsh contrast to the clinical apathy of his actions. The fish swam themselves into his grasp, unknowingly but all so willingly into the jaws of death. It was the end of their lives, soon to meet Albert's knife as they choked on the air.

It's not that Alex didn't feel sympathy for them, nor was it the cool uncaring and un-intrusive thought of a predator. It was simply the necessity of the action. If he could let the fish live, he would. But their canned food supply had gotten so low that their diet now consisted almost exclusively of salmon and the few hardy berries that could survive the cold of this new winter.

It was survival, plain and simple.

Albert, who had grinned when they first split open a fish at this very spot, now took a more clinical approach to their gutting. It wasn't clean, their only knife was essentially a shiv that they had found in one of the cabins, but the way he reduced a once-living breathing creature to its component parts had a process to it now.

It was adaption. It was understanding. It was survival. Not the moral desecration of Marge's old way, or the moral clinging of Isabelle's old way. It was the middle ground, the professional handshake of thoughts that brought together two opposing ideals into something that sacrificed the less convenient parts of each other into something more tolerable.

They weren't saints, and they weren't sinners. The time for that was before, and in all likelihood would come after.

For now, they were just humans, killing and gutting fish because that was the only way either population could live on.

When the bits of meat and guts were properly separated, Alex and Albert carried them down to the impromptu icebox that was intermittently Alex's bedroom, the storage room and the place where each of them let the others go to cry.

They had used the empty cans in an unfortunate way, filling them with snow and using them to hold and cool the viscera of their harvest, removing the possibility of stacking them high as Alex privately wanted to.

What followed was the indignant and unglamorous necessity of filling the cans with fish. It was a bit of an awkward process, and Alex quietly thanked whatever deity still bothered to watch over the planet that they had gloves for the process.

They stacked their collection in neat rows, along with the worn furniture and useless blankets that had been stored here alongside their catch. To Alex, it seemed like that was most of what they gathered. Furniture and blankets. Sometimes books. They found a couple of fishing rods as well, but there wasn't much point to them when they could just dip their nets into the water and collect more fish than they could ever need. So they sat there, leaning against a dresser that Alex figured was way more trouble than it was worth. But Marge had insisted on collecting as much furniture as they could, and with the advent of the snowmobile to help them move bigger ticket items, Alex had started to see why.

It was clear from Ethan and Amanda that trade was going to be a lifeline. The hatchery was rich with food and water, but little else. So interacting with the people of Squamish, that would be their only way to get more specialized equipment. As of now, they only had half a med-kit and a handful of coats. All of their everyday clothing was filthy or the wrong size. As much as they were still essentially living in the apocalypse, Marge wanted to be sure that they had the luxuries to trade once all the tables and chairs down south had been burned as firewood.

She was smart like that. Even now, she had a sense for business. And while she swore to cut off the smugness and the presence that came with the territory, Alex couldn't help but admire the instincts.

Albert finished canning the fish, shivering a little and continuing to rotate his shoulder. "What else do we have on the schedule? We checked the pipes, figured out the problem with said pipes and now we've canned the fish."

Alex scratched his head, trying to remember what had been out of place. "The sunroofs looked a little cloudy. Maybe we could give those a clean?"

"Nah dude, screw that. We did that yesterday. It's Marge's turn to climb up there and scrape all that shit off." He looks around the storage room, considering. "I'm going to see what I can find in here that could be useful tomorrow. Could you give me a hand?"

"Uh… sure." Alex shoved the last bit of fish into the last can, following Albert as he moved deeper into the storage room.

Albert began digging through the miscellaneous junk that they'd essentially dumped into the drawers of the shelves and nightstands that they'd looted. Alex, meanwhile, had an idea that he was ashamed of himself for not coming up with earlier. He started grabbing some blankets, alongside some rusty nails and one of the empty cans. He nearly dropped it all when a loud noise pierced the quiet chilly air. It sounded like an air raid alarm or the scream of some mechanical beast.

He turned, expecting to see the worst, and instead only saw Albert holding up an airhorn with a shit-eating grin. "Dude, look what I found! I thought I lost this!" Albert squeezed the top of the airhorn again, sending another irritating blast into the air of the frozen room.

"How did... why was it in there?" Alex winced, rubbing his ears as if he could massage the noise out of his vibrating skull. "And can you please not use it in here? It's really loud dude."

Albert tooted the horn one more time, pocketing it like a kid in a candy store who'd been told he could take the biggest gobstopper he wanted back home with him. "I guess I threw it in there when I had to carry some shit at some point, then just forgot about it. Lucky break. For all of you." He laughed ominously, smiling that sinister smile that Alex had come to appreciate as being mostly harmless. Mostly. He was a tad worried about what Albert would do when he was granted the power of very loud things in an otherwise very quiet place.

As the man himself cackled at his newfound ability to tease while not *technically* belittling the rest of the group, Albert noticed that Alex was carrying some distinctly non-expedition equipment. "Ok, so what the hell did you find? I don't think we'll be needing a month old empty can of fruit slices on our badass trip to unfreeze the plumbing."

Alex glanced down at his burden, nodding. "Yeah, I'm using these for a... personal project."

Albert shrugged, going back to rifling through the drawers. "Playing house again? Alright. As long as that your microwave made of blankets doesn't rise up as an AI overlord and burn down all our shit again, I'm pretty sure it'll be fine."

Alex wasn't quite sure what to say to that, which tended to be what Albert's jokes resulted in when the other options were anger or admiration. The man walked quite a line.

Laden with the equipment for his personal project, Alex returned to the dorm and got to work. In essence, Albert was right. He was playing house again. But the necessary abandonment of his private room and the increasing tempo of Albert and Isabelle had made sleeping nights and sharing days in one room... uncomfortable.

So, to solve that issue, he stood up on his bed and started nailing the blanket's end to the ceiling with the can. He was partitioning the room, cutting off the small corner to which he'd dragged his bed so that both he and they could have some privacy.

Really, he should have done it sooner. But the rigour of life these days had put him off from it. But now, with the curtain up and the dignity of a private room restored, Alex could lay back on his bed and not worry about glancing upwards and seeing things that would be impossible to unsee.

Another benefit of the end of their essential isolation was the sudden availability of more books. They would find novels and short stories out in the cabins and campgrounds, most of them moulded or rotted from the exposure to the elements. They even managed to snag a Bible. The books available varied wildly. It was essentially a 50/50 split between classics such as Marge's copy of The Old Man and the Sea, to surprisingly modern stories such as the book he was reading right now 'Forgone Spaces'. The result was a wild dichotomy between the more classical tales bound in leather and placed there by Macedon Tours as essentially set dressing, and the modern tales taken to Paradise by enterprising families and woodsmen who wanted to live through the outdoors without entirely leaving behind the comforts of communal imagination. It gave a sense of variety, an alternation between modern content and older tales, each of which could define a mood.

For the rest of the day, he read. While Albert stocked up for their expedition, and Marge took Isabelle out on their own scavenging run, Alex had the time and the space to dedicate to himself. It wasn't the sheer frantic boredom of the weeks isolated. That was a crippling, maddening sort of free time that drove many an entrepreneurial lonesome man or woman to insanity. It was, and rather ironically to Alex, more like having a job. The

9-5 that was too prevalent before the whole world turned on its head. But it was more than that, an evolution of the concept. Or maybe a devolution.

But Alex had work to do, scavenging, cleaning, managing. It was everyone's burden. It wasn't a schedule per se, the regimented world of office hours and bus times, but there was a certain structure to it. If he had been the one to clean the fish filters last, he would be the next to go out scavenging. If he had to scrape the ever-thickening snow off of the sunroofs, he was sure that the next time it got dark inside the farm's floor, he could look up and see someone else letting the light in themselves.

But for now, there was nothing.

So he read, eventually turning on the limited light of the camping lanterns they'd found as night fell over the valley. He watched the sun set behind the swirling clouds above. They looked ominous, and even though the ash and brimstone of the Cascade had long diffused into the atmosphere, these rolling and rumbling storm clouds seemed to carry completely the weight of the almost forgotten plume that had raged across the sky. It would snow heavily tonight.

Alex chose to sleep early as a result, wanting to bypass the whistling of the wind and the shaking of the trees in a way that allowed him to sleep without them haunting his dreams.

***

For the most part, the night was silent. The harsh reign of the snowfall bared down on them with only the faintest of sounds, the chilled wind muffled by the falling snow as it pattered against the windows, settling on the ground as another layer of the stifling blanket laid over the earth. Alex slept almost perfectly throughout, disturbed only by the distant crack of thunderous noise.

It stirred him from his sleep, less a sound and more a feeling. He glanced around the pure blackness of the night, but the noise never repeated itself. He figured it was completely possible that he had dreamed it, and in the midst of the snowstorm he'd woken up with it imprinted on his reality.

But it didn't matter much, and he barely spared it a thought as he returned to sleep without much incident.

24: VEINS

The next morning, the windows were half-buried in snow. Only a sliver of the hazy sun shone through the tops of their frames, and it set a sombre mood inside the dormitory. Alex and Albert woke up early, spending the first few hours of the day trying to dig themselves free from the snow that had jammed the entrance. The good news was that the snow had gotten so high that the fence didn't even need a tarp to be traversed. They essentially just stepped over it. The bad news was, they then had another hour struggling to pull the snowmobile out of the several inches of snow that had covered it. Isabelle helped, using the last of their winter clothing to assist in ripping the vehicle from its snowy prison. Marge watched from the office and Alex hoped that she was sad to be unincluded rather than happy to not have to work. It was laborious, dragging out an entire snowmobile from a mound of snow, but Alex had to think they did a fairly good job. After just a few minutes with the engine block heater going on overdrive, the now extracted snowmobile was ready to ride.

As he watched Albert say goodbye to Isabelle, he shifted uncomfortably under the weight of the rifle over his shoulder. The strap was digging into him a little more that he figured it should be, like the weight of his sins was being carried with him. Making peace with what he'd used the rifle for was part of the process, and since Albert's arm was still unsteady from this very rifle's attack, it came to him to shoulder the load. But understanding the importance of something and trying to accept what it means is one thing.

Being happy about it was something entirely different.

Albert took a moment longer than was strictly necessary to say goodbye to Isa. It seemed rather sweet until Alex spotted the airhorn. He blew it in her ear, grinning as she stumbled back.

"Hey, wha-!" She straightened up, trying to regain composure. "You jerk!"

Albert shrugged, devilishly grinning. "What can I say, it's my charm. You love it!"

"My ears don't, jeez!" She turned around in a huff, heading back to the salmon hatchery.

"Don't I get a kiss goodbye? Come on, it was just a joke."

She made a rude hand gesture at him as she returned to the building, but Alex thought he saw her smile. It was quite a gesture.

"Women, am I right?" Albert snickered at Alex, who was focused on the seat of the snowmobile. He'd seen something there that required more concentration than Albert's antics. He gave Albert the same hand gesture, which made him scoff and crouch next to Alex. "Dick. What're you looking at?"

Alex pointed at a cut in the seat, not very deep and filled with snow. He stuck his finger in the gap, running it down its length to remove the snow inside it. It was about six inches long, 15 centimetres to him. It had cut open the vinyl on the exterior of the seat, revealing the foam-like material on the inside. The shape of the cut brought forward images of claws, of bears and bobcats. But it was a lot cleaner and straighter than he would have expected of an animal. Maybe it was a stray branch that cut a gash as it was whipped around by the wind. But it seemed too deep and precise for that. It was perplexing.

"Alex, dude. What are you looking at?"

"Huh?" Alex snapped out of his inspection, glancing at Albert and gesturing vaguely at the cut in the seat. "This... slice? I'm not really sure what this is."

Albert looked at the cut carefully, seeming like some sort of archeologist appraising a dig site find. "Well, after careful consideration and a lot of analysis, I have to conclude that it may in fact be a cut in the seat."

"You're a dick. I mean I'm not sure why it's here. What caused it? It wasn't here when Ethan gave it to us. I think."

"Is it really that important?" Albert shrugged, standing up again. "It's just a tear in the seat. Shit, the thing was in the middle of a snowstorm. Who knows what sort of bullshit was tearing through the air? Could have been a pinecone for all we care. Stop obsessing over it."

Alex nodded, shaking his head and blinking. He sat down on top of the cut, waiting for Albert to scoot onto the back of the seat before he revved the engine and rode off. He still couldn't shake the feeling that something was off.

***

The world felt like it had been flooded.

Before, the snow had manifested itself as a blanket, a silently suffocating shroud that mirrored the clouds above. It had been simply a layer, an endless field that hid the true ground beneath it. But now, it was something more. It reminded him of what Squamish looked like, back when they first saw it flooded. The buildings they passed were inundated beneath a notable sea of ice and frost. The railway museum was nearly invisible, the weight of this new winter hiding its roof and shoring up its walls. The campgrounds were long submerged, bathrooms and barbeques leaving little but imprints on the snow.

Even the abandoned houses, those forgone memories of the people that used to call this valley home, they were coated in white like the ghostly apparitions they were. Alex considered stopping as they passed the house where he'd seen the snowmobile, but the thing was buried deep enough under the new snowfall that he couldn't even see the imprint of where it would be. The trouble of trying to dig it out right now wouldn't be worth it.

Or maybe Alex just didn't want to stay near the ghost house for long.

Past the disturbingly haunting home, the attractions of the valley petered out. They skirted the river, leaving behind the tourist traps and budget campsites to venture into the rougher terrain of the northern valley. Here, the river started to narrow as it approached the canyons and rock heaps that would define its course for another few kilometres. It would flatten again before the river reached its source, Daisy Lake to the north, which ironically enough was the exact place that the hydroelectric dam that provided them with power was based.

But the hatchery's own source of water was up a small tributary that fed the main river, and unfortunately for them, it was on the opposite bank. The ice had grown over the central channel and the whole thing had been placed under a layer of snow, but Alex didn't feel confident crossing it. He could almost hear the dark water continuing to gurgle beneath the surface, and one wrong step could send him through the snow and into the current beneath the hidden sheet of glassy ice. He shivered, just at the thought.

Fortunately, Albert and the engineers had planned for this. Alex stopped the snowmobile next to a metallic structure that spanned the river. It wasn't a bridge, much to his chagrin, but rather a sort of metallic pulley line that let you cross the river in a small wire mesh basket. Seeing the contraption almost made Alex consider walking across anyways, but Albert had already dismounted and started turning the crank that would bring the precarious basket towards them.

"Why did you put this here instead of a bridge again?" Alex breathed an exasperated breath into the air, watching the slow progress of the basket as it was reeled towards them.

"Well, it didn't need much engineering work, barely any materials and we could sell the thing as an attraction if we ever wanted to. Plus, the whole winch thing goes *weeeee*." Albert gets the basket across, carefully entering the frozen cage with reckless ease. "I think it's fun. Hop in."

Alex is much more careful, wincing when the freezing metal touched the exposed skin of his wrist. The basket sways beneath them, and even though they aren't very high up above the river, a fall would most certainly break the ice.

Albert started pulling the rope to ferry them across, snickering at Alex's clear discomfort. The ride was rickety, and Alex felt like at any moment the metallic superstructure or the rope itself could just… snap. And there he would be, right in that dark river where swimming upwards only struck against solid ice.

The fears were poorly founded in the end, and the two of them disembarked on the other side, with nothing more than embarrassment and lingering fear in Alex's case, and a slight devolution of principal in Albert's. While Alex tried to reinforce his moderately bruised ego and calm his nerves, Albert locked the basket into position so they wouldn't have to worry about it sliding loose on the ice and requiring them to reel it back in. Both tasks accomplished, they started the hike towards the pumping station.

***

This side of the river was technically a provincial park, and the highlands that surrounded the valley jutted up almost abruptly just a little way into the forest. There was meant to be a trail, but the snowstorm had buried whatever markers there had been under several layers of snow. As a result, Alex and Albert had to follow the bank of the river until they found it's tributary, which they then tracked soon after. The stream that they followed wormed it's way upwards towards the cliffs that looked down over the forest they were walking through. The hike was mostly uphill, approaching the highlands on a small slope that lent itself to a climb that sat just on the edge of being fun. Albert ended up snapping a couple of branches off a tree and giving one to Alex, the two of them benefitting from these improvised walking sticks to support the short but arduous ascent.

To make matters worse, the stream was much smaller than the river, and since it had frozen over, they had little to follow for the first few minutes. It was essentially chance, hoping that this small imprint in the snow was the correct small imprint in the snow was almost madness. But apparently, that sort of madness was exactly what they needed.

A rumbling moved through the trees as they followed the stream, gradually growing louder as they got closer and closer to the cliff. Albert seemed to gain confidence at hearing this noise, taking the lead and heading firmly in that direction. Alex followed him, confused by the sound of falling water and by Albert's sudden determination to reach it. This confusion turned to understanding, then amazement as they ascended a small bluff and reached the bottom of the cliffs.

A pool of water lay there, ringed by ice and rippling under the effect of a small waterfall that broke its surface. It was surrounded by snow and trees, a constantly shifting body of pure glacial water, which slowly trickled down under the snow and ice around it. It was an amazing sight, the roaring of the water driving Alex's eyes upwards as he craned his neck to see its source. The sound was so... natural. The water sounded like an ocean or the shores of a lake. It wasn't the constant splashing and jostling of the salmon pools. It was water in motion, a frantic and melodic motion, but one that screamed of the natural beauty of the world. The falls were what made it move, and the falls were what made that movement so exciting. And the roar of the water as it plummeted over the edge of the cliffside and into the pool, it was deafening. Not in the polluted and unnatural way of the snowmobile, but in the fresh and indisputable way of nature. It was a beautiful and impossibly loud sound. Alex just stood at the side of the pond, watching the natural carving of the earth play out before him.

In the meantime, Albert walked a little way off into the woods near the cliffside. A squat concrete shed sat in the shadow of the cascade, topped with snow and ice with its metal door almost entirely buried. He sighed, calling over Alex with the blow of his air horn. Alex winced, dragging his eyes away from the spectacle of nature and following Albert to what he assumed was the pumping station.

"So, shit. This is a problem." Albert gestured at the snow jamming the door, kicking it firmly. "You didn't happen to bring a shovel, or anything did you?"

"No..." Alex didn't like their prospects. It seemed like they would have to spend another few hours digging out another doorway, except this time it would take even longer since they lacked the foresight to bring any tools. He shuddered at the prospect.

"Shit. It'd probably take us less time to go all the way back to the hatchery and grab a shovel than it would deal with this shit. Unless..." Albert's eyes were drawn up to the roof. It was just a little bit higher than they were right now, and Albert seemed to recognize something from that fact. "Alex, boost me up. I want to check something out up there."

"What? What do you think is up there?" Alex followed his gaze, seeing nothing but concrete and snow to explain what would catch Albert's interest like this.

"There's no time to... actually, screw it, not explaining it is stupid. Places like these aren't meant to be accessed a lot, so I doubt they'd think that the snow would magically clear away. Maybe they put a hatch on the roof or some shit." Albert shrugged. "Then again, this is government bureaucracy we're talking about here, so who the hell knows?"

Alex accepted this logic, crouching down and putting his hands out for Albert to use as a step stool. "Wait, didn't we build this?"

Albert used his boost, pulling himself up onto the roof and dusting himself off, before sticking a hand out for Alex to grab in order to pull himself up after him. "Hell no! We funded it sure, but most of this was built by the provincial ministry of the environment. We're not allowed to build in provincial parks, but they are." Once they were both up, he put his hands on his hips and surveyed the small square of snow that they had to dig up. "Margey was real happy with that deal. Now let's find this sucker."

The two of them spent the next five minutes kicking and shoving all the snow off the roof. It was viciously cold, and after just a few minutes of being wrist-deep in the frost, Alex was already doubting that his gloves were even doing their job since the cold embrace of their snowy surroundings still permeated and lashed against his skin. Because of this, the five minutes it took to find the hatch felt more like 5 hours, and Alex was shivering by the time he uncovered the metallic latch that would open up the building below. "Here!"

Albert scampered over from the other side of the roof, grinning when he spotted their entryway. "Hell yeah. I was starting to think we'd wasted our time." The two of them moved onto either side of the hatch, pulling on it for a few moments before it popped loose with a clang. A metal ladder fell out once the lid was off, leading itself into the darkness of the room below.

"Ladies first?" Albert raised an eyebrow, gesturing towards the inside. When Alex shook his head, he scoffed, putting his feet on the ladder and rolling his eyes. "So much for being a gentleman."

Alex watched with trepidation as his friend lowered into the dark room below. He stumbled back onto the snow and cold concrete of the roof, nearly slipping off the edge and into the room as a blood-curdling scream echoed from within. He nearly panicked and booked it in the opposite direction before he heard the resounding laughter of Albert from inside the structure. Carefully, he got to his feet and dusted himself off, heading into the same darkness below.

"You're... an asshole. A really, really big asshole." Alex tried to ignore Albert's snickering as he felt his way along the wall to find a light switch. When he did find the creaky row of switches and turned on the inescapable buzz of the ceiling lights, he found Albert nearly doubled over in laughter from his 'prank'. While Alex was still rather mad at him for scaring him like that, he had to see the funny side just a little bit. It was a well-done prank, and for minimal effort.

It didn't change the fact that he was mad, however. "Dude what the hell! That was such a dick move!"

Albert had finally managed to steady his amusement, leaning against the wall for support as he fought back tears. Now Alex was embarrassed too, imagining what his face must have looked like for the scare to amuse Albert this much. Annoyedly, he shoved past him to look at the rest of the room. "Shut up dude... let's just look around."

The room itself resembled some sort of antiquated mixture of various elements. All at once, it was a fusion of the office back at the salmon hatchery, a cold war era Soviet bunker and a park ranger's station. Dated and specialized consoles dotted the walls, playing a soft sort of hum that was intersected with the occasional smashing noise, presumably the sound of the pump pushing water through the pipes. A desk lay against the back wall, lined on two sides by filing cabinets. On the desk was a map of the Brackendale Provincial Park, outlining its original borders as well as it's 2022 expansion to include the area they were currently in. Alex gave the map a quick glance, but none of it included Paradise so the point of it was essentially null. What was much more interesting and significantly more eye-catching, was the black metallic case emblazoned with the crest of British Columbia and the bold blocky words that said 'SURVIVAL CACHE'.

So while Albert poked around with the consoles and machines,

Alex set the rifle against the desk without much fanfare and opened up the case.

What it was, in simple terms, was a golden ticket. Inside, packed up neatly for ease of use, was a variety of survival supplies. Vacuum dried food, a miniaturized medkit, hand and feet warmers, a rain collector. Simple supplies designed for this very situation, if a lone ranger or visitor was to find themselves isolated at the edge of the wilderness. Most notably, and in Alex's opinion most uncomfortably, there was a folded up survival rifle and a small can of ammo.

This sort of supply package was strange, incredible, and exactly the last thing he'd expected to find here at this lonely pump station. "Holy shit…"

"What?" Albert flicked a switch on one of the consoles, making the blue lights turn red and the green lights turn yellow. Once that incredibly complex series of events was done, the man himself came over to the desk. When he saw what exactly it was Alex had discovered, he had an almost identical reaction. "Holy shit…"

Carefully, Alex closed the case, looking at Albert. "We… we need… are these in all of the park's buildings?" He glanced over the treasure trove of supplies. It had only been a few months, but the idea of food that wasn't fishy or earthen, and medicine that didn't amount to sympathetic feelings was tantalizing. And the possibility that there may be more of these precious care packages? Laid out there in the wilderness where no one would ever even think to look, just waiting for them to swoop in and grab them? That, that was more than tantalizing. That was inspiring.

"I don't know. Shit dude, I didn't even know this was here, and I'm the guy who suggested this whole thing. I think that makes me park Jesus or something."

Alex snorted, closing the case abruptly. "Or we got lucky… still, if there are more of these in the park…" He shook his head, rubbing his neck. "Never mind, that's... that's for Marge to figure out. Did you fix the problem?"

Albert nodded, gesturing at the very confusing set of controls and buttons that lined the console on the wall. "The system's supposed to be automated, but it got jammed or something. All I really had to do was reset the little shit. Our water might taste like Fluoride for the next couple of weeks, but it probably won't kill us."

"Probably?"

Albert winked at him, grabbing the case from the desk and heading towards the ladder. "Probably."

25: DOWNHILL

The wind picked up once the two of them hopped off the roof. Alex pulled his jacket tighter around him, grabbing the walking stick from where he'd leaned it against the side of the building. He waited in the meagre shelter the building provided from the wind, watching as Albert pulled himself out of the snow and offering him a hand.

Albert refused, of course.

Once he *was* out of the snow, Albert glanced off into the woods as he grabbed his own walking stick. "Think we have time for me to take a leak?"

Alex scoffed, shaking his head. "Sure, but it'd freeze off if you tried. Can't you wait until we get back?"

"Hell no dude, I'm busting. That waterfall's basically forcing my hand here. Just a quick leak, then we can head back and test out how our badassery in fixing this thing has made the toilet flush backwards."

"Is that a thing?"

"Hell if I know, I'm not a plumber. Here." He handed over the case of supplies, grinning. "I want to see if I can piss my name in the snow. I'll update you later." Without another word, he turned and headed off into the forest.

Alex could do nothing but shake his head and laugh as he tucked the supplies into his jacket. The man was determined, he could give him that. The crashing of the water made it hard to hear, but he could almost swear that Albert was whistling a tune as he sauntered off. Alex turned away from him and towards the waterfall in question. Even from here, at a strange angle and in a stranger time, it's majesty was inspiring. He found it funny, if not encouraging that despite the rampant chill that had been laid out over this corner of the earth, the flow of fresh water continued. Insomuch as it may soon be polluted, indentured into the rivers lined with the nuclear silt of the Cascade, this spring of fresh, inconceivable water had yet to care for the end of the world. It continued falling, like it always had, in a way that made Alex and his problems seem small by comparison. It was the namesake of the whole event, a Cascade in a more literal fashion than any one name he could ascribe. But still, in this sense of peace, he found it to be everything the Cascade wasn't.

But peace could never last long. Something would always come to break its tranquillity.

At first, it was a quiet noise. Not because of the volume of the waterfall in comparison, but rather because Alex was too enthralled with the presentation of nature to care about the distant and unrecognizable bleating that was trying to draw his attention away. But slowly, not even his airy and distracted tendencies could keep the noise out of his ears. Soon enough he recognized the sound, distant and panicked, repeated loudly as it echoed through the trees.

It was an airhorn. Followed by a scream that turned his blood to ice.

***

Alex ran towards the noise, suddenly and irrevocably focused on the present. The waterfall's thunderous noise faded into the background as his vision sharpened on the world around him. His feet sank into the snow as he ran, limiting his progress as he tried to trace the route Albert had taken into the trees. The screams crystalized, hanging in the air alongside the bleats of the airhorn and an unfamiliarly guttural sound. Alex's fingers fumbled at his shoulder, trying to pull the rifle off and into his hands. He screwed up, dropping it in the snow and wasting potentially precious seconds as he tried to strengthen his grip. The guttural sounds were getting louder, and to his horror, the sounds of the airhorn and the screaming were getting fainter.

He turned a corner, crossing past a tree and witnessing the first sight of a horror scene that would forever play on a loop within his nightmares until the day he died.

A towering, pustule and tumour covered hunk of fur and flesh held Albert's head between its jaws. The bear, or at least that's what he thought it was, had a coating of blood and shredded clothing decorating its coat as it closed its teeth on Albert's skull. It was disgusting, an abomination of nature and it was moments from killing the closest thing Alex had to a friend. He raised the rifle, pointing squarely at the top of its head, past the pulsating growths and the unconscious face of his friend, aiming right for the brain of the beast.

But at that moment, as time slowed and his shot steadied, the scene disappeared. The snow was gone, the beast had vanished, and he was back outside that gift shop, with a man's hands around Albert's neck. He squeezed the trigger, hoping and praying for the shot to fire, to cut down the assailant as it had before. But he couldn't. It didn't. As much as he willed the shot to fire, his finger didn't respond. He was facing his demons now, head on, and his fear overtook him. He shut his eyes, hearing the soft crunch of Albert's head in the beast's jaws, the triumphant roar of the monster's victory and his own heart falling into darkness.

He turned and ran. He didn't look back; he didn't consider what he was doing; he didn't process the truth that his friend had just died in front of him. All he did was run. Because it was all he *could* do at this moment.

With another guttural roar and the sound of crashing flesh, the beast came after him. It seemed to stumble in the snow, not accustomed to the winter weather either. It's lumbering gait still cut a gash through the frozen ground as it followed, unflinching in its determined pursuit. Alex still didn't look back, couldn't ever look back, but just from the sounds alone he knew it was getting closer. While he stumbled and tripped through the snow, the beast used brute force to cut a path. The result was a slow, but noticeable gain on him, and Alex could almost swear he could feel the beast's hot breath on his back.

He considered just giving in. Just crouching down in the snow and letting the monster take him. It would eat well, at least. But something within him kept pushing, even as his legs burned from the exertion of straining so hard against the frozen chains around his legs. Up ahead, the pumping station came back into sight. His heart dropped when he realized that they hadn't left a way to reach the inside without someone's help. He screamed, more out of instinct and pure frustration and anguish than any voluntary action. But then he spotted the hatch and the way it dropped out over the side. They had left it open, and now its edge was just a little bit lower than the roof. The bottom of it had little grooves in it, assumedly to store the ladder. If he could grab onto them, he could pull himself up.

Or so he hoped.

He tried to jump first, but his hands slipped on the ice.

He tried to jump again, but he couldn't pull himself up.

He jumped a third time, just as he heard the beast roar behind him. His hand caught itself between the grooves of the hatch, seizing an anchoring point to grasp onto. His heart pumping with adrenaline and his mind racing with pure terror, Alex pulled himself up onto the roof of the building.

The beast jumped at him, raking its claw down the back of his left leg. He ignored the searing pain, falling nearly headfirst onto the ground inside the room. A small clump of snow had gone down with him but did little to break his fall. He felt a jolt in his arm and a bang in his shoulder, both shooting pain like wildfire through his body. But he wasn't safe yet. He could see the beast's claws gripping the side of the roof, trying to pull itself up and grab him now that he was cornered. With the last of his energy,

Alex pulled himself up the ladder and jammed the hatch shut, leaving him broken and alone inside of a concrete shed.

***

The next moments were just like the end.

Faint flashes of unknown pictures.

A pair of hands fumbling with a first aid kit.

Searing, liquid pain tearing through his leg.

A cold and cozy wrapping of cloth.

Then a dark dream filled with angry beasts and crushed heads.

***

He awoke from the nightmares with a freezing body and a splitting headache. In agony, he clutched his head and tried to stand, the pain within his skull weakening a little as his leg burned with a much hotter pain. He cried out, a broken and pitiful noise that only made him feel more pathetic. He sat back down, leaning against the wall and watching the light buzz above him. He wanted to look at his leg, but he knew the age-old adage that looking at a wound only makes it hurt more. He had to build up the willpower to do it. And all that willpower had gone out the window when he had collapsed here in the first place.

But slowly, inch by inch, he moved his gaze from upwards with the lights to downwards at his leg. His breath hitched as he tried to calm himself, tried to pretend that everything was alright. When he first saw the bloody bandages on his leg, his eyes shot up back towards the ceiling and a wave of phantom pain racked his leg. But slowly, ever so slowly, he looked back down to meet it.

His leg was hastily and unprofessionally bandaged up, clearly done by none other than Alex himself in a daze. The gauze was soaked red, and the remnants of the roll and the alcohol he'd poured on the wound lay scattered across the floor around him, mixing with his own blood.

The sight and feeling almost made him cry. The hopeless agony he felt was nothing less than torture. He knew that focusing on this pain, on the hopeless feelings that welled up inside him, all that would be a greater death sentence than simple inaction.

He had to move, and now. The case of supplies had been dumped haphazardly on the floor. Bags of food had been mixed in atop the blood and alcohol, inspiring disgust and hunger inside Alex's stomach. As revolting as it was to grab dehydrated orange slices out of your own blood and bandages, just like seeing his own wound, the sight of food woke up the primitive desire to eat within him, and he had to lean forward to grab the fuel that would feed the fire necessary to get out of this place.

The food was flavourless, and Alex could barely choke it down. It also brought up that final and scorching necessity, water. The snow that had fallen into the room with him was melted now and mixed with the rest of the fallen liquid to create the disgusting cocktail that decorated the floor. Alex realized this with a sort of sad disgust, figuring out that if he wanted to subdue this newest obstacle, it would mean going back outside.

As tempting as it was to just sit there and waste away, Alex had to focus on survival. That was what mattered now. Not emotion, not pain and not loss. Survival.

First, he organized the supply crate. The bandages and alcohol that could be salvaged were stored carefully in their place. Any loose bits that had fallen out were repacked to the best of his ability. He ended up having to pull the gun out of its place and shove a couple of gauze strips in its stead, since now that they had been pulled out they refused to go back into their proper position.

Second, he unfolded the gun and loaded it. It was a semi-automatic survival carbine, toeing the line between pistol and rifle. It had an orange tip and a plastic body that almost reminded Alex of the plastic dart guns that kids used to run around with. But the bullets he loaded into it were real. And he knew that if he ended up having to use the gun, it would fire just as well as any other rifle.

If he could muster the courage.

Third, and finally, he used the gun's stock to pull himself to his feet. It was dangerous, and halfway through the shaking process of leaning on his good leg, Alex considered unloading the gun so it wouldn't backfire on him. But the determination to stand was greater than the fear to fail, so it was within just a few minutes that Alex was back on his feet, leaning heavily against the wall. A wave of nausea washed over him, nearly sending him teetering back to the floor. But Alex had to keep his strength going. He had to stay upright. He felt his way along the wall towards the hatch, looking upwards at it with his vision tinged by red and black. Closing the hatch had activated some sort of lever, and the ladder was back in place on the underside. He reached up, whimpering as the movement put pressure on his injury, and managed to snag the bottom rung. He pulled down, popping the hatch open and unfurling the ladder with a scattering of snow that landed on his head.

Carefully, he scooped some of it into his hand and took a bite out of it. It was shockingly cold, and it took longer than he'd expected for his mouth to melt the frozen offering into shockingly cold and barely refreshing water. He winced again, holding back tears. It was just another layer of misery to his already broken body.

Climbing the ladder was another issue. He only had the use of his two hands and one of his legs, the other held back from the freezing surface of the ladder. At the very least he had gloves and boots to fight back the chill, but it was slow going regardless. He didn't count the minutes, but the snow in his mouth was completely gone by the time he pulled himself up and onto the roof.

The sky above was still covered in clouds, but the faint imprint left by the sun seemed to be shining from the eastern part of the sky. That meant that Alex had spent an entire feverish night in the pump station and that he'd been gone from the hatchery for more than 24 hours. He couldn't even imagine the looks on the faces of Marge and Isabelle right now. The worry, the fear. And he couldn't anticipate what they would look like when he got back with the news either.

If he got back.

Alex dangled his legs over the edge of the building, gripping the gun tightly. He knew landing on his leg would only make the pain worse, so he elected to essentially fall sideways onto the snowbank. As much as the impact jarred his shoulder, and the impact of his leg on the cold hard snow made him whimper, he couldn't help but feel like it had been the right decision. He used the gun once again to drag himself to his feet. He used it to walk, leaning on it heavily as a replacement for his now-lost walking stick. But instead of following the frozen stream back east towards the river, he instead pulled himself along the furrows that had been left in the snow from the beast's pursuit.

He wasn't quite sure why. He guessed it was a lot of things. A combination of his blood loss, the desire to retrieve the rifle and walking stick, maybe even just a need to confirm that what he'd seen had been real. That Albert really had died here, less than a dozen hours ago.

He turned around the tree that he'd first bypassed to see the scene. He was wincing, half wishing nothing was there, half wishing for a definite closure. Instead, he found neither.

Snowfall had obscured the scene, but it was easily discernable that someone had been attacked there. Tainted red snow peeked out from under the fresh fall and bits of fabric and plastic were scattered around the small clearing. There was no body, at least no discernable one, and a faint furrow tainted with red seemed to go deeper into the woods. The beast must have dragged Albert off, to feast on him somewhere else. A tear spilled from Alex's face when he realized the fate of his friend, leaving behind it a trail of stingingly cold water. He nearly broke down again, collapsing into the snow as he perhaps should have done in the first place. He'd been pushed far past the breaking point, and now it seemed much easier to just lie down and let the cold winter's blanket roll over him.

But that wasn't the deal. That wasn't the deal at all. He wasn't strong, far from it. And maybe an Alex from just a few months ago would have given in. But his commitment was to try, and goddamnit if that meant giving up. Carefully he wiped his eyes as more tears came, secretly glad nobody was around to see him weep. With a strained gasp, he reached into the snow where he'd discarded the rifle, picking it up and slinging it over his shoulder once more. The walking stick had been lost in the new layer of snow, but Alex could barely notice. He turned around, limping his way back towards the pump station and away from the scene of the phantom carnage.

He didn't promise that he would avenge his fallen friend. He didn't draw up convoluted plans to return one day and track the monster to its lair so he could slay it singlehandedly in a tale worthy of song.

Instead, Alex Park walked alone and wept, the tears freezing over the path behind him.

26: VANISHINGS

Descending down the slope towards the pulley system that bridged the river, he started to hallucinate. It's a hard thing to realize, but there comes a point where it becomes clear that the world around you had shifted from what was real. At first, it was the small things. A distant caw of a crow that sounded far too loud, a tree that looked particularly like sasquatch looming before him, the creek beneath him starting to bubble as if it wasn't covered in a layer of ice. The blood loss was really getting to him now, and he realized that he had to make it back home before it got worse. It did leave him a little panicked, knowing that he couldn't trust his eyes and ears anymore. He stumbled along in a woozy state, battling his cognitive functions to stay on track. He was somewhere in the state between being awake and dreaming, with each blending over each other. The clouds above swirled faster than possible, the ground beneath his feet tilted at raw and impossible angles. A faint buzzing permeated his hearing now, and it was driving him nearly mad to be aware of it all.

Nearly without noticing, he slammed into the basket for the pulley, the impact rattling his bones with undue force. He struggled to climb in as the shock sent the world spinning. His leg sent another fiery burst of pain through his body as it collided with the cold metal of the basket. The sudden pain made him cry out, but the intensity of the experience helped him focus. Numbly he wrapped his hands around the rope and pulled, playing his own Charon across the river as the distance across seemed to grow longer.

On the other bank, he fell to his knees and had to drag himself to the snowmobile. The cool snow scraped at the bandages over his wound, providing some relief with its cool embrace even as the gouges it left exposed his still tender flesh to the elements. The wound bled even more as he mounted the snowmobile, starting it while the edges of his vision turned a worrying shade of black.

It was tunnel vision now, and as he revved up the vehicle and pulled his way into the forest, all Alex could comprehend afterwards was a series of images that flashed through his mind. A tree trunk the size of a building. Drifts of snow piled up like pyramids in the desert of Giza. The red snowmobile of the abandoned house, unearthed and waiting outside of its ghostly dominion. A distant train making it's way down the abandoned railway, leaving huge plumes in its wake.

He knew none of it was real, but each image stuck with him like the imprint of light when you closed your eyes. Time lost meaning, and all he knew was that he had little of it left by the time he pulled up outside the hatchery's gate, slumping over the controls of the snowmobile as his leg trailed a scarlet groove in the snow. A distant sound of a door opening drew upon what little attention he had left, and somewhere faintly in his mind, he knew that he could be saved.

Arms wrapped around him and pulled his limp body back towards the hatchery. Worried expressions danced around his vision, faint imprints of people he knew. Marge and Isabelle, each in their own way letting him know he was safe. With that in mind, he finally let go and fell into a deep sleep.

27: FAINTLY

The recollection of his ride through the forest, of the trek down the hill, it all came back to him in a single moment.

It had been a few days since the incident. Alex had spent that entire time in bed, faintly aware that he was in some other place than his dreams. As far as the distant form of consciousness that manifested in this time was concerned, he could stay that way forever. But some things were wrong. Heat in his legs, freezing in his feet, small pinpricks of needles in his arms that roused a distant sense of what pain was.

And then, light.

Alex sat up suddenly, eyes wide with shock and confusion. He looked around wildly, unaware of where he was, mind filled with the numbing images of his memories and dreams. A light shone through a frosted pane of glass, illuminating the small space in which he found himself. Recognition washed over him as he realized he was in his makeshift room back at the hatchery. The faint smell of mildew and the distant hum of machinery had never made him more relieved. Carefully, he laid back down, gasping from the pain and frailty of movement. He'd been in that position for a while, and although he couldn't count them, the days had taken their toll. His spine ached, his forehead burned and his leg still hurt like the embers of a once raging bonfire. But he was alive, and at least moderately able, so he knew something must have gone right.

He stared at the ceiling a while, trying to reconcile the images in his mind and the pains in his body. The trip to the pump station seemed unreal now, a horror film that he'd watched in reverse.

Hallucinations, imagination and reality all blended together into one confusing image, and he knew that some of it had to be true. The red snowmobile, for one, seemed more real than fake. But then again, so too did the Sasquatch tree. That's the danger of shattering the wall between reality and fabrication, when you pick up the bricks to build it again, the pieces will be all mixed up.

And what about the beast? He hadn't had any blood loss yet, but the image of a cancerous and gigantic bear had persisted from just the encounter with the monster. Was it real? Did the radiation act on it so quickly, turning a timidly native creature into an image of hell? Or was it just the first of many illusions that would haunt him that day?

Alex didn't know.

The door to the dorms on the other side of the blanket walls opened, and a soft click seemed to resound unreasonably loudly through the walls. Alex woozily tried to focus on the footsteps that originated from the entrance, fighting off the marauding fear that tried to take root and make him believe that it was just another monster behind the curtain. His heart skipped a beat when the presence beyond the curtain started to pull it back. The tension had mounted like a rocket, and Alex felt like he would shatter from the mere sight of whatever it was on the other side of that curtain.

As a result, he was almost disappointed when it turned out to just be Marge. "Holy shit, you're awake." She laughed with astonishment, sitting at the end of his bed. "How the hell are you?"

Alex blinked, shaking his head. He was still trying to make peace with the fact that it was Marge at the foot at his bed and not a flesh-eating terror from his nightmares. She fit the bill, seeming to have all of Marge's facial features and none of the gnashing teeth that would fit a monster's profile. But she looked older. More tired. Like some more weight had settled onto her shoulders. He knew that it had been just a few days, less from any telling features of the world and more so from the simple chronology of the mind, but Marge looked like she had aged several years. And poorly, at that. Her eyes were more sunken, her hair more frazzled and her posture weaker. Maybe it was just the effects of a post-Cascade world, but Marge looked more like a zombie than a person of flesh and bone. Maybe that was part of why he was on edge.

Alex realized that he hadn't spoken a word, and it had been at least a minute since Marge had asked her question. He cleared his throat, voice coming out hoarse and grated as he tried to respond. The first attempt equated to hot air. The second attempt resembled a growl more than it did a statement. But with the third, he managed to croak out something a little more considerable than nothing. "Good…"

Marge shook her head, smiling weakly. It was a pained look, and didn't serve her in trying to look non-threatening to Alex. It didn't seem genuine. She scratched her head, focusing her attention on the ceiling briefly before turning back towards him. She quivered ever so slightly as she spoke. "Well, shit, I'm glad you've been good. Because these last few days have sucked ass."

"They were bad?" Alex tried to sit up, leaning against his pillows. "How…"

"Really bad." Marge chuckled softly, an uneasy noise that cracked something and let out some of the pain inside her. "After you and Albert didn't come back, Isa started losing it. And when you came back alone, trailing blood and whispering about ghosts and snowmobiles, she figured out that Albert probably wouldn't be pulling up behind you."

"Albert… he's…" Alex couldn't finish the sentence. It was hard to remember what had happened on their expedition, sort out the memories from the fabrications. But this difficulty in expression didn't stem from that. It came from the disbelief that it could be true.

"Dead." Marge nodded, glancing downwards. "Yeah. As I said, we figured that out. Isa took it pretty badly. She locked herself in my room with a bunch of fish and some buckets of water. It's been… shit, I don't know. A while. It's been a while since I've seen her. So I've just spent these last few days running this damn place all by my goddamn self."

"Is… is that it?" Alex blinked, lying back down on his back as a wave of nausea took over him.

Marge hacked out a laugh. It was an unhinged sort of sound, the laugh of someone with one foot out of their proper mind. "Yeah, that's it. Since Albert's gone and Isa's catatonic, I've had the pleasure of doing every goddamn thing around here plus taking care of you." She waved her hand at nothing, a purely symbolic action. "It's not been a good time. So don't go begging for excuses or anything, because none of us have had a good time."

"Excuses? Marge I…" Alex didn't really know what to ask. Marge didn't seem entirely there, and he knew for sure that he wasn't either. "How am I even alive?"

Marge shrugged. "Fairies and pixie dust I guess. Somehow all your blood just teleported back into you, spick and span." She deadpanned a moment, rubbing her eyes. "Ok, really, it was a terrible trade. You were lucky as hell that Ethan ended up riding up here just as we were putting you to bed. That asshat saved your life. Isa had already started hoarding and I have no clue what the difference between a bandage and a gauze is, but he brought up his 'doctor' friend and got you stable alongside some blood bags to keep you going. It cost us a shit ton of fish though, so I *really* hope you can pick up some of the crushing weight that has been dropped on my shoulders."

Alex tried to sit up again, sending a silent thank you to Ethan from his bed. He knew it wouldn't do and that a proper thank you was due in the future, but for now, he hoped that whatever spirit lay in the sky above would be able to pass it along. It wasn't quite a prayer, and he wasn't quite happy with it, but there were more pressing matters to attend to as he refocused on Marge. "Are you ok? You seem..."

"Stressed? Yeah, no shit." She nodded, wiping her forehead. "I'm really hoping that you pull through this shit quickly because there's no way in hell that I'm going to keep carrying this whole team for much longer. It feels too much like being back at the office if you know what I mean."

"Marge, I... I'm sorry." As unreasonable as it may be, Alex felt guilty. Their expedition had left Marge back with the weight of the world placed squarely on her shoulders, and with everyone else out of commission, it was a weight that she had to carry alone.

"Hey, you don't be sorry. It's Isabelle I'm pissed at. We're in this shit together, she can't lock herself up to cry about it." Alex was surprised at how vicious Marge was being. It reeked of the ghosts they'd tried to drop, of the barbed personality that they elected to deny.

"Marge, Albert is... he's dead. He and Isabelle were forming a pretty big bond. I don't think I could keep it together if I was her. Shit, I don't know if I... I..." The tidal wave of emotion hit him again. Albert was dead, and that was an inevitability. Denial would do it no good, and refuting it wo-

"Snap out of it!" Marge seemed to hold herself back from smacking him, eyes flaring. "I just said I'm not going to tolerate this shit. For God's sake, we have to accept this bullshit. I'm sad too, of course I am damn it! I'm not heartless. But this is exactly the sort of thing I was worried about, and we can't hang on to 'feeling bad.' This is goddamn survival, and life goes on. So keep your head on your shoulders Alex or I swear I'll knock it off."

"Yes, Marge. I'll yeah..." Alex nodded, starting to bottle up his emotions again. Slam the door shut to his self-acceptance and go back to denying that the sun had to go down every day. But that wouldn't work either. It would just make it worse when it resurfaced later. Alex had to face his feelings and as unpleasant as that may be, he would have to do it soon. Maybe not right now, but he had to work through it. "...I just need some time."

Marge grimaced, nodding. "Sure, whatever. You'll need to rest a while anyway, since, you know, your leg got shredded." She stood up, cracking her knuckles. "I'll give you about a week to sort your shit out. But then we're getting back to work. Because now that I've seen what being the *only* one keeping us all alive is like, I'm not sure how illustrious this whole leader nonsense is. So, Alex, to sum it all up for you: get the hell better, right the hell now."

Marge ducked her way back through the curtain, moving the blanket walls aside a little more forcefully than necessary. It reminded Alex of a door being slammed, and the windows shook in tune from an unrelated wind.

Topical.

***

The next week was almost darker than the days following the Cascade. Addressing each individual evil of this newer world had been rough in their own right. But Albert's death was like a combination of everything that had previously made Alex break.

It was the raw and unfiltered brutality of the end of the world, it was the dark and sombre desolation of a lonesome death. It was the failure of his own hands to save someone else, and it was the tragedy of the snuffed out light that once shone in their lives. All in all, it would be enough to spiral anyone, let alone someone so close to Albert. Alex understood why Isabelle wasn't able to handle it. He couldn't either. If he was able, he was sure that backing down and crying himself to sleep would be far easier than trying to overcome his issues. But he was afforded no quarter. No space to breathe. The people left still needed him. So as much as he would never be able to fully surpass the grief in his heart and carry his friends singlehandedly over the finish line, he could damn well cry.

It was three days until he could walk again. His leg screamed at him like a banshee of hell, but he was determined to walk and not drag himself to the bathroom. The great success of his single trek was enough of a morale booster to let him try again. By the fifth day of the week, he had started exercising his legs again. It was an improvised physical therapy, and he was sure that it wasn't doing much but strain his healing. Still, it was routine. It was confidence. It was a defiance of the horrors beyond the hatchery's walls that tried to keep him down.

By the sixth day, he'd started helping Marge with chores again. She tagged out rather happily, nearly falling to sleep on her feet when he offered to take the reigns of work. The aching in his body and his soul didn't disappear, but the occupation of other things in his mind let the darker aspects of the current state wash on him like waves on a beach. He wasn't ignoring them, but the memories of Albert and what had happened to him ended up settling more amicably when he didn't have to confront them head-on.

It was on the seventh day that he addressed Isabelle. Marge had tagged back in that morning, after sleeping 16 hours straight. That left Alex with the free time to sit by her doorway and try to talk to her. "Isa?"

No response.

"Isa, it's me. It's Alex. I…" He trailed off, trying to find the proper words to comfort her somehow. He knew it would be impossible. The relationship Alber and Isabelle had wasn't long-lasting, hell she'd hated him just a few months ago. But they'd gotten closer, in a way he still wasn't able to grasp. Spewing ideology at her wouldn't work, and trying to coax her out of there would only make her draw herself closer in. So instead he decided to bridge the gap. "Did you know me an Albert went to university together?"

Alex leaned against the door, staring at the ceiling as he talked. "UBC. We weren't very close back then, just neighbours down the dorm hall. I was studying Speech Sciences, he was studying… Math I think? Anyways, we didn't have a lot of crossovers, but we hung out from time to time. Like buddies. It was actually… actually me who suggested that we should hire him after I got a job at Macedon Tours. Marge never forgave me for it." He chuckled uneasily. He wasn't sure where exactly he was going here, and Isabelle hadn't said a word. But he didn't want to just stop.

"He's always been a trickster. One time he told me about some big festival going on across campus. I don't know why, but I believed him. So I went over there, across the entire two kilometres of campus, and of course… nothing." He shrugged, although he wasn't quite sure why. "By the time I got back, he'd helped some of my other friends throw a surprise party. All he'd been told was to keep me distracted, but that was enough to get him to send me all the way across campus. That's who he was, he liked to joke around, but he did it right." Alex smiled at the memory, shaking his head fondly.

Isabelle still didn't respond, but he could feel the door shake a little behind him, as if she'd leaned against it or something. He almost tried to speak, to draw her out. But he realized it would be better to do it slowly. Rome wasn't built in a day, and hearts weren't healed in an hour. "I'll… see you later Isabelle. I'll be back tomorrow if you want."

As he stood up, he could swear he heard a faint yes from beyond the doorway, a voice filled with pain and misery, but flickering with a spark of commemorated joy.

Maybe it was worth something to talk at the walls.

***

Much to Marge's chagrin and Isabelle's satisfaction, Alex sat next to the door once more on the next day. Quietly and hesitantly he began to tell more stories. Things he'd known about Albert for the last decade or so that they had known each other. They weren't always close for most of those years sure, but

Albert got up to enough antics that there was a wealth of stories that Alex could tell. He came back the day after that as well. Then the day after that. And slowly, as his leg healed and the grief of Albert's shocking fate began to fade, Alex comforted Isabelle. At first, she was silent, then she would communicate by knocking or banging on the walls. Soon enough, she was whispering to him in a hoarse and unused to ask questions and learn more about the man she had once despised.

Alex had to work doubly hard elsewhere to keep Marge off his back to do so. She advocated for kicking down the door and putting Isabelle to work, so he had to do Isabelle's assignments as well to compromise. It was worth it though, in his eyes.

It was another week afterwards when Isabelle asked him the question he'd dreaded. "How did it happen?"

Alex sucked in a breath, looking at the ceiling. He wasn't sure if he should be honest or not. Isabelle deserved to know the truth, but the truth was violent, non-comforting and uneasy. A simplified lie, that he had died quickly and painlessly would be best, some form of comfort that she could hold onto in knowing that Albert hadn't suffered.

But that wasn't something Alex could do.

"It... it was a bear. I think it was a bear. It was covered in tumours and rot so I'm not quite sure. I think it must have been hibernating or something. But when the winter didn't end, it had to wake up and... it needed food." He paused for a moment to listen to Isabelle, but she didn't make any noise. "He went off to go to the bathroom. Neither of us thought there would be any trouble, so when I heard the airhorn going..."

Alex had to stop, wiping the tears from his eyes. Being strong was a necessity right now, as hard as it may be. "I tried to save him but... well I was too late. I froze up on the shot. I missed. His head was already in its jaws and he... he went quickly." He shook his head again, trying to scatter the memory as it hardened once more. "It couldn't have been more than a minute Isa. Couldn't have. He didn't suffer long."

There was silence, and Alex strained to hear what Isabelle was doing. It was concerning to thusly hear... nothing.

It was about a minute before the door clicked softly as the lock turned, and Isabelle jumped out and hugged Alex with tears streaming down her face. Alex nearly jumped back in surprise, hugging her back gently. She was even more dishevelled than Marge, having locked herself in a single room for two weeks without a shower and nothing to eat but fish. The pungent odour she emitted as a result wasn't important however, as it was eclipsed by the pure display of grief before him. He rocked her gently shushing her and trying in vain to comfort the poor woman as she wept. It was a difficult couple of minutes, with Isabelle's own reaction nearly compromising the aloof immunity to Albert's death that Alex had built up over this time.

Isabelle finally pulled back, sniffing and wiping her eyes. She wobbled to her feet, leaning on Alex for support. She leaned back on the door pushing it slightly back into position. "Thank you Alex. That was... that must have been hard for you. But I appreciate it. I'm glad he didn't have to go out... alone. Especially with such a good friend."

She turned to head back into the room, pausing when Alex put his hand on her shoulder. "Isabelle?" She turned her head, looking at him blankly. Alex hesitated, clearing his throat. "Are you going back inside?"

She nodded, smiling weakly. "I am. Just tell Marge I need more time, alright?"

Alex protested, trying to hold her back. "Isa, we can't do this without you for much longer. It's gotten to Marge, and it's going to start getting to me too. Please, I know... shit, I know you got hit hard, but we need to keep surviving."

Isabelle turned back towards the room, shaking Alex's hand off. "Just a little more time Alex. I promise. I'll come back out to help soon. I just need a little more time."

She walked into the room, pulling the door shut behind her. She locked it with a click, leaving Alex all alone again.

28: RED

Early in the morning in what was meant to be the early days of summer, Alex felt something was off. It was a regular day by all accounts. The clouds were hanging heavy over the valley and the snow was as soft and cold as it had ever been. There was a crick in his back that he had been trying to work out, twisting and turning his shoulder to try to wrangle the muscle back into place. His leg still throbbed painfully every time he moved it, but it had reached the point that combating its stinging complaints was more a chore than an obstacle. Aside from that, the world was about as amicably peaceful and uninteresting as someone could hope for.

Still, Alex couldn't shake that feeling of irregularity. There had been a tension, a maintained thread since he'd returned from the pump station. It should have been gone, disappeared like a ghost exorcised by peace. But his hairs still stood on end, his eyes still darted around the room and the storm overhead still brewed. He was in the office, trying to learn the suite of tools and logistics that had let Albert run the place. It looked like an assorted jumble of letters and numbers to him, but he'd started to find the patterns and parameters that made them move around. It was like playing a game, in a way. Just an assortment of rules that he had to learn. He felt like he was close to cracking it.

Marge wasn't helping matters, playing on his nerves and sense of unease with her silent and judgmental stare from her spot near the back of the room.

"Hey Marge, could you stop staring at me? Please?"

Marge spat at the wall, standing up. "Sure. I'll just hand overseeing your ass off to Isa. Oh wait, you let her lock herself in again, so the only other person who can do shit is me. Oh well!" She sat back down, leaning on her elbow grumpily.

"Look, Marge, I don't want to fight." Alex put the computer in sleep mode, scooching his chair around so he could face her. "I know it's been rough, but just a few more days and she'll..."

"Just a few more days? She's had a few days asshat. She's had weeks! Shit, this is the exact sort of thing we agreed to *stop* dwelling on. I gave a whole speech and everything. I'm the damn leader, she should listen to me when I tell her to stop crying like a little... damn it!" Marge stood up, kicking the chair and leaning on the wall. "I shouldn't be talking like this. I need to take responsibility and not be such an ass. But shit, she needs to step up, ok?"

"You're trying. That's what matters." Alex stood up, tentatively putting a hand on her shoulder. "She's trying too. It's just... harder for her."

"Yeah. Yeah..." Marge sat back down, rubbing her head. "It's just frustrating. Like a corporate guideline that none of the sh- employees try to follow. Now there's an analogy that's relevant to the post-Cascade hellscape we live in, huh?"

Alex tried to suppress a chuckle, which made Marge snicker and slowly devolved into shared laughter. It was nice, to say the least. The part of Marge that he'd worried would be lost forever when they adopted this new outlook on life. But no, she was still there. She could laugh occasionally, if prompted.

It just happened that the world made laughter a little harder than he would have liked.

Sitting back down, the humour faded and left Alex uneasy again. He looked past Marge and at the darkened shadows beneath the tree's shade. There was nothing there, nothing noteworthy anyways. Just pine needles and older snow. But still, he couldn't shake that ghost of an idea that something was off.

"Hey." Marge brought him back to the present, reaching into the pocket of the scavenged and oversized denim shirt she was wearing. "I found your little secrets." She pulled out the photographs that Alex had found in the cabins months ago. The fishermen by the river.

"Secrets? Oh, those? I don't know why I kept them..."

"Probably to frame them. Or because you're weirdly sentimental." Marge shuffled through the crinkled bits of film, inspecting them. "I recognize some of these people." She showed Alex the pair of pictures. Alex focused on the second one, catching sight of the woman at its foreground. There was still something about her that he thought was familiar, although he still couldn't place it.

"Who were they? Guests?"

"Technically." She pulled the photos back, snapping Alex out of his wonderings once more.

"A few of them used to live here. We bought off all their land, but I guess some of them still liked the place. They came up for the grand opening. Pretty sure the poor f... uh... suckers regretted selling. Mr. Donahue wanted to give them discounts on their admission as extra compensation. I advised against it." She slumped her shoulders a bit.

A faint rumbling took hold in Alex's ears. He looked around to try to find a source, but it was impossible to locate just where it was coming from. He figured he must be imagining it since Marge didn't react and his psyche was more than a little damaged. Still, imagined or not it put him on edge. He cleared his throat, shaking his head to try to clear away the unreal noises.

"Did you give them a discount? Why'd you advise against it?"

Marge shrugged, gesturing vaguely. "We didn't. And we didn't for the same reason that I said we shouldn't. They had already been paid, and the park was already turning less of a profit than we'd expected. It didn't make sense financially." When Alex narrowed his eyes at her, she scoffed. "What? I had to keep our business going. It's not like it was unethical. Amoral maybe, but we'd done everything by the book and by the law. For all I know, that shit could have gotten us sued."

Alex sighed, looking down at the photos once more. The woman caught his attention again, and he gestured at her, looking over at Marge. "Do you know who that is?"

Marge raised an eyebrow, looking down at the picture again. "Her? Shit, I do but I can't really… oh! Right, damn." She shook her head. "That's Mrs. Young. She was one of the most troublesome residents. She *really* didn't want to sell, but her husband did. Even after they signed the papers and got the money, she was *pissed*."

"She seems familiar…"

"I doubt it. You've probably never met her. They moved down to Squamish I'm pretty sure, so unless you've been sneaking off to meet Ethan without my permission, I doubt you would have met them. Shit, they probably lived in the flooded area if we're being honest." Marge shrugged, glancing out the window. "Good riddance as far as I'm concerned."

"Marge! That's disgusting!" Alex was shocked that she would speak so casually about death. It was one thing to acknowledge the fate of the world's population count, but it was entirely another to *hope* that more people had died.

"What?" She shrugged, wincing a little and peering out the glass. "It's not like I'd kill her personally if I saw her. It'd just be better for us if we didn't have someone else vying for Paradise Valley as well, you know? It's like a… what the hell is it in those stupid movies that used to be so popular? It's like a pretender to the throne or some shit. We don't need it."

Alex shook his head, staring at the floor. Marge's logic was sound, but it was a harsh thing to hear. There was a substantial difference in calculating simple numbers and wishing death onto someone who had a face you could see. She was someone's wife, someone's friend. But here they were hoping she was a washed-up corpse, just because she could have notions of claiming the valley.

Was that survival? Was that adapting to this new world?

The questions that ate him up before started to rise again. There was no safety in it, no simple solution. It was the complexity of ideology that went past the direction of their existence. The rumbling in his ears got louder, and he was sure now that it was a reflection of his own turmoil.

Only it wasn't.

Marge narrowed her eyes, looking down the road. "I think that's Ethan coming. I'm pretty sure he's early, but it seems right that you could use that spare time to thank him for his help in keeping you alive."

Alex looked up, getting to his feet woozily and stumbling over to the window. He peered out at the snowy expanse beyond the hatchery walls, noticing the plume of snow that was rising up down the valley's thoroughfare. "Is it? I thought I was imagining the sound…"

"You were probably… distracted. You were probably distracted. Go get the fish we packaged up, come on. I'll get the winter wear ready." She gestured towards the door to the hallway, moving away from the window and stepping through. Alex took another moment to watch the plume rise into the air and fall to the ground before turning and following Marge.

Together, they walked towards the storage room, each giving a different glance towards the locked door where Isabelle was still hiding. Alex was sympathetic, Marge was coldly angry. Through the farm's floor and past the bedrooms, they split up only when they reached their quarries. Alex bent down to sort the cans of fish into one bucket, glancing concernedly at just how many empty and unfilled cans there were. They would need a definite restock soon. As Marge pulled on her snow pants and puffy jacket, Alex still couldn't shake the rumbling from his ears. It wasn't *just* the snowmobile now. He was sure of it. Maybe it was a lingering effect of his own blood-loss induced insanity. Maybe it was just plain madness. But he couldn't shake it, and he was sure now that it wasn't something physical. It was something inside him, his own rhythm inside his own body.

"Hey, I know it's your thing, but could you stop staring at a wall? We're on a timetable here." Marge patted his back, bringing Alex back into focus. He stood up, grabbing the bucket full of fish and following her. With his free hand, he gently worked his finger inside his ear, trying to dig out the rumbling and the mounting sense of unease. Their march back in the quiet of the hatchery's interior kept getting disrupted by these phantom feelings, and Alex could barely stand it anymore. It was like a little drummer was beating away at the inside of his skull, and the little drummer couldn't actually play the little drum with any skill.

Marge went back to the window as Alex set the bucket down and tried to turn on the computer to take one more crack at figuring out its configurations and secrets. She watched the snowmobile approach with disinterest, barely focusing on it as she checked her disgustingly dirty nails and pulled a glove over them. It was only after she looked up and took true stock of the situation that she panicked.

Quickly, dropping to the floor behind the cover of the windowsill, she whisper-shouted at Alex. "Alex! That's not Ethan! Shit, that's not Ethan!" Alex blinked, turning to look at her with confusion, rubbing his eyes and focusing on the brighter world outside the hatchery.

Barreling towards them on a faded red snowmobile, a woman decked in winter clothing was making a beeline towards the gate. Alex gasped, ducking down with Marge and peeking back over the rim of the window. It was hard to tell from this distance, but it looked like the snowmobile from the abandoned house that he'd passed. The one that had been buried, but then unearthed in his hallucinations.

"Get down you idiot!" Marge yanked him back down as the woman closed on the gate, cutting off Alex's view and dragging him into the closer confines of the floor. "Don't let them see you! Maybe they don't know we're here."

Alex nodded, rubbing his head. The rumbling was even louder, and this time he knew it was physical. He glanced at Marge, who looked somewhere between panicking and calculating, trying to determine a course of action to take on this sudden and unknown threat. She stayed in that state for what felt like minutes, the moments dragging on and the unknown rider getting closer. Finally, she seemed to come to a conclusion. "Alex, you need to go grab one of the g- "

A wrenching screech hit the air, like the sound of broken stone and bent steel. Alex instinctively peeked over the windowsill, tracing the noise as the rumbling came to a sudden end. The woman had crashed her snowmobile into the top of the gate, bending it inwards with the force of her acceleration and sending up another plume of snow as she spiralled to a stop in the parking lot. The front of the vehicle had crumpled from the impact, and their new visitor was holding onto the handlebars with a death-defying grip. She looked up towards the hatchery, ski goggles the fiery reflective colour of fresh blood.

Alex ducked back down as the goggles seemed to focus on him and the woman stumbled off of the snowmobile. Marge facepalmed, then stood up and dragged Alex back to his feet. "There's no point now you moron, she already saw you. Stop grovelling and go grab a goddamn gun!"

She shoved Alex away and towards the hallway. The blood rushed into his ears as he hit the door hard, fumbling for a moment with the handle. His hand slipped on the cool metal a few times before he got a grip. He couldn't focus, enraptured by the conflict going on behind him. Even as he finally pushed the door open and fell to the ground with an oomph, he kept his eyes on the stranger. Marge did as well, standing upright behind the window with a determined look in her eye and an unflinching resolve to stand her ground.

Her eyes were locked on the face of the stranger, concentrated solely on the covered visage of black cloth and blood-red goggles. She was meeting the gaze of this new unknown, trying to communicate that she wasn't going to back down for whatever reason this stranger had barged down their gate. The emotionless mask of the invader didn't leave anything to discern, but Marge stared with enough intensity to make Alex flinch. But it was too strong, and he realized with horror that Marge's intense focus on their face had let the woman reach into her coat and pull out a shiny silver revolver.

"Marge! Duck!" Alex found himself screaming, struggling to his feet as the pain of the wound in his leg incited itself under the pressure of the situation. There was a monumental bang and a crashing of glass as the bullet fired from the gun and pierced the window with shocking speed. It flew inches over Marge's head as she ducked down beneath the sudden hail of razor-sharp glass. Alex's warning had easily spared her life, as the bullet whizzed and imbedded itself in the wall at the same level as where Marge's heart would have been.

"Damn it!" Marge stumbled over to Alex, ducking as another bullet fired more wildly in her general direction. Alex watched the glass crumble beneath her feet and felt the cool winter's wind wash over his face as the stranger lined up a third shot. Marge dove into the doorway, scrambling past Alex as he slammed it shut behind them. Another resounding bang shook the world as Alex helped her to her feet, limping alongside her as their assailant jumped down into the office behind them. They were almost at the end of the hallway when Alex heard the door handle turn behind them.

Time seemed to slow as the door opened behind them. His leg seemed to stretch forever as he crossed the threshold to the farm. As the door swung open behind them, he knew that they wouldn't make it. The gun was already swinging into position, lining up on him with startling swiftness. The spots of blood left on the ground from the glass cuts along Marge's arms seemed to form a trail, leading a path from their assailant back to them. It was essentially inevitable, their fate almost sealed as the trigger was pulled back to fire. There they were, so close to safety. Marge seemed to realize it too, both in the inevitability of their demise and just how close they were to avoiding it.

She dove into him as the cascading sound of the gun echoed down the hall. The sound seemed to vibrate deeper than his bones, rattling his brain and sending him spiralling. At the same time, the impact of Marge's shove sent him careening towards the floor of the farm. A scream ripped through the air, and Alex expected to feel the hot sting of lead somewhere inside him. Instead, he felt the much broader pain of the concrete floor as he crashed into the ground at the foot of the steps that lead up to the doorway.

Marge was on top of him, and he realized that it was her that was screaming. It was full of pain and rage, the sound he'd expected of a banshee. Quickly he tried to disentangle himself from her, noting the blossoming of blood that emerged on her lower back. A stark realization hit Alex. The bullet was headed right for him, probably destined to hit somewhere vital. But Marge had jumped in the way as she shoved him to the ground, and now she was the one with a bullet lodged in her spine. Alex felt a sudden wave of relief and thankfulness. It wasn't exactly the sort of thing he'd expected from her.

Not that it mattered.

The assailant was standing in the doorway, looking down at them with the gun in her hand and the same masked and faceless expression on her visage. She levelled the gun at the screaming Marge and the cowering Alex, stopping and pausing when she realized their predicament. Alex had the same realization: he and Marge weren't going anywhere. She was still screaming bloody murder, and he was pinned beneath her. The woman seemed to realize that too, holstering her gun and striding down to them. She moved to Marge's head, silencing her with a vicious strike of the boot in her face. It was an unpleasant sight and an even more unpleasant sound. But it shut her up.

With that done, she turned her attention back to Alex. And he was absolutely terrified. There were no heroics here, no defiant questions or unflinching bravery. Alex was just plain scared, and it was as simple as that.

The woman slowly pulled off her ski goggles, then her mask. She blinked in the light of the factory floor, rubbing her face and smiling down at Alex with a distinctly insane grin. Her face was dirty, her hair was falling out and her teeth were starting to suffer from decay. But Alex recognized her almost immediately. She was the woman from the same picture Alex had in his pocket.

29: REVENGE

There was a moment there, quiet in the shadows of the room. Alex was wide-eyed and terrified, staring in horror at who was beneath the mask. She, on the other hand, seemed to be relishing it. She started laughing, a distinctly unnerving sound that only served to freak Alex out even more. It was a rough bout of laughter, and by the end of it she was nearly doubled over. She wiped a tear from her eye and smiled once more at Alex. She shook her head slowly, relishing the moment. "Oh Macedon, I can't tell you how much I've *waited* for this moment. Ever since you kicked me out of here, I've been *waiting.* And my God it's paid off."

She waited for a response, crouching down next to Alex. When all he did was shy away, she grabbed him by the chin and forced him to look at her. "Do you know who I am? Do you? So many people you crushed here, I doubt you took the time to memorize each of them. But oh, I doubt you took the time to *really* ruin their lives like you did mine." She waited a few more moments before pulling out the revolver again and pointing it at his head, the cold steel pressed to his temple as tears started falling from his eyes. "Do you know Macedon?! Do you know who I am?!"

Alex nodded slowly. He did know. He did. "Mrs… Mrs… Young. You used to live here…"

The gun pressed a little deeper into his skull a moment before she pulled it away. "You've got it sweetie. That's exactly who I am. Call me Clara, that's my name after all. But let me tell you why I'm more than that." She reached into the pockets of her coat, searching for something. Alex took the opportunity to look for a way out, an escape route. But his vision was blurring from the tears, and he was still pinned down by Marge, who he could only hope was still alive. Her groaning and laboured breathing seemed to indicate that she was, but if there was anything Alex knew now it was that he couldn't be sure of anything.

Finally, she seemed to find what she was looking for. A grimy photograph emerged from her pockets, and she shoved it in his face. It was of course as dirty as its proprietor and the tears made it nearly impossible to discern certain aspects of it. Still, in due time Alex recognized what it was. It didn't pop out at him anymore, didn't scream at his demons and bring up his darkness. But the sight still defined something inside him.

It was the man he'd killed.

He was sitting in front of a fireplace, comfortably placed in a pleasant rocking chair. He looked happy, distinctly jolly and entirely different from the person who once haunted Alex's dreams. But he was still obviously the same man. And even more obviously, the younger woman in the chair next to him was the same woman with a gun to his very own head. It was Clara. The man was Mr. Young. And Alex realized that the very reason he'd recognized her in the first place was because he'd seen that very picture back in their home. Tears came to his eyes and the manically insane woman above him cackled like a harpy.

"You see now? You killed him, Macedon. You bastards killed Steven, the love of my life. You tempted him, exiled him and executed him. You broke our marriage you sick sons of bitches. You ruined everything and all that I loved." Clara slowly stood up, reaching for her pistol. "I've spent months waiting for this moment. Watching you from the woods. Tracing your tracks. Fixing that old snowmobile just so I could get through the gate. Weeks upon weeks of eating berries and drinking the poison water. Watching my hair fall out and my teeth rot. I can feel the tumours killing me inside even right now Macedon. But it's all worth it, just to kill you. Thank you for the opportunity." She reached for the gun, and Alex shut his eyes tightly. This was it. After all they'd done and everything they had struggled for, their end wouldn't be infighting or the harsh cold grip of winter. It would be a crazy woman with a gun, and as her finger clamped down on the trigger Alex descended into despair, enveloped by the shroud of darkness.

In truth, maybe he would have accepted the inevitability of his own death.

But the flash of light, the boom of the gun, the advent of darkness, it all didn't come. Instead, a resounding clang came from somewhere above him, accompanied by a broken cry and the woman falling down on top of him. He forced his eyes open, trying to understand just what had happened. Through the tears and wooziness of his fallen grace, he saw Isabelle, clutching a trash can above her head and bringing it's stark metal surface down to bear once more onto Clara's head.

This inexplicable sight digested and the sudden wooziness of his fall striking him at once accepted, Alex dove deep back down into the darkness of unconsciousness.

***

This time, it didn't take days to come back to the surface. It took minutes. Still, the world around him was almost equally unrecognizable.

He had been leaned against the wall of the farm's floor, legs splayed out in front of him. Directly next to him was Marge, laid out on her stomach with a definingly big hole in her back and Isabelle crouched over her trying to bandage it up. The sudden sight almost made Alex lose his lunch, and he gagged audibly as Isabelle put the last bit of gauze around the gaping maw of Marge's wound.

Groaning, he tried to pull himself to his feet, trembling as he found purchase on the smooth concrete floor at the edge of the water. Isabelle was too preoccupied and Marge was too unconscious to deal with what had happened, so he realized that it was up to him to manage the invader. To decide what to do with Clara. She was unconscious on the floor, still slumped in place where Isabelle had knocked her over the head. Blood oozed from the wound slowly, leaking ever so slightly into the salmon pools and leaving a distinct impression in the water. Isabelle barely seemed to register that Alex was moving, even as he made his way over to their attacker. He scooped up the discarded gun as he hobbled, half-tempted to just take it and fire at her until it was empty. Instead, he sat her up against the wall and shakily levelled it to her head.

It was entirely possible that he could have pulled the trigger right then and there, a gentle squeeze of the cold steel that would snuff her out just like he had her husband. A single resounding sound that would shake him to his core, then haunt him, then eventually just like all the others, fade into simple acceptance and regret.

But instead, her eyes flickered. A little bit of humanity shone through in the hazel coloured windows to her soul. Alex pulled his finger off the trigger. Suddenly what had been the simple chore of execution had turned into a moral quandary. It wasn't clinical, and it wasn't just survival. It was a human being, missing her hair and teeth and sporting a viciously vengeful attitude, but she was a person nonetheless. And insomuch as she was willing to pull the trigger on his own head after a brief monologue, Alex wasn't sure if he could do the same without summoning up the same level of mania.

So instead of ending her right here and right now, Alex crouched in front of her and levelled the gun. It was a twisted mirror of the situation just a few minutes ago, but instead of insanity, or hatred, Alex just felt embarrassed. Mournful. Maybe even regretful. He couldn't find a way to summarize all of his tumbling feelings into a proper question. Instead, he chose to just ask the first thing that came to mind. "Why?"

Clara sat up, keeping her eyes firmly on the gun. The blood started dripping down her face from the abrasion on top of her head. It was a rather haunting image, and almost brought Alex's lunch back to the doorstep. She chuckled, coughing with the laughter. It was a disconcerting sound. "I already told you. You... monsters. You threw me out of my home, you turned my husband into an abusive ass, and then to top it off, you killed him. You ruined everything. Everything!"

"I'm sorry, but..."

"Sorry? You're sorry?" She choked back another laugh, tears in her eyes. "You ruined everything. Me and Steven, we were happy. Everyone thought it was wrong, that he was too old for me, or that I was too naïve for him. But we were happy. Damn it we were happy! We had our little house in the woods and we were happy!"

Alex lowered the gun a little. It was still pointed at her, but it was aimed more towards the stomach than the face. "Why did you sell then?"

She spat at him, the gob of saliva landing on the floor between them. "Why do you think?" She nodded at Marge, who was only just regaining consciousness and seemingly sobbing from the sudden pain she was in. "That bitch lured him in. I begged him not to sell, I begged. But he grew up poor so there wasn't really much I could do. It's was like holding a steak in front of a starving man. It was just cruel. Just cruel Macedon, just cruel."

Alex wasn't pointing the gun anymore. It was at rest. The woman's tears mixed with her blood now, a combined river of diluted red that fell to the floor in small little droplets. She was defeated and broken. It was hard to even think that she was the same person who'd held him in this exact position moments ago. The fight had gone out of her, and it had gone out fully.

"Steven realized that he'd made a mistake after we bought our new place down in Vancouver. Took him a month to realize he'd been duped. He pissed away all that cash on gambling and booze. Started getting angrier and angrier. He tried to buy the place back you know. It's still there. But you monsters wouldn't let it out of your... meaty disgusting claws. We moved back up here. To try to recapture the magic and all. But it was gone. Steven broke down. You broke him." She wiped the blood and tears from her eyes, sniffing. "And then you killed him."

Alex had a lump in his throat now. Somehow this defeated misery was worse than the terrifying anger. He wanted to hug her, wanted to apologize for what they'd done. He felt like a monster. Even still... "He attacked us. He tried to kill Albert."

"And what, that makes it ok? He was defending our property. I wasn't there, but I know for a fact that Steven wouldn't do anything he didn't think was right. He made bad decisions, but he thought he was saving us by taking us out of there. He was a damn fool. But he was my husband, and you *bastards* just killed him!" She shook her head, looking at the floor. "I should have been there. I should have helped him rip your throats out as soon as you showed up."

She sighed quietly. "But instead, I was stuck in Vancouver. I watched the world end right in front of my own eyes. Saw my hair fall out of my head. Saw all the burned and broken bodies that got torn apart by the blast. But you know what Macedon? That shit was nothing compared to what you did. I spent a week trudging down the highway past psychos and maniacs to get back home to Steven. A *week*. And what the hell did I find?" She sobbed, tears flowing freely now. "I found a grave. A goddamn grave. I almost gave up right there. I just... laid on the grave and cried."

Alex paused for a moment. He glanced over at Isabelle and Marge, the latter of which was trying to sit up. He caught her eye, seeing the anger in it and looking away. It was unsettling. "I... I get that. Why didn't you?"

Clara laughed again, a sad chocking sound with more pain than humour. "Because you had to suffer for what you did. Your trail wasn't hard to follow. I'd just come from Squamish, and the only other place you could go was here." She snorted. "I didn't think it would be the great employees of Macedon *themselves* huddling in this shithole. It was the first bit of luck I'd had since the blast. I could avenge my husband *and* myself. The only shame about it all is that I didn't manage to get your other friend personally."

Alex felt a surge of anger, lifting the gun again. "How the hell did you know Albert died?"

Clara guffawed, staring daggers at Marge who was trying to stand despite Isabelle's protests. "I've been watching you this whole time. Waiting for you to slip up. I couldn't get in when you had the gate locked up, and I didn't have a gun. But time solved that. I came up here all the time after you kicked us out. I knew who had guns I could use. I knew who had snowmobiles I could fix-up. The tools were all there. All I had to do was wait..." She glanced at the gun again. "You made it easy. I ran some sabotage too. Tried to break your snowmobile during the blizzard. I missed. Didn't plan to screw up again, so I just screwed with you however else I could. I doubt the bears were pleased with all that stomping I did on top of their den, but they sure were hungrier than happy."

"You... you killed Albert?" The anger mounted, and once again he had his finger on the trigger. He realized that she had been there all along. The shadows he'd seen in the woods late at night. The ghosts that he swore still haunted the houses. The gun that had disappeared that was now levelled at her head. The old red snowmobile, appearing suddenly and disappearing just as quickly. Things that he'd assumed were tricks of the mind or echoes of the past, all of them leading up to the single moment where the objective embodiment of their sins could end them in peace. And worst of all, she'd already gotten Albert.

"Shoot her Alex." Marge had stopped struggling to stand, letting Isabelle work but watching the entire exchange with an unflinching gaze. "That bitch has screwed us over. She's attacked us, and we can't let that slide. Survival, remember?"

Alex started to squeeze the trigger, thinking about what she'd done. She'd chased them, and haunted them, and hurt them, all because she couldn't let go. She'd tried to hurt them so badly, and she'd succeeded too. Pulling the trigger would be peace for Albert. Peace for Marge, who didn't look too good. Peace for the Valley.

But what had that done for her?

Alex looked at the sunken and broken eyes on the other end of the barrel, and he just couldn't do it. As much as he may have wanted to, and as much as it may give them peace and security, it wouldn't change what had happened. It wouldn't help them.

He lowered the gun with a sigh, fumbling to pocket it. "Get the hell out."

Both Clara and Marge looked over at him, shocked. "What?"

"I said..." He looked between the two women, gathering up courage. "Get out. I want you to leave Clara, and never come back. Get on your snowmobile and get out. I'm letting you live."

"Alex!" Marge tried to scramble to her feet again, sliding to the ground in pain as she did so. "I said shoot her! What the hell are you doing?"

"I'm letting her go." Alex tried to offer Clara his hand, but she just stared at it in hollow shock. "You can go. I'm not going to stoop to your level. That's not what we're about here Clara. We're here to survive, not kill. So get out of here."

She stood up alone, spitting on his hand. "You're an idiot. And I hope you all freeze to death in this waste of time and life. I'll be back if you don't."

"No. No, you won't." Alex took a deep breath, then sighed. "Clara, we'll never forgive you for what you did. And we don't want you to forgive us either. Because we well and truly screwed each other. Me killing you now? That's revenge. That's... wrong. We've been going back and forth and we didn't even know it. The only way for both of us to move on is for you to leave and never come back. Because if you do, *you're* the one who's screwing us. *You're* the one who's started it. I'm letting you go to end this. And if you don't take the chance, I'm sure Marge will be happy to end it another way."

Clara glared at him, then at the other two. She slowly backed off, limping away and towards her battered up snowmobile. Alex followed carefully after her, glaring daggers at her as she mounted her machine and sputtered away down the thoroughfare. The plume of snow behind her quickly hid her from view, but he knew she would leave. She had to. Or there would be hell to pay.

Alex turned back to the hatchery, letting out a deep sigh.

The ghosts would certainly persist.

The memories would never vanish.

But now, Alex Park could stand simply in the snow and enjoy the silence.

EPILOGUE.

Alex was laid in his bed.

                                        "Alex?"

There would be shouting later.

                                        "Yeah, Isa?"

Anger, disappointment, rage.

                      "I'm… I'm glad you decided to spare her."

Marge would shriek and scream.

                          "That means a lot coming from you."

He'd brought that on himself.

                         "Yeah. She was hurt but… yeah."

But for now, she was asleep.

                                "What's wrong?"

The thoughts of the past would swirl around him.

                    "I'm scared. I think I found something."

The ghosts of the present would haunt his thoughts.

                                        "What?"

The fears of the future would permeate his vision.

                            "Put your hand here."

He let them swirl around and around.

                         "Your stomach? Why?"

There would be a time to deal with them later.

                  "Just do it. Do you feel that?"

Because right now?

                            "It's your heartbeat."

Right now Alex was in the eye of the storm.

"I know. I know. Just... listen to it."

A heartbeat.

"Isa, really, I don't see what this could..."

Two heartbeats.

ABOUT THE AUTHOR

Kai Hugessen

Kai Hugessen is an uninteresting social recluse living in the shuttered up guest room of his parents ocean-view villa at the southern tip of the Baja California Peninsula.
His hobbies include videogames, speculative thought experiments and bizarre phases of obsession with hybrid vehicles.
For more information, please email him at: theworldmakesense@gmail.com
To ask about his views on auto-insurance, please email him at: thisaintmysenseofhumor@gmail.com

ACKNOWLEDGEMENTS:
To Mom
To Dad
To Jack
To Uncle Mike
Thank you, all of you, for taking the time to read my silly little stories. You alone inspired me to keep at it as long as I have. They should put your names on the cover.

Manufactured by Amazon.ca
Bolton, ON